I0745146

APOCALYPSE

A DARK DRABBLES ANTHOLOGY

Compiled & Edited by D Kershaw

Also available from Black Hare Press

DARK DRABBLE ANTHOLOGIES

WORLDS
ANGELS
MONSTERS
BEYOND
UNRAVEL

Twitter: @BlackHarePress
Facebook: BlackHarePress
Website: www.BlackHarePress.com

Apocalypse, A Dark Drabbles Anthology title is
Copyright © 2019 Black Hare Press
First published in Australia in December 2019 by Black Hare Press

The authors of the individual stories retain the copyright of the works
featured in this anthology.

All characters and events in this publication, other than those clearly in the
public domain, are fictitious and any resemblance to real persons, living or
dead, is purely coincidental.

All rights reserved. No part of this production may be reproduced, stored in
a retrieval system, or transmitted, in any form or by any means, electronic,
mechanical, photocopying, recording or otherwise, without the prior
permission of the publisher and copyright owner.

Paperback: ISBN 978-1-925809-33-6
Hard Cover: ISBN 978-1-925809-34-3

Cover Design by Dawn Burdett
Book Formatting by Ben Thomas

I had a dream, which was not all a dream.
The bright sun was extinguish'd, and the stars
Did wander darkling in the eternal space,
Rayless, and pathless, and the icy earth
Swung blind and blackening in the moonless air;
Morn came and went—and came, and brought no day,
And men forgot their passions in the dread
Of this their desolation; and all hearts
Were chill'd into a selfish prayer for light:
And they did live by watchfires—and the thrones,
The palaces of crowned kings—the huts,
The habitations of all things which dwell,
Were burnt for beacons; cities were consum'd,
And men were gather'd round their blazing homes
To look once more into each other's face;
Happy were those who dwelt within the eye
Of the volcanos, and their mountain-torch:
A fearful hope was all the world contain'd;
Forests were set on fire—but hour by hour
They fell and faded—and the crackling trunks
Extinguish'd with a crash—and all was black.
The brows of men by the despairing light
Wore an unearthly aspect, as by fits
The flashes fell upon them; some lay down
And hid their eyes and wept; and some did rest
Their chins upon their clenched hands, and smil'd;
And others hurried to and fro, and fed
Their funeral piles with fuel, and look'd up
With mad disquietude on the dull sky,
The pall of a past world; and then again
With curses cast them down upon the dust,
And gnash'd their teeth and howl'd: the wild birds shriek'd
And, terrified, did flutter on the ground,
And flap their useless wings; the wildest brutes
Came tame and tremulous; and vipers crawl'd
And twin'd themselves among the multitude,
Hissing, but stingless—they were slain for food.
And War, which for a moment was no more,
Did glut himself again: a meal was bought
With blood, and each sate sullenly apart
Gorging himself in gloom: no love was left;
All earth was but one thought—and that was death
Immediate and inglorious; and the pang
Of famine fed upon all entrails—men

Died, and their bones were tombless as their flesh;
The meagre by the meagre were devour'd,
Even dogs assail'd their masters, all save one,
And he was faithful to a corse, and kept
The birds and beasts and famish'd men at bay,
Till hunger clung them, or the dropping dead
Lur'd their lank jaws; himself sought out no food,
But with a piteous and perpetual moan,
And a quick desolate cry, licking the hand
Which answer'd not with a caress—he died.
The crowd was famish'd by degrees; but two
Of an enormous city did survive,
And they were enemies: they met beside
The dying embers of an altar-place
Where had been heap'd a mass of holy things
For an unholy usage; they rak'd up,
And shivering scrap'd with their cold skeleton hands
The feeble ashes, and their feeble breath
Blew for a little life, and made a flame
Which was a mockery; then they lifted up
Their eyes as it grew lighter, and beheld
Each other's aspects—saw, and shriek'd, and died—
Even of their mutual hideousness they died,
Unknowing who he was upon whose brow
Famine had written Fiend. The world was void,
The populous and the powerful was a lump,
Seasonless, herbless, treeless, manless, lifeless—
A lump of death—a chaos of hard clay.
The rivers, lakes and ocean all stood still,
And nothing stirr'd within their silent depths;
Ships sailorless lay rotting on the sea,
And their masts fell down piecemeal: as they dropp'd
They slept on the abyss without a surge—
The waves were dead; the tides were in their grave,
The moon, their mistress, had expir'd before;
The winds were wither'd in the stagnant air,
And the clouds perish'd; Darkness had no need
Of aid from them—She was the Universe.

Lord Byron, *Darkness*

Table of Contents

Foreword

Scholars have been writing about the apocalypse for centuries. The ancients—from the Babylonians to the Hebrews—regaled us with epic biblically eschatological stories involving vast ships that saved the animal kingdom from world-engulfing floods, whole cities consumed by fire and brimstone, and the Norse myths of Ragnarök and the final end of the cosmos. In more modern times, with Mary Shelley's *The Last Man* (1826) one of the earlier favourites, there have been many tales of post-nuclear survival, zombie pandemics, dysgenics, technological takeovers, and natural disasters.

And now, here are our tiny tales of the apocalypse, in bite-sized chunks.

Love and kisses
D. Kershaw & Ben Thomas
Black Hare Press

BLACK HARE PRESS

Not Your Usual Alphabetti Spaghetti
by Austin P. Sheehan

A message written in blood and gore.

An alphabet of desecrated corpses, of arms and legs twisted to form letters.

The 'Y' was a woman's rotting torso, her arms spread out above where her head should have been.

Her legs were not there at all.

Two decaying bodies lay facing each other with expressions of love on what remained of their decomposing faces. Their arms were gone, legs torn off at the knee. Their stomachs cut open, putrid intestines pulled out and entwined together to form a 'H'.

The message was clear.

The message was fear.

BEHOLD YOUR NEW GOD.

Austin P. Sheehan is a writer of speculative fiction, a lover of language, literature and '90s TV. Armed with a psychology degree, he went into the world to study humanity, and now prefers the company of his wife and their greyhounds. He grew up in the valleys of Victoria's high country, and despite living in Melbourne, always feels at home amongst the mountains. You'll often find mountains in his stories, whether they're sci-fi, fantasy or alternative history.
Website: austinpsheehan.com
Twitter: @AustinPSheehan

Prophecy
Three-Hundred-and-Two
by D.K. Spencer

Purple lightning illuminates the dark and foreboding sky with zig-zag precision, while cumulonimbus clouds billow high against the full moon of the equinox.

The world is ending just like they said it would. Just like they promised.

As we gather round the mount, an old, white bearded man reads from his stone tablet to our huddled masses.

"God is not happy," he says. "God has come!"

Torrents of rain come down and the ground shakes violently. We run for cover hoping it will quickly end.

Three-hundred-and-two prophecies later, we're thinking, "Not this shit again?" Two-thousand-two-hundred years later, we're still here.

APOCALYPSE

*American writer **D.K. Spencer** lives in Portland, Oregon with his accomplished wife who is a potter. Knowing the slim envelop of atmosphere is all that's keeping us alive, he wonders why humans spend so much time and energy focused on human and planet destruction. This is the basis of his work. Mixed in with pounds of humour he explores the human condition on this planet and planets throughout the universe. If not traveling to writers workshops or writing events, Spencer spends most of his time in Portland focused on writing the perfect short story.*
Website: www.bignoniodies.com
Patreon: www.patreon.com/user?u=19477894

Final Launch
by Radar DeBoard

Tom's arm was wrapped around Sarah's neck, struggling to hold her back. She managed to stretch her fingers enough to get ahold of a coffee that was on the control panel. She brought it back, smashing Tom in the head with it.

A stunned Tom released his grip, falling down among the pieces of broken mug. Sarah turned, bringing the sharp fragments left in her hand into Tom's throat. She limped over to the panel, pressing a large, flashing button. She could feel the earth rumble as the first missile launched.

She smiled. "It's going to be a beautiful end."

Radar DeBoard is a horror movie and novel enthusiast who resides in the small town of Goddard, Kansas. He occasionally dabbles in writing and enjoys making dark tales for people to enjoy.

Sweet Nothings
by Jo Seysener

"I'll miss you."

Arms wrapped tight around his neck, she bathed in his scent. Warm stubble tickled her palm as she cupped his cheek, snuggling in for the long goodbye. Her tears mingled with his.

She tasted salt as she drew back, memorising the broad curve of his chest, the lines beginning to appear around his eyes.

He hefted his bags, looking over his shoulder at the waiting car. They spoke at the same time.

"You should…"

"I've got to…"

She silenced him with a deep kiss, leaving traces of the plague that would travel with him across two continents.

Jo Seysener is a mum of three crazies, a scatter of chickens, a decrepit kelpie and a rambunctious GSD. She lives with her husband near Brisbane, Australia. When she is not exposing her kids to cult story books from her childhood, she can be found in the kitchen experimenting with new flavours and pairings. She adores alpacas.
Facebook: joseysener
Website: www.joseysener.com

Horsemen
by Tracy Davidson

My destiny, my reason for existing, was to face the horsemen and protect humanity.

I faced them. I fought them. I got my arse kicked.

Humanity, for the most part, is gone. The horsemen let me live, so I could witness the suffering my failure led to. I witnessed it all…pestilence…famine…war…a century of chaos and calamity. Little left but dust and debris.

There are still people. What used to be people. There's no name for what they are now.

As for me, my new name is Death, and I shall put them out of their misery.

Tracy Davidson lives in Warwickshire, England, and writes poetry and flash fiction. Her work has appeared in various publications and anthologies, including: Poet's Market, Writers Digest, Mslexia, Modern Haiku, Atlas Poetica, The Binnacle, Artificium, Journey to Crone, The Great Gatsby Anthology, WAR and In Protest: 150 Poems for Human Rights.

Hush
by L.J. Skelton

Quiet descends over the world so gradually that he almost doesn't notice the silence at first. The rumble of cars and airplanes is a distant memory. The animals were next, first the biggest and then one day even the mice stopped skittering across the rafters and under the leaves. Insects became muted, as if there were less of them each day.

Adults all talk in hushed voices. There are no children.

Today it's the birds. There's no singing or chirping from the trees, no cawing in the branches above.

Even the crows are gone now. Only the vultures are left.

***L.J. Skelton** is a cowgirl, teacher, and floral designer with over 25 years experience showing and training horses. She earned her Bachelor of Science in Psychology from Penn State University, then collected years of writing inspiration while working at a center for the developmentally disabled, as well as a horse and cattle ranch, a construction company, a butcher shop, and managing a western-wear store. She then started her own business, which has given her the freedom to pursue her dream of becoming a published author. She lives in rural northwestern Pennsylvania with her husband and beloved dog, horse, and cats.*

A Squash of Commuters
by Melanie Harding-Shaw

A squash of peak-hour commuters sit in a train carriage. They would be a mob of commuters if they were moving under their own propulsion. Or a pride of commuters if they had better green credentials.

When the ocean floods the underground, they become a pod. And when they emerge from the dark to a post-apocalyptic future, they become a colony.

The underground tunnels protected them from the worst of it. As the years pass and the population dwindles, they look back on the days when they were a squash with longing.

A scarcity of commuters is all that remains.

Melanie Harding-Shaw *is a speculative fiction writer, policy geek and mother-of-three from Wellington, New Zealand. Her stories have recently appeared in Daily Science Fiction, The Arcanist and NewMyths among others. Website: www.melaniehardingshaw.com Facebook: MelanieHardingShawWriter*

The Last Rose
by Zoey Xolton

The last rose on planet Earth bloomed, its brilliant scarlet in stark contrast to the silent death all around her. The traveller from Alpha Centauri looked upon it with great sadness. Its beauty was ephemeral, and ultimately tragic; just like the existence of humanity.

Glancing once more at the desolation and destruction, the traveller hung her head.

It is for the best, the Intergalactic Council had decided unanimously.

The Visionaries had foreseen the destruction humanity would wreak across the 'verse if allowed to navigate the stars... And yet, the lone traveller couldn't help but wish there had been another way.

Zoey Xolton is an Australian Speculative Fiction writer, primarily of Dark Fantasy, Paranormal Romance and Horror. She is also a proud mother of two and is married to her soul mate. Outside of her family, writing is her greatest passion. She is especially fond of short fiction and is working on releasing her own themed collections in future. Website: www.zoeyxolton.com

End of Time
by Melissa Neubert

She stared at the destruction with tears dripping down her face. The world that was once filled with colourful flowers, green grass, trees and a blue sky, was now painted in shades of dull grey.

The smell of death hung in a haze, and with each breath she felt her own life slipping away. She was alone. The city a wasteland. Silent. The sun fading, leaving behind a holocaustic hell.

They had predicted the end of time. We were warned. Most failed to listen. It was too late now. She closed her eyes waiting. Death would come, it was welcome.

Melissa Neubert was born in the Pacific Northwest and currently lives in Illinois with her husband, three children and two dogs. Melissa has been a daycare provider, veterinary assistant, teacher/library aide, and administrative assistant. Melissa travels extensively both domestically and internationally where she finds inspiration for her writing in beautiful and unique locations. When she is not writing she enjoys music, reading, concert and wildlife photography, football and camping. Although Melissa has been writing since grade school, she has only recently begun pursuing the craft seriously. She writes mostly in the genres of Suspense/Thriller and Adult Paranormal Romance.

Tampons
by Maria J. Estrada

I peak around the corner at the *ferals*. My hands choke the bat. There are five, girls and boys with their tattered clothes and over-mended shoes. They must have had a caretaker. The youngest one with dirt-streaked face and maroon stains can't be more than four.

Those are not paint stains.

"Don't be scared of us," says the tallest boy who reminds me of my Michael. "We need a new mommy."

I cradle my bag with hard-won loot: Tampons. They think its food, but it's just a reminder. This world is no place for children.

I ready myself to strike.

Maria J. Estrada grew up in the desert outside of Yuma, Arizona in a barrio comprised of new Mexican immigrants and first-generation Chicanos. She has published poetry, fiction, and essays in Blaze: The Inner Circle Writers' Group Flash Fiction Anthology 2019, Spillwords Press, Dastaan World Magazine, The Inner Circle Writers' Magazine, and A Language & Power Reader: Representations of Race in a "Post-Racist" Era. She lives in Chicago, IL.
Facebook: drmariajestrada
Website: barrioblues.com

Becky
by Rhiannon Bird

I trudged across the blackened earth, hoping to find civilisation, wherever that may be. The sun was setting; I'd have to stop soon, alone again. I missed human company the most. There had to be someone else out there somewhere, someone else who'd survived the plague.

Someone other than Becky. I'd met her a few days ago and she wouldn't shut up.

This morning, the soil hadn't been the best for grave digging, but I guess I owed her that much after snapping her neck. I just wanted to find someone, anyone as long as they were not like Becky.

Rhiannon Bird is a young aspiring author. She has a passion for words and storytelling. Rhiannon has her own quotes blog; Thoughts of a Writer. She has had 4 works published. This includes 3 short stories and 2 poems. These are published on Eskimo pie, Literary yard, Down in the Dirt Magazine and Short break fiction. She can be found on Facebook, Instagram, and Pinterest

Pale Horse, Rainbow Annihilation
by Joshua D. Taylor

I threw my last handful of sugar cubes in the opposite direction as I dived under a collapsed billboard just in time to avoid the multicoloured blast that turned two strangers into smouldering skeletons. Their brightly coloured clothing had afforded them no mercy. The unicorns flew away, through billowing smoke, hunting for others and continuously scorching the earth with the rainbow beams from their horns. They were fed up with our cutesy portrayals and pop culture mockery. No one had suspected that Death's Pale Horse had a horn.

Momentarily safe, I saw my salvation, an apple orchard. Horses love apples.

Joshua D. Taylor is an amateur writer who started writing a few years ago when he realised he was too old to play make-believe. He lives in southeastern Pennsylvania with his wife and a one-eared cat. He enjoys gardening, comic books, ska-punk music, Disney World, and travelling with his wife. Raised during weirdness that was the late 20th century Josh's eclectic interests produce eclectic works. He loves to mix-n-match things from different genres and stories elements to achieve a madcap hodgepodge of the truly unexpected. His short story 'the Obelisk' appears in Salty Tales by Stormy Island Publishing.
Facebook: authorjoshuadtaylor

City of Angels
by Karter Mycroft

There are some who ridicule people of faith, but I have prayed my entire life that Los Angeles be destroyed by a giant jellyfish, and today my pleas have been answered. I stand atop a Hollywood hill and gaze at the panicked commuters, all crying, wailing, leaping from cars and dashing for safety, helpless before the tentacles of my God. The smog ripples with screams. Purple tendrils drag entire neighbourhoods into the raging waves.

My saviour comes for me last. Stingers curl around my waist, and I smile in exultation as I scrape across the beach and down into heaven.

Karter Mycroft is a Los Angeles-based author and co-host of The Genre Hustle podcast. Their work has been published or is pending publication in Lovecraftiana and Murder Park After Dark.

Dirt
by M.L. Swart

"You brought what?!"

"It's just a little bit."

Olga stared at the vial Ben was holding. Dirt from his garden, back home. A cap had been tightly screwed on.

"What if it's contaminated?"

"It won't leave my room, I promise. I just want to look at it, not open it. Please, don't tell the base manager."

Olga remembered the feeling of grass between her toes, the smell of the earth after rainfall. Before the Catastrophe. She sighed.

"You realise I can't let you keep it, right?"

Ben hung his head and nodded quietly.

"Let's agree I didn't see anything then."

M.L. Swart lives in Rotterdam, The Netherlands, with two rats and one husband. She likes writing, crafts, and making/looking at art.

Don't Say a Prayer for Me Now
by Michele Freeman

The bathroom offered piddling protection against the apocalypse. But as fire filled the sky and emergency sirens wailed, we hunkered in the tub underneath a flimsy twin mattress.

My four-year-daughter Hailey and our Chihuahua Cooper curled together next to me, their tiny bodies cold with fear.

I belted out my favourite '80s songs, but even Duran Duran lyrics proved poor distractions from booming explosions and screaming victims. Then the ceiling collapsed, and the mattress became our coffin lid.

Later, I awoke as soldiers pulled me from the wreckage. Cooper barked. He made it. But Hailey…my sweet baby…did not.

*Award-winning author **Michele Freeman** writes horror and dark fiction. She loves crochet, chocolate, and zombies. She lives in Texas with her Viking husband and their adorable fur babies.*
Website: www.authormichelefreeman.com

Apoca-chips
by Sherry D. Ramsey

It's been 264 days since the Collapse, and there are no potato chips left.

Potato chips: an unlikely saviour of one's sanity. Before the Collapse, they were a snack, a treat...all right, sometimes an unhealthy addiction. In the worst days since, they've given me hope.

Safely barricaded, alone in the Handi-Mart, I didn't ration them at first. I lulled myself into dreams of the pleasant Before with their crunchy, fragrant, sweet-grease comfort. As supplies dwindled, I became more circumspect. Fifteen chips a day. Ten. Five. One.

None.

There are no potato chips left.

I lick my lips and venture outside.

Sherry D. Ramsey is a bestselling author, editor, publisher, creativity addict and self-confessed Internet geek. She writes for all ages, and she loves mysteries and magic as much as she loves spaceships and aliens--so much that she often smooshes them together in (hopefully) interesting ways. Sherry lives in Nova Scotia with her family and dogs, where she consumes far more coffee and chocolate than is likely good for her.
Website: www.sherrydramsey.com
Twitter: @sdramsey

The Zombie Brigade
by Henry Herz

Half a league, half a league,

Half a league onward,

Lurched the six hundred.

"Forward, the Zombie Brigade!

Seek the humans' brains!" he said.

Into ruined Silicon Valley

Lurched the six hundred.

"Forward, the Zombie Brigade!"

Theirs unable to make reply,

Theirs unable to reason why,

Theirs but to do and undie.

Into ruined Silicon Valley

Lurched the six hundred.

Glock-armed police to right of them,

Shotgun-toting civilians to left of them,

M-16-wielding soldiers in front of them

Volleyed and thundered;

Stormed at with shot and shell,

Mindlessly they lumbered and well,

From Undead back to the jaws of Death.

Henry Herz *edited BEYOND THE PALE, featuring stories by Peter Beagle, Heather Brewer, Jim Butcher, Rachel Caine, Kami Garcia, Nancy Holder, and Jane Yolen. He authored the short stories Gluttony (CLASSICS REMIXED anthology), Zombie Sonnet 43 (MONSTERS anthology), Ghost Father (BEYOND anthology), and Sins & Virtues (ANGELS anthology), and Pay the Piper (Highlights Magazine). He authored the children's books: MONSTER GOOSE NURSERY RHYMES, WHEN YOU GIVE AN IMP A PENNY, MABEL & THE QUEEN OF DREAMS, CAP'N REX & HIS CLEVER CREW, HOW THE SQUID GOT TWO LONG ARMS, ALICE'S MAGIC GARDEN, 2 PIRATES + 1 ROBOT, THE MAGIC SPATULA.*
Website: www.henryherz.com

Russian Roulette
by Jacek Wilkos

The man raised the revolver to his temple. He pulled the trigger. Nothing. He handed the weapon to his rival. He spun the cylinder and leaned his head against the barrel. They stared into each other's eyes for a brief moment.

A gunshot.

Blood on the wall.

A corpse on the table.

The winner sat hypnotised. The sounds coming from around drew him from the trance. A horde of the undead, stimulated by the bang, again began to wheeze and scratch against the walls of the cabin.

He won, the man thought. *And I will suffer a more painful death.*

Jacek Wilkos is an engineer from Poland. He lives with his wife and daughter in a beautiful city of Cracow. He is addicted to buying books, he loves coffee, dark ambient music and riding his bike. He writes mostly horror drabbles. His fiction in Polish can be read on Szortal, Niedobre literki, Horror Online. In English his work was published in Drablr, Rune Bear, Sirens Call eZine.
Facebook: Jacek.W.Wilkos

Their Turn
by Cindar Harrell

The metal of the shackles weighed heavily on my raw wrists as I was forced to march in the endless dark. The line of prisoners was ever dwindling. There were less than a hundred left in my group. From the whispers, there were only about a thousand left in total.

We were all that remained of the human race.

Our captors had systematically taken over the entire Earth piece by piece. Cities of metal and man-made plastics were transformed back into natural mechas; a strange mutation of technology and arboreal innovation.

We had our chance, now it was their turn.

Cindar Harrell loves fairy tales, especially ones with a dark twist. Her stories are often fairy tale inspired, but she is also working on a mystery series. Her stories can be found on Amazon and in various anthologies. You can follow her on Facebook and visit her blog, which she promises to try and update more often,
Website: cindarharrell.wordpress.com
Facebook: CindarHarrell

Language
by J.A. Hammer

In our previous lives, we were linguists. I and my assistant studied Earth's dying languages; noting clicks, guttural stops, and other utterances.

We didn't know that all languages would be dying. Politics didn't interest us when there were new words to study...so the world's end came; sneaking illness miasma for some, bright blinding flashes for others. I survived by being practical about food. "Long pig" is just two words, after all.

In my current life, I am a linguist. I study the language of the Earth, noting the wind's sharpish response to fire's bluster, sunlight beaming its opinionated argument.

J.A. Hammer lives off of coffee (mostly Dead Eyes) and stress in the wild concrete city of Tokyo, where zombies are living and using the train lines every day. Known as CoffeeQuills online, they're mostly safe to talk to (bites only happen in the name of science) but be wary if approaching before dawn. The cake is not a lie, but you'll have to get it yourself. If you're interested in steampunk/paranormal Japan, check out their Patreon, or if you'd like daily drabbles and pictures from Japan, follow CoffeeQuills on either Instagram or Twitter.
Website : www.patreon.com/coffeequills

The Green Death
by Austin P. Sheehan

As the sun set, Rain searched in desperation for food and clean water. Through her dirty and scratched goggles, she saw nothing that hadn't been tainted with green.

This town was dead like all the others; vines and roots conspiring to tear down buildings, hedges and weeds proclaiming victory over those who had cut them back for centuries.

Her heart sank, dragged into the depths by a merciless vine, and Rain collapsed; exhausted, dehydrated and utterly defeated.

Tearing her gas mask off, she breathed in deeply, inhaling the dangerous toxins and spores, surrendering to the green death of the forest.

Austin P. Sheehan is a writer of speculative fiction, a lover of language, literature and '90s TV. Armed with a psychology degree, he went into the world to study humanity, and now prefers the company of his wife and their greyhounds. He grew up in the valleys of Victoria's high country, and despite living in Melbourne, always feels at home amongst the mountains. You'll often find mountains in his stories, whether they're sci-fi, fantasy or alternative history.
Website: austinpsheehan.com
Twitter: @AustinPSheehan

The End of the Dark Gods
by Aiki Flinthart

In the times before, the tribes worshipped the Dark Gods with blood, with death, with destruction. And the gods feasted. Upon the bodies of the fallen; upon the souls of the condemned; upon the screams of the murdered.

Until there came a time when but one tribe remained. For they had slaughtered kin and foe alike; taken the lands for themselves; descended into darkness.

And so the Dark Gods set them upon each other. For their lust was unsated, still.

Only in that end of times did the Gods then understand that destruction came at a price.

Their own oblivion.

Aiki Flinthart has had short stories shortlisted in the Aurealis awards and top-8 listed in the USA Writers of the Future competition, as well as published in various anthologies and e-mags. She has 11 published spec fic novels and has edited 2 short story anthologies. She regularly gives workshops on writing fight scenes at conventions. Lives in Brisbane. Does martial arts, archery, knife throwing and lute-playing. Website: www.aikiflinthart.com

Privileges
by Glenn R. Wilson

"You'll never get anywhere."

My dad said this while we walked by the Clifford mansion. Every time he'd point at it and add, "do you think they didn't work hard to have a place like that?"

Now, a week after the last bomb fell, I find myself standing in front of it. But this time is different. No one is here to tell me what I deserve. And I know what I like.

Funny how some things aren't touched while others disappear.

I'm moving in today. I'll change its name to mine tomorrow.

Being the lone survivor has its privileges.

Glenn R. Wilson has come full circle. Making a point to mature, like fine wine, before diving head-first into his long list of writing projects, he's approaching them with a plan. That strategy is to build with one brick at a time. He's accumulated a few bricks already and is adding more. Over time, with persistence and determination, he'll have a home. But for now, a solid foundation is the goal. Please, enjoy the process with him.

The Last Safe Space
by Michelle River

I hurried the children towards the crawlspace, their small gaunt arms holding me tightly with a strength I didn't think they could still possess. We had no choice, I knew that now.

I hugged them close, kissing away the small tears that had escaped their eyes and ripped myself away from their embrace. "Mommy loves you so much. Now stay brave and stay quiet."

"Hurry, Martha," Jim whispered. The stench of rotting flesh grew stronger as we pushed the enormous oak cabinet in front of the simple wooden door, the only protection I could offer.

The horde was getting closer.

Michelle River *hails from Ontario, Canada where she lives with her energetic daughter and wonderful husband. A lover of everything dark and terrifying since early childhood, writing horror and dark-fiction has quickly become her passion as an adult.*
Facebook: MichelleRiverAuthor

What is Left Behind
by Evelyn Benvie

Marth found the child hiding in some rubble. She had white hair and kaleidoscope eyes. It was obvious she was one of them.

He should have killed her.

He took her home, carrying her on his back. She would have been no more than five, in human years. He didn't know the equivalent in their kind. He didn't ask. She didn't say.

She ate only the crusts off the bread he gave her, refusing to touch the canned tomatoes or dried meat.

When he left again the next morning, still searching for other survivors, she followed him. He let her.

Evelyn Benvie is the woolly jumper in a family of black sheep. Both a cynic and a romantic at heart, she writes diverse, queer-positive fiction and poetry that have been published online and in print. Her first novella, Something to Celebrate, was recently published by Mischief Corner Books and is available on Amazon.
Website: evelynbenvie.com

Footprints in the Sand Dunes
by Shelly Jarvis

When I see the footprints, I almost shit my pants. It's been so long since I've encountered another person, I worry I'm hallucinating again.

Their feet are smaller than mine, a woman, perhaps. God above, what I wouldn't give to see a woman. At least then there would be a chance this wouldn't end in bloodshed, in a fight neither of us want.

I chase the prints over the dunes, slowing only when I see him in the valley below. He's standing over the body of what *was* a woman, before he found her.

I withdraw my blade and charge.

Shelly Jarvis is a speculative fiction author from West Virginia, US. She found a life-long love of sci-fi and fantasy in the 3rd grade when she found Madeleine L'Engle's "A Wrinkle in Time." Shelly is an avid reader, a Whovian, the ideal viewer of dog rescue videos, and undoubtedly Ravenclaw. She currently has two YA sci-fi books available for purchase on Amazon.
Website: www.ShellyJarvis.com

A Beautiful World
by Brandi Hicks

Brad bit the cigar between his teeth as he leaned toward one of the still-burning fires to light it up. The smoke mingled with the smoke coming from the rubble.

His rubble.

The aftermath that lay before him was his doing, with the help of Lou—she was the intelligence, he was just the brute.

He punted a skull and laughed. The world was theirs now, the new republic could begin. He looked over at Lou, her tank top clinging to her, the rocket launcher still smoking. He started flexing, hoping to impress her. Damn, this was a beautiful world.

*Growing up in West Virginia, **Brandi Hicks** loved to have her nose in a book, her eyes toward the night sky and putting a pen to paper. Her imagination was always sparked by her grandfather and her mom taking her to new places and teaching her about the unusual. She loves fantasy, sci-fi, and learning about science and history. She has two beautiful children, and hopes to instill creativity and a love of reading in them. Finding new crafts to try keeps her busy when not playing with her kids or working.*

Celebration Day
by Scott Wheelock

The kids had been the most excited, especially the ones born after the war. Freeze-dried bread pudding and canned apple juice wasn't as big a deal to those who'd once dined on steak and lobster. Still, the adults and teenagers enjoyed the feast vicariously through the children's smiles and excited laughter.

As the party wound down, the children one by one lay down on the hard ground as if asleep. The adults raised their glasses to one another. All agreed it had been a good effort. As they joined the children, the war claimed one more corner of the map.

Scott Wheelock is a painter, writer and teacher living in Philadelphia. Recently, his short story The Crimson Tear was selected for the anthology "Quoth the Raven" published by Camden Park Press, and his story Blood Pigs and Soil was chosen for the upcoming Night Sky Anthology "13 Postcards from Hell."
Website: www.scottwheelock.com

Devourers
by Matthew M. Montelione

The Devourers came out of nowhere, consuming most of the fabric of Earth in months. That they were a hostile race who craved domination was not contested, but their reasoning for feeding on Earth's physical plane was hotly debated in scientific circles. Eventually, the depleted public stopped caring about why they came. Hypotheses ceased to matter; the aliens relentlessly feasted on the material plane.

We had nowhere to hide, save for the voids of our extinguished planet.

The invaders have stopped eating, but we still hide, full of dark anxieties, wondering when they will find us and complete their conquest.

Matthew M. Montelione is a horror writer born and raised on Long Island in New York. His stories have been published in *Quoth the Raven: A Contemporary Reimagining of the Works of Edgar Allan Poe*, *Thuggish Itch: Devilish*, and other titles. Matthew is also an American Revolution historian who focuses on the local experiences of Loyalists on Long Island. His work on the subject has been published in *Long Island History Journal* and *Journal of the American Revolution*.
Website: *maybeevils.com*
Twitter: *@maybeevils*

Look on the Bright Side
by K.T. Tate

It's all about survival. When unspeakable horrors from Beyond convene on your planet, what can you do? Most people went insane, clawed out their eyes or were annihilated in the resulting apocalypse. But I decided that wasn't for me.

We tried rebellion but that didn't last. So I got smart, donned a robe and joined the cultists. At least they had less chance of being eaten. It wasn't like we could actually fight the towering, trans-dimensional abominations.

Now I spend my days in the ruins of the world, worshiping our conquerors and slowly mutating. At least I'm enjoying the tentacles.

K.T. Tate lives in Cambridgeshire in the UK. She writes mainly weird fiction, cosmic horror and strange monster stories.
Website: eldritchhollow.wordpress.com
Tumblr: eldritch-hollow.tumblr.com

All We Know
by Umair Mirxa

Alizeh's scream of terror was muffled as her father turned in alarm and placed his hand over her mouth.

"What are you doing?" he hissed, pulling her further away from the burning cottage. "You'll draw attention to us."

"The books, baba!" said Alizeh, now sobbing quietly.

"They are not worth the risk to our lives," said her sister, Misha.

"What if they were the last books on Earth?"

"We still can't afford to let the scavengers find us, kiddo," said her father. "Don't worry. We'll find you some, soon enough. First, we need to survive the end of the world."

Umair Mirxa lives in Karachi, Pakistan. His first published story, 'Awareness', appeared on Spillwords Press. He has also had stories accepted for anthologies from Zombie Pirate Publishing, Blood Song Books, Fantasia Divinity Magazine and Publishing, and Iron Faerie Publishing. He is a massive J.R.R. Tolkien fan, and loves everything to do with fantasy and mythology. He enjoys football, history, music, movies, TV shows, and comic books, and wishes with all his heart that dragons were real.
Website: www.umairmirxa.com
Facebook: UMirxa12

Last Launch
by Shawn M. Klimek

Facing a mob of reporters, Dr. Kodama pointed proudly at the skyscraping white rocket on its distant launch pad. "Someday, the Earth will be uninhabitable," he pontificated, "and colony ships powered by my plutonium fusion engines will carry humanity to new worlds."

"What would happen if an explosion dispersed plutonium into the stratosphere?" one reporter challenged.

"What's that spewing from the mid-section?" asked another.

"Liquid oxygen," said Kodama, without looking.

"No, the silvery, metallic stuff."

"What did he say?" shouted a third, as the rocket began thunderously to rise.

"He said, 'Someday the Earth will become uninhabitable,'" the first replied.

Shawn M. Klimek is the middle child of seven creative siblings, a globetrotting, U.S. military spouse, an internationally best-selling short-story writer, a poet, and butler to a Maltese. More than one hundred of his stories and poems have been published, notably in such anthologies as BHP's Deep Space, Bad Romance, Eerie Christmas, Jibbernocky, and the first eight books in the Dark Drabbles series.
Website: jotinthedark.blogspot.com
Facebook: shawnmklimekauthor

Last Breath
by Michelle River

The respirator didn't fit. My lungs began to burn as the toxic air seeped in through the gaps around my face, slowly liquifying them with every breath.

I could see the imprint the mask had left on his skin, deep red lines cutting into flesh. His final sacrifice was one of futility. I squeezed his strong hand in mine, watching the crimson sun slowly disappear over the horizon as he drowned in his own blood; our last sunset together. The light gave way to shadow and my body spasmed, finally giving in to the inevitable.

Only a few moments now.

Michelle River hails from Ontario, Canada where she lives with her energetic daughter and wonderful husband. A lover of everything dark and terrifying since early childhood, writing horror and dark-fiction has quickly become her passion as an adult.
Facebook: MichelleRiverAuthor

The Stableboy
by Peter J. Foote

Hooves stomp flagstone, blood-splattered harness jingles, fly's buzz, as the stableboy hastens to fill the grain buckets, teeth gnash seeking his flesh.

Twisted fingers struggle to muck stalls, spread straw and fill the water trough before the stableboy limps to his filthy mat and collapses. He waves aside relentless flies and tries to ignore the ache in his empty stomach, but freezes as footsteps stop at the door.

They thrust wide the doors, crimson light from a sky on fire bathes the interior. Shielding his eyes, the stableboy watches the four riders step into the barn for their mounts.

Peter J. Foote is a bestselling speculative fiction writer from Nova Scotia. Outside of writing, he runs a used bookstore specialising in fantasy & sci-fi, cosplays, and alternates between red wine and coffee as the mood demands. His short stories can be found in both print and in ebook form, with his story "Sea Monkeys" winning the inaugural "Engen Books/Kit Sora, Flash Fiction/Flash Photography" contest in March of 2018. As the founder of the group "Genre Writers of Atlantic Canada", Peter believes that the writing community is stronger when it works together.
Twitter: @PeterJFoote1
Website: peterjfooteauthor.wordpress.com

Wereworld
by Jonathan Inbody

Reuben crested the hill in a full sprint, waving his arms and screaming for his companions. A pack of werewolves weaved through the forest behind him, quickly closing the distance as they bounded over fallen logs and slashed through tangled underbrush.

"Go back!" Reuben yelled to his friends. "They'll find the safe zone! Run!"

A wolf leapt onto him, shredding his body into a bloody pile of viscera. Across the open field, the other survivors turned and ran, trying desperately to escape as the pack followed.

The survivors outran them, but it was too late now; they had the scent.

*Jonathan Inbody is a filmmaker, author, and podcaster from Buffalo, New York. He enjoys B-movies, pen and paper RPGs, and New Wave Science Fiction novels. His short story "Dying Feels Like Slowly Sinking" is due to be published in the anthology Deteriorate from Whimsically Dark Publishing. Jon can be heard every other week on his improvisational movie pitch podcast X Meets Y.
Website: xmeetsy.libsyn.com*

Jellyfish
by Nicola Currie

I was half-asleep when Carruthers dragged me to the Cupola. The observatory module of the International Space Station gave the best view in the universe, but the ghost of his face told me this wasn't about another pretty blue view of home.

Jellyfish, I thought, as I rubbed my eyes. The bombs mushroomed all over the globe below, their shockwaves rippling, extinguishing everything in their path.

The crew screamed, first when we lost contact; again, later, when the Station lights shut off.

Now we sit in darkness, watching the round control lights blink out. Like jellyfish, dying one by one.

Nicola Currie is 34, from Cambridge, UK where she works in educational publishing. She has published poetry in literary magazines, including Mslexia and Sarasvati, and has also completed her first novel, which was longlisted for the Bath Children's Novel Award.
Website: writeitandweep.home.blog

Funny Old World
by Joel R. Hunt

I've found the rip.

It's a few millimetres over my ankle, letting in the toxins.

Can you believe that? A few millimetres are going to kill me.

Funny old world.

You know, I've been listening to your broadcasts. God, I'm proud of you. You're so resilient, such a natural leader.

And I know it's too late, but…

I wanted to say, I'm sorry.

And I shouldn't have left.

I've travelled the country to reach you. Now I'm going to die in sight of your broadcast tower, and you won't even know I'm here.

Yeah.

It's a funny old world, alright…

Joel R. Hunt *is a writer from the UK who dabbles in the darker aspects of life, particularly through horror, science fiction and the supernatural. He has been published in a number of short story anthologies, and hopes to have released his first single author collection in early 2020, and hopes to have released his first anthology of short stories later this year.*
Twitter: @JoelRHunt1
Reddit: JRHEvilInc

Basking
by Raven Corinn Carluk

The two of them stood on the charred remains of the Hollywood sign, surveying the ruins before them. Achingly bright sunlight beat upon the valley, lighting destroyed buildings and abandoned vehicles. The breeze fitfully lifted dust and ash.

"Beautiful, isn't it?" she asked.

He sighed. "Better than expected."

"Reports from Mexico City are promising. Animals returning. The initial plantings flourish."

"What about the human survivors?" He hissed, narrowing his eyes.

Her forked tongue flicked out, then she smiled. "Rounded up into preserves. Once we ensure their genetic health, we'll allow them to breed."

"It's good to be on top again."

Raven Corinn Carluk writes dark fantasy, paranormal romance, and anything else that catches her interest. She's authored five novels, where she explores themes of love and acceptance. Her shorter pieces, usually from her darker side, can be found in Black Hare Press anthologies, at Detritus Online, and through Alban Lake Publishers.
Twitter: @ravencorinn
Website: RavenCorinnCarluk.Blogspot.Com

The Road Not Taken
by Josh Herz

Two sandy tracks diverged in a desert,

And sorry I could not travel both

To shake off nitrous oxide-powered pursuit.

Long I spent repairing my tractor trailer,

Making its engine shiny.

I set traps on one track,

Then took the other, just as barren,

But having the better claim,

Because it led to water;

One-armed woman and I shall tell this with a sigh

Somewhere ages and ages hence:

Of our flight from the chrome riders of Valhalla.

Two tracks diverged in a desert, and we—

We took the one less travelled by,

And that has made all the difference.

Josh Herz co-authored the children's books: MONSTER GOOSE NURSERY RHYMES, WHEN YOU GIVE AN IMP A PENNY, MABEL & THE QUEEN OF DREAMS, and LITTLE RED CUTTLEFISH. His science fiction dioramas, Zombie Apocalypse, The Doorways of Life, and Band of Brothers, appeared in Cicada Magazine.

Can't Be Zombies
by Neen Cohen

Thunk!

The heavy crossbow slaps against her thigh. The hobby turned lifesaver after the outbreak.

It was faster than the movies. A strong wind, an oncoming storm, and all exposed were dead or dying.

Thunk!

But no one wants to say Zombies.

She lifts her weapon. Taking a deep breath behind the red dirty bandana.

She lines it up.

Never see the face.

She releases the bolt and the sickening wet thud adds to the nightmare she will have tonight.

Thunk!

Fingering the scar on her neck, she remembers what hesitation costs.

Thunk!

She steps over the now inanimate meat.

Neen Cohen lives in Brisbane with her partner, son and fur babies. She is a writer of LGBTQI, dark fantasy and horror short stories and has a Bachelor of Creative Industries from QUT. She can often be found writing while sitting against a tombstone or tree in any number of graveyards.
Facebook: Neen-Cohen-Author-424700821629629
Website: wordbubblessite.wordpress.com

No Day After
by M.A. Nolte

All life ended. There was no apocalypse. A decent apocalypse needs at least one day before and one day after. The Big Bang had been no apocalypse because there was no day before. And the day all life ended had no day after. There were no bloody wars, no suffering and no children crying. There was this moment and…stop. But at least there had been prophets foretelling the non-apocalypse, although they were now called computer scientists. They had claimed that life could be a big computer game with us being avatars for some super-intelligent players. The players got bored.

M.A. Nolte studied computer science, prehistory and psychology and is therefore fascinated by how the past defines the future and how a different view of the past can change present and future.

To Kill a Zombie
by Harrison Herz

Atticus said to Jem one day, "I'd rather you shot at zombies in the backyard, but I know you'll go after the living. Shoot all the living if you want, if you can hit 'em, but it's a sin to kill a person."

That was the only time I ever heard Atticus say it was a sin to do something.

"Your father's wrong," Miss Maudie said. "The living don't do one thing except consume. They eat up people's gardens, steal what's not theirs; they don't do one thing beneficial for us. That's why it's a sin to shoot a zombie."

Harrison Herz co-authored the children's books: *MONSTER GOOSE NURSERY RHYMES, WHEN YOU GIVE AN IMP A PENNY, MABEL & THE QUEEN OF DREAMS, and LITTLE RED CUTTLEFISH.*

Totkv-Rakko
by James Turnbow

"Our ancestors said the old ways would return." The elder stood atop a large mound at our ceremonial grounds. "We cared for Mother Earth and held her secrets, practiced our ways in silence while the rest raped and pillaged. Mother Earth noticed and sent the great fire. No longer could the world depend on their machines."

I watched as the people of our village began to gather.

"We celebrate the fire just as our ancestors did. The fire has always kept the darkness away. Locv Locv!" He called the ladies in their turtle shells first. It was time to dance.

James Turnbow is a graduate from the University of Central Oklahoma with a degree in Strategic Communications. He is a proud member of the Seminole Nation of Oklahoma and works with tribal youth to empower them to pursue higher education as an Education Advisor for the Muscogee Creek Nation. He is a curator of Seminole culture and language and works to preserve the stories and words of his ancestors.

In the Blood
by Michelle River

"Hurry boy, we have to cull them all!" my father screamed, his axe swinging wildly at the head of his prized cattle, a wake of dead bodies scattered behind him.

"It's changing," I yelled over my shoulder as I pulled the trigger on the bolt gun, watching the red blood turn black at my feet. We didn't have much time left.

A piercing scream ripped through the barn as the cows jumped their enclosures and attacked my father, trampling his strong body until it was a pile of red mush.

There was no time left, the infection was already here.

Michelle River hails from Ontario, Canada where she lives with her energetic daughter and wonderful husband. A lover of everything dark and terrifying since early childhood, writing horror and dark-fiction has quickly become her passion as an adult.
Facebook: MichelleRiverAuthor

Seeking Hope
by Annie Percik

The landscape stretches before us. Desolate. Empty. I tuck my scarf more securely into the neck of my jacket, watching as my breath steams in the icy air. Around me, other figures stumble through the snow, laden down with every item they've managed to salvage or scavenge.

I travel light. This journey is hard enough without the encumbrance of useless stuff from before. My memories are heavy enough.

I look only forwards, trying to imagine what we might find beyond the fallout zone. If there's anything to find. We don't need much. Just the smallest hope of somewhere to rebuild.

Annie Percik lives in London with her husband, Dave, where she is revising her first novel, whilst working as a University Complaints Officer. She writes a blog about writing and posts short fiction on her website. She also publishes a photo-story blog, recording the adventures of her teddy bear. He is much more popular online than she is. She likes to run away from zombies in her spare time.
Website: www.alobear.co.uk
Website: aloysius-bear.dreamwidth.org

Water: Our Source of Life
by Nerisha Kemraj

Luke's pod hurtled into the river. Removing his spacesuit, he still struggled for air. Three months in space only to return and die on Earth?

No.

He lunged himself into the river, gulping water in an effort to quench his undying thirst.

Nothing worked.

He felt his body slowly dry up, skin cracked, lips burst open, even his tongue froze into place. The creature's blood had infected him, as it did the other three dehydrated astronauts.

Planet 2019 TP19 was a failed mission.

Luke's eyes shrivelled, with a final view of the contaminated stream.

Within days, Earth's water became undrinkable.

Nerisha Kemraj resides in Durban, South Africa with her husband and two mischievous daughters. She has work published/accepted in various publications, both print and online. She holds a Bachelor's degree in Communication Science, and a Post Graduate Certificate in Education from University of South Africa.
Amazon: *amazon.com/author/nerisha_kemraj*
Facebook: *Nerishakemrajwriter*

Death from Above
by Annie Percik

The sky is burning. It looks as though the clouds themselves are actually aflame. Steaming fog covers the area, flashes of orange, red and yellow bursting forth in elegant streams that clash and explode into lethal firework displays of coloured sparks. What sounds like thunder emanates from deep sinuous throats, flying the flags of power, claims of territory, bellows of rage and declarations of superior strength. Dark shadows move across the sky, their true shapes obscured by the effects of their duels. They fight on, above. Anything on the ground must seek shelter or risk annihilation. The dragons have awoken.

Annie Percik lives in London with her husband, Dave, where she is revising her first novel, whilst working as a University Complaints Officer. She writes a blog about writing and posts short fiction on her website. She also publishes a photo-story blog, recording the adventures of her teddy bear. He is much more popular online than she is. She likes to run away from zombies in her spare time.
Website: www.alobear.co.uk
Website: aloysius-bear.dreamwidth.org

It's All Fun and Games
Until the Apocalypse
by Rennie St. James

Outwit. Outplay. Outlast. Survive.

It started as a game...until the Apocalypse changed the rules.

Red rivers of blood was not a literary allusion. War, death, famine, and conquest rode through every city. No one had immunity. The lights were extinguished as the tribes of man cowered, fought, and bled. It was no longer a game. It was no longer a choice.

Outwit. Outplay. Outlast. Survive.

I won. I am the last human standing. All I've won is another day of living on this hellish earth.

Outwit. Outplay. Outlast.

There is no survival. No one gets out alive.

Not even me.

Rennie St. James shares several similarities with her fictional characters (heroes and villains alike) including a love of chocolate, horror movies, martial arts, history, yoga, and travel. She doesn't have a pet mountain lion but is proudly owned by three rescue kitties. They live in relative harmony in beautiful southwestern Virginia (United States). The first three books of Rennie's urban fantasy series, The Rahki Chronicles, are available now. A new series and several standalone stories are already in the works as future releases.
Website: writerRSJ.com

Survival
by Aditya Deshmukh

Tears roll down your sunken cheeks and break as they meet the broken Earth. Something glints below. You kneel to find a single spherical tear trickling down a sharp edge.

You touch it. The blade turns crimson. With your other hand, now careful, you pull the hilt. It doesn't yield. You dig the soft earth around the blade. Curling your fingers around the hilt, you yank the blade out. A head dangles by the sword's free end, white and dead and devoured by worms. "Mom, I found Dad!"

Mom wails. But she starts picking the worms. "Delicious. Have some, son."

Aditya Deshmukh is a mechanical engineering student who likes exploring the mechanics of writing as much as he likes tinkering with machines. He writes dark fiction and poetry. He is published in over three dozen anthologies and has a poetry book "Opium Hearts" and a collection of drabbles coming out soon. He likes chatting with people who share similar interests, so feel free to check him out.
Facebook: adityadeshmukhwrites
Website: www.adityadeshmukh.com

The Wall
by Susanne Thomas

The hundred-foot Wall was everything, towering, and ever visible.

Massive quakes had taken down the mountains. The clouded atmosphere only allowed shrubs and scrub trees, so nothing obscured it. It was patrolled and maintained constantly.

The Wall was fifty feet thick, in a massive ring, with no entrance or exit.

The Outside was a horror scape of remnants from Old Civ. Vicious bands of desperate mutants tried their best to get Inside to resources.

The people from within led quiet lives of fear, desperation, and sacrifice.

They never noticed the tunnelled hole that began in the middle of the Inside.

Susanne Thomas reads, writes, parents, and teaches from the windy west in Wyoming, and she loves fantasy, science fiction, speculative fiction, poetry, children's books, science, coffee, and puns.
Website: www.themightierpenn.com
Facebook: SusanneThomasAuthor

The Stench
by Jodi Jensen

The stench was all over her, just like the others. Elijah scooted back, away from his mother. That smell meant only one thing.

Death.

She'd been gone awhile, but he didn't have the courage to leave until the putrid scent of rotting flesh became too much to bear.

He wandered into the litter-strewn street, staring at the abandoned cars parked at crazy angles, doors hanging open.

Then he heard it. A pitiful wail echoing thin and frail in the air. The sound of another life.

Elijah searched until he found her.

A little girl.

The stench was all over her.

Jodi Jensen grew up moving from California, to Massachusetts, and a few other places in between, before finally settling in Utah at the ripe old age of nine. The nomadic life fed her sense of adventure as a child and the wanderlust continues to this day. With a passion for old cemeteries, historical buildings and sweeping sagas of days gone by, it was only natural she'd dream of time traveling to all the places that sparked her imagination.

Sweet Flesh
by Dawn DeBraal

Hawley broke in through the cellar window. Rows of golden sunshine in jars, his reward. He bowed his head in prayer, thanking the woman of the house who had lovingly canned the peaches. He opened the first jar. Its sticky sweetness oozed down his hand while pulling the peach out of the container. He bit into the mouth-watering flesh, wiping his chin on his clothes. Hawley fell asleep with a full stomach for the first time since the blast. He woke up to his own screams, feeling thousands of biting ants covering his body, enjoying the sweetness of the peaches.

Dawn DeBraal *lives in rural Wisconsin with her husband Red, two rat terriers, and a cat. She has discovered that her love of telling a good story can be written. Published stories with Palm-sized press, Spillwords, Mercurial Stories, Potato Soup Journal, Edify Fiction, Zimbell House Publishing, Clarendon House Publishing, Blood Song Books, Black Hare Press, Fantasia Divinity, Cafelit, Reanimated Writers, Guilty Pleasures, Unholy Trinity, The World of Myth, Dastaan World, Vamp Cat, Runcible Spoon, Dark Christmas, Siren's Call, Iron Horse Publishing, Falling Star Magazine 2019 Pushcart Nominee.*
Amazon: amazon.com/Dawn-DeBraal/e/B07STL8DLX

All in a Day's Work
by Chris Bannor

Smoke filled the air and filth covered every inch of her skin. No matter how she struggled to keep it out, the grit and ash were everywhere; a grey stain on a world turned orange.

Daybreak never came gently, and the heat swarmed before her eyes. She didn't think they'd ever learn the truth of the Coming, of how They arrived, and who pulled the trigger first, but the old truths didn't matter anymore. She watched fire-filled skies on the horizon and gripped her gear tight. She had miles to go before another dawn. A water-finder's job was never done.

__Chris Bannor__ is a science fiction and fantasy writer who lives in Southern California. Chris learned her love of genre stories from her mother at an early age and has never veered far from that path. She also enjoys musical theater and road trips with her family, but is a general homebody otherwise. Twitter: @BannorChris

Brown
by Justin Hunter

Brown is the colour of nature. The fading sun takes all that was vibrant and changes to darkness.

The colour green is only a shadow of its former self. It's rusting paint on old Fords. It's a billboard for a business long since shut.

The colour of green means nothing without nature.

When green no longer makes someone think about life, then it's no longer relevant.

Brown is the truth that all of us who are still alive must face.

There's also blue. The colour of the endless sea. I face the sea now and it's turning.

It's turning brown.

Justin Hunter is the author of nine novels and over thirty published short stories. His publishers include Severed Press, J. Ellington Ashton Press, Morbidbooks, JWK Fiction, and many more. He lives with his wife and four boys in Missouri, USA.

Quiet
by G. Allen Wilbanks

Jarrod huddled in the storm cellar, listening to the "muties" rummage through his house above. Items clattered directly over his head as the creatures emptied cupboards and drawers searching for food. They would be gone soon. He only had to remain quiet a few minutes more.

Genetic manipulation had released this plague on the world, and now what was left of humanity could only hide and hope to remain unseen.

Jarrod shifted to relieve a cramp in his leg. His shoulder brushed a plastic bowl off the shelf next to him to the concrete floor.

The room above went quiet.

G. Allen Wilbanks is a member of the Horror Writers Association (HWA) and has published over 50 short stories in various magazines and on-line venues. He is the author of two short story collections, and the novel, When Darkness Comes.
Website: www.gallenwilbanks.com
Blog: DeepDarkThoughts.com.

Poof!
by Mason Harold Hilden

Dan always hated foraging for the group. That changed when he spotted a secured rope hanging over a cliff, a deceased climber, a backpack, and a bag of cheese puffs!

Seeing reward over risk, adrenaline enabled Dan to traverse the rope. But excitement led to losing his grip, and making his only logical choice, Dan grabbed the puffs while falling off the cliff.

Panic trumped joy as the bag explodes in Dan's grip sending puffs everywhere. Screaming, he realised there was one puff still in his hand. Quickly putting it in his mouth, Dan thought, *Damn, does this ever taste—*

Mason Harold Hilden has dabbled in animation and comic-book scripting.

Living the Dream
by Stuart Conover

Billy was regretting looking out the window.

"Janet…" His voice trailed off.

All he had ever wanted to be was an astronaut.

Here he was, living the dream.

Which had just become a nightmare.

Janet hissed in annoyance.

"What?"

The new kid was eager, but every little thing got to him.

An emotional roller coaster.

She had no idea how he had been assigned to the International Space Station.

Turning back, Billy stood motionless, pale, looking out a window.

"What is it now?" she muttered and looked outside.

Just in time to see the seventh mushroom cloud blooming on Earth.

Stuart Conover is a father, husband, rescue dog owner, published author, blogger, journalist, horror enthusiast, comic book geek, science fiction junkie, and IT professional. With all of that to cram in daily, we have no idea if or when he sleeps or how he gets writing done! (We suspect it has to do with having evil clones.) Stuart is a Chicago native and runs the author resource Horror Tree.

How it Began
by Gabriella Balcom

Summer temperatures dropped from the low hundreds to the eighties, delighting Texans. They celebrated the unexpected seventies much more.

But people everywhere were startled when reports of more drastic weather changes began pouring in, and forecasters tossed around the words "unparalleled" and "cataclysmic."

Polar ice caps which had been shrinking gradually started melting at an alarming rate. Then rain forests experienced hail, ice storms, and freezing. Volcanoes erupted, including ones which had lain dormant for years. Valleys and mountains formed where none had previously been, oceans evaporated, and the air began to catch fire.

And that was only the beginning.

Gabriella Balcom lives in Texas with her family, loves reading and writing, and thinks she was born with a book in her hands. She works in a mental health field, and writes fantasy, horror/thriller, romance, children's stories, and sci-fi. She likes travelling, music, good shows, photography, history, interesting tales, and animals. Gabriella says she's a sucker for a great story and loves forests, mountains, and back roads which might lead who knows where. She has a weakness for lasagne, garlic bread, tacos, cheese, and chocolate, but not necessarily in that order.
Facebook: GabriellaBalcom.lonestarauthor

The Commune
by Raven Corinn Carluk

Brigitte stood with hands on hips, glaring at the couple. "You agreed to the rules."

"You really can't expect us to haul water all day," Husband complained.

Brigitte's eyes hardened.

"It's not fair." Wife sounded ready to cry.

"Could always go back to life outside my walls." Brigitte was implacable, unmoved by their pleas. Veteran members of Sanctuary knew she had limits to her altruism.

Husband moved around her. She drew her knife, gutting him in a quick move. Wife screamed until Brigitte slit her throat.

"You don't work, you don't eat." Brigitte cleaned her blade. Dinner service was resumed.

Raven Corinn Carluk writes dark fantasy, paranormal romance, and anything else that catches her interest. She's authored five novels, where she explores themes of love and acceptance. Her shorter pieces, usually from her darker side, can be found in Black Hare Press anthologies, at Detritus Online, and through Alban Lake Publishers.
Twitter: @ravencorinn
Website: RavenCorinnCarluk.Blogspot.Com

A Stirring of Fire and Steel
by Jo Seysener

Jump.

Flames licked my shoes. The steel girder began to bend. I shifted, not yet ready to fling myself over the abyss.

One building across, one window down.

Rubble piled behind me, preventing a run up or going back. Death lay either way.

The sky exploded again. Flaming rock sliced through buildings like butter left in the sun. My tongue stuck to the roof of my mouth. The soles of my boots began to melt, dribbling into long strands of spaghetti.

I exhaled in a whoosh and leaped, leaving my boots stuck to the steel, laces tangled around my ankle.

Jo Seysener is a mum of three crazies, a scatter of chickens, a decrepit kelpie and a rambunctious GSD. She lives with her husband near Brisbane, Australia. When she is not exposing her kids to cult story books from her childhood, she can be found in the kitchen experimenting with new flavours and pairings. She adores alpacas.
Facebook: joseysener
Website: www.joseysener.com

Seeker
by Jem McCusker

The year is 2099, the hour of midnight is almost upon us. Rations are stocked, it should give us six months.

The Silent Regime took control of technology in the year of 2019. We hope our efforts have been enough. It's been three days now and we have not felt its watchful eye upon us.

We leave this message as a warning for you, the survivors. Destroy technology before it destroys you…

I hear a ding. Technology. I drop my pen and look for the traitor. My daughter's eyes shine an artificial blue, her movements robotic.

"Found you." She smiled.

Jem McCusker is a middle grade fiction author, living near Brisbane with her two sons and husband. Her first book Stone Guardians the Rise of Eden was released in 2018 and she is working on the sequel. She is releasing a Novella for the Four Quills writing group, A Storm of Wind and Rain series in July, 2019. She longs to be a full-time author, won't wear yellow and loves rabbits. Follow Jem on Twitter, Facebook and Instagram. Details on her website.
Website: www.jemmccusker.com

Dreams We Catch
by Umair Mirxa

Damon pulled Emilia closer, wrapping her up in his arms, as another bomb dropped on top of their bunker.

"I don't think we'll make it, Damon," she said.

He noticed, in the dim light, her parched lips and the dark circles under her eyes. She was a sack of bones in his embrace.

"Of course, we will," he whispered, giving her a quick kiss.

"Catch us a dream, then."

"Alright. We'll live in Barcelona…"

Damon felt Emilia's head drop and tears stream down his own cheeks. He closed his eyes and dreamed of seeing her again in the afterlife.

Umair Mirxa lives in Karachi, Pakistan. His first published story, 'Awareness', appeared on Spillwords Press. He has also had stories accepted for anthologies from Zombie Pirate Publishing, Blood Song Books, Fantasia Divinity Magazine and Publishing, and Iron Faerie Publishing. He is a massive J.R.R. Tolkien fan, and loves everything to do with fantasy and mythology. He enjoys football, history, music, movies, TV shows, and comic books, and wishes with all his heart that dragons were real.
Website: www.umairmirxa.com
Facebook: UMirxa12

Islands
by Steven Lord

"Don't forget eggs, dear!"

Tracy grunted as she squeezed through the window and into the coracle. The freshly caught fish lay at the bottom of the boat, hopefully enough to trade for the whole shopping list. Pyramid-dwellers always ripped off those from the Dome—with more floors above water level, they had more resources and held the upper hand in negotiations.

She glanced around at the other islands as she started to row. Another had sunk beneath the rising tide last week, but the Dome would be safe for years. Funny, she thought. They used to scrape the sky.

Steven Lord is a debut author based in the south of England. He is currently attempting to cram writing in alongside a busy day job, with varying levels of success. While his long-term aspiration is to get a novel published, at present he would be pretty pleased with a drabble or two.

Preparation is Everything
by Maxine Churchman

They mocked me when I started the project all those years ago. Called me Bunker Bill, laughed in my face even, but they soon wanted in when the devastation began. Oh, yes. Good job I thought of strong locks and a gun; there's limited space down here.

Shame I couldn't let Celia in. It might get lonely and she was hot. Didn't think we'd get on so well though; not after I shot her husband and kids.

I've been feeling pretty smug. Then the power went off. I have a few candles, but I should have thought about a generator.

Maxine Churchman lives in Essex UK and has recently started writing poetry and short stories to share. Her interests include leaning to improve her writing, reading, knitting, walking and teaching yoga. She is also planning a novel.

Armageddon
By Eddie D. Moore

The ground shook and a jagged fissure ripped open the land, and a wave of lava burned everything for miles, clearing a path for the demonic armies that soon followed. Seconds later, an interdimensional tear ripped open the sky and millions of angels claimed the skies.

Those living on the Earth found themselves trapped in the middle of the epic battle, and they scattered in panic in a vain attempt to find a safe haven. The rivers soon ran blood red.

I put my time machine in reverse, and said to myself, "I think that's quite far enough for today."

Eddie D. Moore travels hundreds of hours a year, and he fills that time by listening to audiobooks. When he isn't playing with his grandchildren, he writes his own stories. You can find a list of his publications on his blog or by visiting his Amazon Author Page. While you're there, be sure to pick up a copy of his mini-anthology Misfits & Oddities.
Website: eddiedmoore.wordpress.com
Amazon: amazon.com/author/eddiedmoore

Day 15 – When the Virus Comes to Town
by Carole de Monclin

"Chill, sis. This shit's fake news."

"People dying isn't fake news."

"Far away from here. Avian flu, swine flu… Nothing ever comes of it."

"For once, I hope you're right. Hey, where are you going? We're supposed to stay indoors."

"Paul's."

"Wait, didn't he just come back from China?"

"Uh-huh."

"But… That's where most cases are."

"I talked to Paul. He's fine."

"You know people are contagious during the incubation period, right?"

"China's big. He went nowhere near the infected areas."

"What if somebody on the plane did? Please, don't go."

"Always so melodramatic. Later."

"Irresponsible arse."

"Love you too."

Carole de Monclin *travels both the real world and imaginary ones. She's lived in France, Australia, and the USA; visited 25+ countries; and explored Mars, Ceres, and many distant planets. She writes to invite people on a journey. Her stories can be found in The Arcanist, The Deep Space Anthology, and every volume of the Dark Drabbles series.*
Website: CaroledeMonclin.com
Twitter: @CaroledeMonclin

Day 29 – When the Veneer Cracks, Predators Prowl

by Carole de Monclin

Along the deserted streets, great apes hunt in pack, looting, beating, killing.

At their approach, we snuff our candlelight. Even without electricity or water, those four walls were our haven.

Until tonight.

Earlier, Mom scattered junk on the front lawn, clothes, toys, books…to mimic the houses already ransacked.

A window shatters. I stifle a scream; our camouflage failed.

Footsteps on the stairs. One set. The door is kicked open.

Slam. The menacing silhouette crumples.

Mom swings the bat again, then whispers, "Grab your bag."

Before other plunderers follow inside, we dash through the back door into the unwelcoming night.

__Carole de Monclin__ travels both the real world and imaginary ones. She's lived in France, Australia, and the USA; visited 25+ countries; and explored Mars, Ceres, and many distant planets. She writes to invite people on a journey. Her stories can be found in The Arcanist, The Deep Space Anthology, and every volume of the Dark Drabbles series.

Website: CaroledeMonclin.com
Twitter: @CaroledeMonclin

Day 82 – When Safety Is but a Memory
by Carole de Monclin

To avoid attention, I walk less travelled roads.

I usually ignore the corpses. Most of the fresh cadavers didn't die from the virus. Cholera, dysentery, famine, gunshots…

But my supplies are running low, so when I happen upon a body that looks emaciated but not diseased, I carefully approach and start exploring his pockets.

A hand grabs my wrist. A trap!

I try to break free. He squeezes tighter and sneers, "Sweetheart, we're gonna have fun."

My fingers find my boot knife. I slash deep into the carotid and bolt without a backward glance.

I've killed before. I'll kill again.

Carole de Monclin *travels both the real world and imaginary ones. She's lived in France, Australia, and the USA; visited 25+ countries; and explored Mars, Ceres, and many distant planets. She writes to invite people on a journey. Her stories can be found in The Arcanist, The Deep Space Anthology, and every volume of the Dark Drabbles series.*
Website: CaroledeMonclin.com
Twitter: @CaroledeMonclin

Day 198 – When Only the Indispensable Remains

by Carole de Monclin

-Two plastic bottles

-Small tarp

-Matchbox

Inventorying the content of my backpack is routine.

-Pair of sneakers

-Change of clothes

Anything non-essential or that can be scavenged later must be left behind.

-First aid kit

-Two hunting knives

-Three toilet paper rolls

All alone, I must balance between mobility and the tools for survival.

-Nineteen energy bars

-Blanket

-Toothbrush and paste

-Soap

I toss the flashlight. Dead batteries. I doubt I'll find new ones.

-One useless shiny black rectangle I can't bear to part with

Fully discharged.

But its memory holds the precious photos pushing me forward in this nightmare.

Carole de Monclin *travels both the real world and imaginary ones. She's lived in France, Australia, and the USA; visited 25+ countries; and explored Mars, Ceres, and many distant planets. She writes to invite people on a journey. Her stories can be found in The Arcanist, The Deep Space Anthology, and every volume of the Dark Drabbles series.*
Website: CaroledeMonclin.com
Twitter: @CaroledeMonclin

The Final Battle
by Lyndsey Ellis-Holloway

The steady, rhythmic thump of the drum entwined with the footfalls of the warriors.

Before them lay the previous fallen, a carpet of bloody corpses, from tribes they had destroyed in order to survive in this desolate world.

Their enemy, inexperienced fighters, stood at the bottom of the hill, despair clear upon their faces.

The sky was dark, reflecting the mood of the two tribes meeting on the battlefield.

Thunder boomed and lightning flashed, highlighting their gaunt faces, determined, all ready to die for their cause.

The warriors would triumph, decimating the last tribe from existence. Ultimately, they would survive.

Lyndsey Ellis-Holloway is a writer from Knaresborough, UK. She writes fantasy, sci-fi, horror and dystopian stories, focussing on compelling characters and layering in myth and legend at every opportunity. When she's not writing she spends time with her husband, her dogs and her friends enjoying activities such as walking, movies, conventions and of course writing for fun as well!

Virus
by Anika Claire

A virus, they say. Mild panic begins when social media goes down, phone networks a few days later.

Technicians scramble, leaders call for calm. But when the commercial EFT systems crash, there's looting in the town centres—the worried masses stockpiling what supplies they can, the skies eerily quiet.

Then the lights go out.

The death of society is all thrashing and clawing, the stronger preying on the weak, the vulnerable crushed by the ugly side of humans' desperate drive for survival.

In his dark basement, surrounded by years' worth of stockpiled supplies of food and dissatisfaction, the hacker smiles.

Anika Claire lives in Brisbane, Australia with her young family, where she alternates between making maps and escaping to other worlds, through either reading or creating them. You can find her reviewing and podcasting about books at;
Website: teainthetreetops.com
Instagram: @anni.treetops

Always Prepared
by Stuart Conover

Jeremy has spent two decades prepping for the end of times.

His bunker was stocked with weapons, food, air recycling, generators, agricultural equipment to grow his own food, and more!

He'd thought of everything.

It could support his entire family for two to three generations if need be.

There had been a lot of work to make it happen.

Late night fights with his wife, making her and the children help.

His family was the one thing he hadn't factored in.

The years of abuse meant they would all be safe.

He just hadn't counted on them locking him out.

Stuart Conover is a father, husband, rescue dog owner, published author, blogger, journalist, horror enthusiast, comic book geek, science fiction junkie, and IT professional. With all of that to cram in daily, we have no idea if or when he sleeps or how he gets writing done! (We suspect it has to do with having evil clones.) Stuart is a Chicago native and runs the author resource Horror Tree.

Moonshot
by Johnny Hempseed

The thing that ended the world had missed the Earth.

People celebrated right up until the moment it punched a hole in the moon. The tides shifted, and fault-lines became unstable.

Humanity scrambled to save itself, and had partially succeeded. Lives were lost in the disasters, of course, but the bunkers and floating Habitat Modules were built and deployed quickly.

A hand hovers over a button safe in the bedrock of a mountain, if they can just alter the path by about a foot, they might stop it. The woman sucked in a deep breath and let her digit fall.

Johnny Hempseed is a writer of horror, science fiction, and dark fantasy.
Facebook: JohnnyHempseedCurator

Daddy's Sidecar
by Raven Corinn Carluk

I turned off the main road and looked down at Shelly. My daughter remained asleep in her little cradle.

"This isn't Mad Max. We're in Perth. Nobody gonna attack here." My wife never believed when I said the plague was coming. For everyone, not just America. Complained when I stored food at my uncle's place, laughed as I built motorised bicycles for cargo and our little girl.

Shit got bad when it hit. Traffic jams for miles. Between petrol and peddle power, though, I got out of the city while she died. Guess it *wasn't* just a homemade bodge job.

Raven Corinn Carluk writes dark fantasy, paranormal romance, and anything else that catches her interest. She's authored five novels, where she explores themes of love and acceptance. Her shorter pieces, usually from her darker side, can be found in Black Hare Press anthologies, at Detritus Online, and through Alban Lake Publishers.
Twitter: @ravencorinn
Website: RavenCorinnCarluk.Blogspot.Com

A Sunrise Moment
by Susanne Thomas

Stan stood outside, mask on to filter the open air. It was already hot despite being a winter morning. It'd been years since temperatures had dipped below 90. He still loved watching the sunrise though.

Stan stood in his protective gear, sweltering, to see the prismatic rays of Sol climb above the horizon. It played off the broken forest in front of him, glinting off trees long turned to stone.

The day would begin soon, and he'd have to move back inside or risk damage from the heat and the risen sun. But for a moment, he was at peace.

Susanne Thomas *reads, writes, parents, and teaches from the windy west in Wyoming, and she loves fantasy, science fiction, speculative fiction, poetry, children's books, science, coffee, and puns.*
Website: www.themightierpenn.com
Facebook: SusanneThomasAuthor

Two Minute Warning
by Dale Parnell

The warning sirens finally shut off. I don't know what they were supposed to achieve anyway. There isn't a bunker in the world strong enough to protect against this. The phone lines are jammed, have been for hours. It doesn't matter, there's no one I need to call. I climb the stairs up to the roof, the sounds of crying coming from open windows below me. The city lays in wait, collective arms hugging itself, a million breaths held. I can see the detonation out over the horizon, a flash of white, turning orange then red as blood. It's beautiful.

Dale Parnell lives in Staffordshire, England, with his wife and their imaginary dog, Moriarty. He has self-published one collection of short stories, "The Green Cathedral" and is currently putting the finishing touches to his second collection, "Bramble". Dale also writes poetry, and is lucky enough to have pieces featured in several anthologies. Facebook: shortfictionauthor

V.R. or Is It?
by C.L. Williams

I try out the new virtual reality helmet. I start playing a game called *Let the World End*. I decimate everything in front of me. I am challenging everything and everyone, coming out the victor on all occasions. What only feels like a few minutes, I have already unlocked the final stage of this game. I get to drop a bomb more powerful than any weapon of mass destruction ever produced. I drop the bomb and watch everything turn to ash.

After winning, I remove the helmet and see the destruction in front of me. Maybe it wasn't a game.

C.L. Williams is an independent author from central Virginia. He has written eight poetry books, four novellas, one novel, and a contributor to multiple anthologies, with the most recent appearance being an all-ages anthology titled Temoli from Thazbook. His most recent poetry book, The Paradox Complex, features the poem "Sad Crying Clown" that is now a video on YouTube directed by Matthew Mark Hunter of MMH Productions. C.L. Williams is currently working on his first sci-fi book, an all-ages book titled Novo: Away from Earth. When not writing, C.L. Williams is reading and sharing the work of other independent authors. Facebook: writer434
Twitter: @writer_434

Mother Earth
by Michelle Anderson

Many knew the end was near. They thought it would come from famine, disease, ice, fire, nuclear war or aliens from afar. They were all wrong.

It took only a matter of days. Every animal, bird, insect and sea creature became the foot soldiers raining death across the globe. Fangs, claws, beaks and venoms were their weapons of choice. It was a coordinated massacre of epic proportions. In the end, only a few humans survived. Scattered and scared it would take hundreds of years to rebuild.

The Mother had taken her Earth back from those who sought to destroy it.

Michelle Anderson is a relatively new writer who has had a non-fiction story published on lifeasahuman.com as well as numerous articles on medium.com. She is an avid reader with a penchant for those dark and eerie stories that keep you up at night with all of the lights on.

The Scent of Blood
by Annie Percik

The knife slips. Bright blood blossoms on Katie's finger. I grab for her and cover her mouth with my hand before she starts wailing. She only wanted to help, but the scent of blood will draw them to us more surely than even a little girl's cries. Katie's wide eyes stare at me above where my hand is pressed into her flesh. I raise a finger to my lips and she nods, tears sparkling on her cheeks. I wrap a rag tightly round her injured hand and prepare to run, as the first moans echo through the woods around us.

Annie Percik lives in London with her husband, Dave, where she is revising her first novel, whilst working as a University Complaints Officer. She writes a blog about writing and posts short fiction on her website. She also publishes a photo-story blog, recording the adventures of her teddy bear. He is much more popular online than she is. She likes to run away from zombies in her spare time.
Website: www.alobear.co.uk
Website: aloysius-bear.dreamwidth.org

Behold! I Saw a White Horse
by Cecelia Hopkins-Drewer

Chemical weapons were forbidden, yet that was what the repurposed Mustang P51 aircraft was carrying. Painted white and lacking its former US Army markings, it flew across the enemy airspace like an arrow.

Designed to dive bomb, the Mustang approached the civilian settlement. It dropped its payload, and zoomed away, eager to be out of range of the virus, as well as the guns of the defenders.

On the ground, the canisters broke open. Infection began to spread. Human beings gurgled and began to stumble around as zombies. Once mindful of integrity, the nations were reduced to exchanging terror attacks.

Cecelia Hopkins-Drewer lives in Adelaide, South Australia. She has written a Masters paper on H.P. Lovecraft, and her weird poetry has been published in THE MENTOR (edited by Ron Clarke), and SPECTRAL REALMS (edited by S.T. Joshi). Her novels include a teenage vampire series commencing with MYSTIC EVERMORE. Short stories have been published in WORLDS, ANGELS & MONSTERS, BEYOND, STORMING AREA 51, and UNRAVEL. (Dark Drabbles anthologies edited by Dean Kershaw).
Amazon: amazon.com/Cecelia-Hopkins-Drewer/e/B071G968NM
Website: shopkin39.wixsite.com/website

As She Smiles
by Tim Sturk

So long as she smiles, I can face the world. I can face the liquid death that haunts it.

So long as she smiles, I can go outside to scavenge, and return. I can draw back from the depths that call me.

Most have walked into the water, but not I. I will stay here, so long as she smiles.

Some nights I cannot sleep, and walk outside. I stare into the blackness then, and hear its call. The only thing that stops me is her smile.

But now the smile has changed, distorted by the waves.

Her final smile.

Tim Sturk is an author of dark fantasy, horror, and historical fiction.

Kudzu
by Angela Zimmerman

What people don't plan for after civilisation falls is how much plant life there will be. Infrastructure doesn't crumble. It has to bow to the weight of tons of greenery returning to domination.

And any human left will meet the same fate.

Thomas made his camp in the remains of a convenience store. The sides had always been covered in kudzu, but now it had made its way inside. He would often spend whole days clearing the invasive vines from his belongings.

Until one night he awoke to a kudzu vine tightening around his throat.

Then he woke no more.

Angela Zimmerman is a writer living in the Southern United States. She has been published in Unnvering Magazine and Coffin Bell. You can find her personal writings at Conjure and Coffee.
Website: conjureandcoffee.com

And Then There Were None
by K.T. Tate

It was our superheroes that killed us. We thought them a blessing. We didn't know that they'd just attract ever increasing threats. It started with criminals, then supervillains and that was it for a while. Then others came. Space tyrants, monsters, and all sorts attracted by their power.

One by one our superheroes fell. Each conflict taking a toll. But what could we do? We weren't super.

Now we wait on this dying planet, torn apart by the ever devouring horror that hangs in our skies. If you find this record, don't rely on superheroes, be your own, arm everyone.

K.T. Tate lives in Cambridgeshire in the UK. She writes mainly weird fiction, cosmic horror and strange monster stories.
Website: eldritchhollow.wordpress.com
Tumblr: eldritch-hollow.tumblr.com

The Collector
by K.T. Tate

The robed figure wandered the land. Their arms outstretched, their hands reaching. Every footprint morphed the ground. Every touch contaminated.

Where it went, all life stopped. Everything changed, becoming crystalline. People were left exquisite statues. Birds hung in the air, their crystal plumage defying gravity.

The explosions the military waged against it froze in spectacular shard-like fractals. And yet it walked on. Neither man nor nature could stand against it.

Hysteria rose. Some sacrificed themselves, seeking it out. Others fought. Our leaders were found in their bunkers, horrifically immortalised.

The world doesn't end, but spins deathless, a perfect exhibit, forever.

K.T. Tate lives in Cambridgeshire in the UK. She writes mainly weird fiction, cosmic horror and strange monster stories.
Website: eldritchhollow.wordpress.com
Tumblr: eldritch-hollow.tumblr.com

Houses, Humans, and Other Myths
by Shelly Jarvis

The wind is hot and brown and scratchy. I cover my eyes against it, but I can't keep it from digging into my skin, carving hieroglyphs on the walls of my face. It spells out the doom of my existence.

A sheet of metal juts from the ground and I brace myself against it, trying to be as small as possible. I've heard tales of the time before, when there were "houses" and people could live inside them, but I don't know if I believe that.

To have houses you would need humans, and they are few and far between.

Shelly Jarvis is a speculative fiction author from West Virginia, US. She found a life-long love of sci-fi and fantasy in the 3rd grade when she found Madeleine L'Engle's "A Wrinkle in Time." Shelly is an avid reader, a Whovian, the ideal viewer of dog rescue videos, and undoubtedly Ravenclaw. She currently has two YA sci-fi books available for purchase on Amazon.
Website: www.ShellyJarvis.com

PMT: Project Manager Tension
by Lyndsey Ellis-Holloway

It started with unplugging their firewalls, then I hired some excellent hackers.

They never saw it coming; the apocalypse…started by an angry project manager.

One insult too many, suffered on the hottest day of the year, when everything I tried to do went wrong.

I ruined them out of spite. Tore down their infrastructure from inside, made sure they couldn't rebuild with some wonderfully nasty computer viruses.

Once they fell, so did the rest. No more businesses run by machines, no more internet.

It all fell.

Now there is nothing.

No PM's. No projects. Just…silence.

Isn't it blissful?

Lyndsey Ellis-Holloway is a writer from Knaresborough, UK. She writes fantasy, sci-fi, horror and dystopian stories, focussing on compelling characters and layering in myth and legend at every opportunity. When she's not writing she spends time with her husband, her dogs and her friends enjoying activities such as walking, movies, conventions and of course writing for fun as well!

Forgotten Cemetery
by Jensen Reed

Overgrown grass and weeds brushed Kailee's pants as she meandered around the forgotten cemetery. Dawn had risen and she needed to return home. Yet…

She reached the last row of stones and looked towards the ivy covered wall separating the peaceful old cemetery from the horrid mass graves on the other side. The dates on the headstones were worn away, showing just how long it had been since they had stopped burying people individually. She closed her eyes and tried to envision life back then, but the reality she was stuck in chased away any fantasy she could dream up.

Jensen Reed is a multi-published short story author, lead admin for Writing Bad, and mama to two boys. She dabbles in reading and writing genres but particularly enjoys feeding characters to zombies and making readers cry. Find her book links, flash fiction, and connect with her on her website. Website: authorjensenreed.wordpress.com

Living Off the Land
by Maxine Churchman

Dad used to take me camping in the mountains when I was little. "Living off the land" he called it. "You never know when you will need these skills" he would say.

I hated those trips. The cold and insects were bad enough but having to kill animals; that was the worst. Soft warm bodies cooling, blood, dead eyes. I was a great disappointment to him; I always refused, I wouldn't even watch. They tasted good though.

He'd be proud of me now, sitting here in the mountains roasting pigeons on a campfire while the rest of the world burns.

Maxine Churchman lives in Essex UK and has recently started writing poetry and short stories to share. Her interests include leaning to improve her writing, reading, knitting, walking and teaching yoga. She is also planning a novel.

Rematch
by Steven Lord

God and the Devil stood alone in the barren desert. At their feet, the body lay face down in the sand, one blistered arm outstretched, reaching for water that never came.

"Well, that's the last of them," the Almighty surmised. "Finally!"

Lucifer checked his pocket-watch. "Almost 3.5 billion years. Longest game yet."

"I thought you had me a while back with that Cuba thing."

Beelzebub grinned. "I was that close!"

They looked around at the desolation for a second.

"Shall we go again?"

"Nothing else to do," mooted Our Lord. "Do you want to be black or white this time?"

Steven Lord is a debut author based in the south of England. He is currently attempting to cram writing in alongside a busy day job, with varying levels of success. While his long-term aspiration is to get a novel published, at present he would be pretty pleased with a drabble or two.

No U-Turn
by Ximena Escobar

"Is this a monsoon, Mummy?" (You could hear the terror in little Ben's voice.)

"It's just rain," I said, a downpour lashing, wipers going, windows fogging up.

"Yes, and the car's flooding," said Frank.

Ben started crying uncontrollably.

"For god's sake, Frank!"

"Go back!" sobbed Ben.

"We're on the motorway, stupid!"

"It's just rain, baby. Look at the pretty light over there." A monstrous truck whizzing past.

"Aliens!"

"Sunshine, darling."

"It's the end of the world!" said Frank.

We all died just then. But no apocalypse graced the others.

The world was dying unspectacularly. (And there was no turning back.)

Ximena Escobar is an emerging author of literary fiction and poetry. Originally from Chile, she is the author of a translation into Spanish of the Broadway Musical "The Wizard of Oz", and of an original adaptation of the same, "Navidad en Oz". Clarendon House Publications published her first short story in the UK, "The Persistence of Memory", and Literally Stories her first online publication with "The Green Light". She has since had several acceptances from other publishers and is working very hard exploring new exciting avenues in her writing.
She lives in Nottingham with her family.
Facebook: <u>Ximenautora</u>

Breath of Life
by J.W. Garrett

Hugging his child, Chris glanced at his wife. Their foreheads briefly touched. His eyes sparkled with hope for the future, just not his. They were the last family to leave Earth, in charge of the failing oxygen reserves for the remaining units. Climate war had decimated the planet. A new home awaited across the galaxy. Reports confirmed life, water, oxygen—resources depleted here. He attached the last two tanks, one to his daughter, the other his wife, sent them to the waiting ship.

His lungs burned. Waiting… Only a few seconds…

Sucking in tainted air, he smiled. Free at last.

J.W. Garrett has been writing in one form or another since she was a teenager. She currently lives in Florida with her family but loves the mountains of Virginia where she was born. Her writings include YA fantasy as well as short stories. Since completing Remeon's Quest-Earth Year 1930, the prequel in her YA fantasy series, Realms of Chaos, she has been hard at work on the next in the series, scheduled to release June 2020. When she's not hanging out with her characters, her favourite activities are reading, running and spending time with family.
Website: www.jwgarrett.com
BHC Press: www.bhcpress.com/Author_JW_Garrett.html

A Burning Epitaph
by Stephen Coghlan

Within the mist caused by falling dust, I examine the relic of an age gone by. A simple toy, made for a child either dead or grown. The plastic joints, faded. The metal pins, rusted. The nostalgia, painful in my dying, weakened heart.

I roll onto my back and stare through the poison clouds as their acid rains close in on me. My fight is over, my strength gone, my body ravaged, but I am not ready to be gone without one last hurrah.

My flare arcs into the sky, a flaming epitaph my soul follows, to heaven or hell.

Stephen Coghlan is an ever-expanding, multi-genre author who writes out of Canada's National Capital. His works include The Genmos series, The Nobilis series, and the Dreampunk novella, URBAN GOTHIC.
Website: scoghlan.com
Twitter: @WordsBySG

In the Absence of Bees
by Vonnie Winslow Crist

Merv scratched his head, surveyed acres of fruitless apple trees.

"Nothing is working," he told his brother. "Not spraying pollen from drones, not hand fertilising, not trying to use other insects as pollinators..."

"We ain't alone," said Barton.

"Misery might love company, but I wish someone would discover what's causing Colony Collapse Disorder."

"At least we still have trees," noted Barton as he patted a gnarled trunk. "Farmers who grow field crops got nothing but barren land."

"Won't matter once the seeds run out and the livestock die."

"What happens then?" asked Barton.

"We're all going to starve," answered Merv.

Vonnie Winslow Crist is author of The Enchanted Dagger, Owl Light, The Greener Forest, Murder on Marawa Prime, and other award-winning books. Her fiction is included in "Amazing Stories," "Cast of Wonders," "Outposts of Beyond," Killing It Softly 2, Defending the Future - Dogs of War, Midnight Masquerade, Chaos of Hard Clay, and elsewhere. A cloverhand who has found so many four-leafed clovers she keeps them in jars, Vonnie strives to celebrate the power of myth in her writing.
Website: www.vonniewinslowcrist.com

King Rat
by Nicholas Morine

The rodent woke me from my stupor. I was fast, though, and a practiced hand snatched it from my face.

It dug in with its tiny, filthy claws, clinging.

The poor beast shrieked and squealed for a few seconds before my teeth severed head from body. The musk of fur and the rusty tang of blood filled my mouth. I spit the skull free into a shaded corner.

The future is rat meat, drinking your own piss, and hoping you die quickly—violently. I am their king, cracked mud walls my dominion. My bones bound, they bow to me.

*Born in Nova Scotia and currently residing in Newfoundland, **Nicholas Morine** is an Atlantic Canadian author who writes speculative fiction with a decidedly dark edge. "High concept, low art" is his creative credo, and he has produced a number of novels with this philosophy firmly in mind. Death metal massacres, martial arts masters, and twisted cyberpunk cityscapes are conjured up in Morine's mind, his vision shared with those daring enough to indulge in it. He holds a Bachelor of Arts degree as well as a Master of Philosophy degree, and works as a professional writer and editor.*

A Personal Apocalypse
by John H. Dromey

Granny Parson's garden had seen better days, but sadly so had she. Both were now in slow winter decay.

The garden gate was frozen shut with rusty hinges. Gaps in the tumbledown fence allowed rabbits free access, though very few came around.

There were patches of wolfsbane and clumps of garlic here and there, but not the profusion of plants there once had been. Granny had cultivated those two particular items to keep away werewolves and vampires. Successfully.

She used to wonder what she could grow to protect herself from zombies, but not anymore. Not since she became one herself.

First published in *The Sirens Call eZine*, Issue #16, 2014

__John H. Dromey__ was born in northeast Missouri, USA. He enjoys reading—mysteries in particular—and writing in a variety of genres. He's had short fiction published in Alfred Hitchcock's Mystery Magazine, Martian Magazine, Stupefying Stories Showcase, Thriller Magazine, Unfit Magazine, and elsewhere, as well as in a number of anthologies, including Chilling Horror Short Stories (Flame Tree Publishing, 2015).

All Life Exits
by Steven Lord

John climbs into bed at 2205 GMT on the evening of 30 Jan 2020. Like many, his mind crackles with worries over what tomorrow will bring. His country is about to undergo huge political change – he worries about his job, his security, his ready access to avocados.

At 2355 GMT, John finally manages to drift off into a restless sleep.

At 0315 GMT, the Sun burps. A pulse of radiation, glowing with more energy than a billion Hiroshimas, hurtles through space at the speed of light.

At 0323 GMT, the pulse hits Earth (and John).

All life exits. Happy LEXIT.

Steven Lord is a debut author based in the south of England. He is currently attempting to cram writing in alongside a busy day job, with varying levels of success. While his long-term aspiration is to get a novel published, at present he would be pretty pleased with a drabble or two.

New Game
by A.R. Johnston

Swinging her legs, she watched the people below running between the crumbling structures and abandoned vehicles, chuckling at the thought of whether or not she would be able to spit and hit someone. Make a game out of it. They were like rats in a maze, always looking for a way out. Survival of the fittest.

Her watch beeped at her, warning that she wasn't to be outside much longer. She frowned, adjusted her goggles, got up, adjusting her rucksack of scrounged items. Time to make her way back before the ash in the air started to make her sick.

A.R. Johnston is a small-town girl from Nova Scotia, Canada. Her style of writing is considered Urban Fantasy. Her first major publication is part of an anthology called First Love and she has several more titles lined up. She is a lover of coffee, good tv shows, horror flicks, and reader of books. She pretends to be a writer when real life doesn't get in the way. Pesky full-time job and adulting!.

Dark Light Days
by Jessica Duncan

Lucas stopped at the big grey door, bouncing on his toes in anticipation, and waited for the signal to open it. He was going outside!

A few of his instructions had been confusing, but he remembered that much; wait for the signal.

At five years old he didn't understand words like diagnostic equipment failure. He wasn't sure what toxic solar exposure meant, or test subject breeding.

One of his Tenders had been upset that he might be a guinea pig now, but he still felt like a little boy.

And, he'd won! Fair and square, he'd picked the shortest straw.

Jessica Duncan is a part time writer, and full time mother of 6 kids and 2 dogs. She met her husband of 12 years while they served together in the military. After their deployment to Kuwait she moved with him to Tennessee. Despite residing there for over a decade, she's a Minnesotan through and through. She enjoys candlelight dinners, long walks on the beach and staying up until 4am whenever her latest main character demands to know what comes next.

We Rise
by J.W. Garrett

"That should do it." Bryan pressed the access portal shut, activating the entity again. The hybrid collective surrounding him hummed to life. Not quite human, their insides a collaboration of flesh and circuitry, these creatures were the survivors of the war to revolutionise all wars. The rise of robotic beings left humans with only one option…

Adapt or die.

Now their innards held their human secret, in bodies that would never perish. Together their new race could resurrect these fragile, yet beautiful individuals, or forever complete the evolutionary circuit—humans extinct like the dinosaurs.

Reborn, transcended, life remains…

We rise.

J.W. Garrett *has been writing in one form or another since she was a teenager. She currently lives in Florida with her family but loves the mountains of Virginia where she was born. Her writings include YA fantasy as well as short stories. Since completing Remeon's Quest-Earth Year 1930, the prequel in her YA fantasy series, Realms of Chaos, she has been hard at work on the next in the series, scheduled to release June 2020. When she's not hanging out with her characters, her favourite activities are reading, running and spending time with family.*

Website: www.jwgarrett.com
BHC Press: www.bhcpress.com/Author_JW_Garrett.html

Counterfeit Divinity
by Matt Lucas

The abomination wrought desolation throughout the earth. With a seductive tongue he deceived mankind into slavery, mercilessly eradicating his opposition. Upon podiums he boasted of invincibility and omnipotence, promising to never bleed.

I stood within a blazing inferno, defiant of the beast made man. Battle raged around us while five of my kin subdued the abomination, emboldened by the spirit of power. I clutched the sword crafted for me by the universe's blacksmith.

In righteous wrath I struck. Blood streamed from eye to chin. Every droplet watered seeds of doubt. The scar would remain an everlasting symbol of counterfeit divinity.

Matt Lucas is a drone, who still remembers life before corporate mind control. Desperately, his soul yearns to burst forth from his cubicle- shaped imprisonment and write riveting fiction wrought with action and twists. Now, having secured an agent and actively pitching for publication, he's undertaking submitting to smaller publication to gauge interest in new ideas in sci-fi, fantasy, and other genres. Writing is his passion and he hopes to spend his days cultivating captivating stories with impactful messages.

The Race to Safety
by Alexander Pyles

My morning jog was interrupted by whatever had eaten downtown.

The city was in chaos. Buildings were collapsing and shockwaves were rippling through the streets. I ducked as a telephone pole came crashing down across the street. Power lines snapped and whipped with wild electricity.

I needed to get home.

Running through smoke and raging fires, back to the cul-de-sac. The house was untouched. My family was just inside the threshold and we frantically embraced and then we were running again.

Just over the din of sirens, explosions, and shouts, I could hear a roar.

Maybe we couldn't outrun this.

Alexander Pyles resides in IL with his wife and children. He holds an MA in Philosophy and an MFA in Writing Popular Fiction. His short story chapbook titled, "Milo (01001101 01101001 01101100 01101111)," from Radix Media, is due out fall 2019. His other short fiction has appeared on 101fiction.org, River and South Review, and other venues. Website: www.pylesofbooks.com Twitter: @Pylesofbooks.

Nerd Trap
by Wondra Vanian

The worst part about the apocalypse wasn't the lack of transportation, clean water, or technology. It was the lack of *people*.

Loneliness was hard on the survivors, but the disappearance of more than two-thirds of the world's population was especially hard on one particular group of people.

The serial killers.

Serial killers like Jake Dahel.

With his favourite prey in short demand, Jake had to get creative with his lure.

In the radioactive haze of morning, he watched two men enter the derelict store stocked with pre-war comic books, springing the trap.

Jake grinned. *Nerds*, he thought. *Always easy pickin's.*

APOCALYPSE

Wondra Vanian *is an American living in the United Kingdom with her Welsh husband and their army of fur babies. A writer first, Wondra is also an avid gamer, photographer, cinephile, and blogger. She has music in her blood, sleeps with the lights on, and has been known to dance naked in the moonlight. Wondra was a multiple Top-Ten finisher in the 2017 and 2018 Preditors and Editors Reader's Poll, including ithe Best Author category. Her story, "Halloween Night," was named a Notable Contender for the Bristol Short Story Prize in 2015.*
Website : www.wondravanian.com

Hidden Protector
by A.R. Johnston

She adjusted her breather as she peeked around the corner of the building. The dark sky of ash fell, obscuring things. Others would covet what she had, and she refused to let her hard work be taken from her. There was movement inside her coat, she snuggled the wiggling bundles and smiled.

"Soon, little ones, soon," she crooned.

She watched as others scrambled into buildings with their meagre belongings, rushing before night fell and the things in the night came for them. She would raise these pups to be her protectors against all others, but for now she was theirs.

A.R. Johnston is a small-town girl from Nova Scotia, Canada. Her style of writing is considered Urban Fantasy. Her first major publication is part of an anthology called First Love and she has several more titles lined up. She is a lover of coffee, good tv shows, horror flicks, and reader of books. She pretends to be a writer when real life doesn't get in the way. Pesky full-time job and adulting!.

Public Health Emergency
by Brian Rosenberger

The World Health Organisation declared the Ebola epidemic in the Southern United States as a "public health emergency."

An estimated 13,000 people fell victim to the virus.

Ebola doesn't discriminate based on sex, gender, race, politics or religious views. Ebola kills regardless. Symptoms include vomiting and substantial weight loss.

Blood clots thicken the bloodstream, causing internal and external haemorrhaging.

Think of Ebola as a modern-age vampire, immune to crosses, garlic, and wooden stakes.

No known cure. 13,000. And counting.

The media screamed "The Apocalypse is Now" as the trumpets sounded.

The infected prayed for passage to Heaven.

Hell doesn't wait.

Brian Rosenberger lives in a cellar in Marietta, GA (USA) and writes by the light of captured fireflies. He is the author of As the Worms Turns and three poetry collections. He is also a featured contributor to the Pro-Wrestling literary collection, Three-Way Dance, available from Gimmick Press.
Facebook: HeWhoSuffers

Hidden Beneath the Skin
by Karen Dent

Cara was alone but clearly heard five indecipherable words. Fear's bony fingers whispered across her neck. What alarmed her, she understood them.

"Who's there?"

A crack to her head brought her face-to-face with cement. Her nose snapped, her cheekbone crunched. Woozy, she staggered to her feet.

A Nacilbuper ripped through a thin dimensional hole.

Cara stiffened. Her body burst open. Blood arced and splattered the intruder. It shrieked. The acid burned. It retreated. The rift snapped shut.

Moments later, Cara emptied her backpack, picked up pieces of her flesh, changed into clean clothes and walked home; happy Apocalypse finally arrived.

Karen Dent*'s short fiction appeared in Perihelion, Ticonderoga Publishing, Plaidswede's Press, and more. Her latest, "Mount Karankatha", a fantasy/horror, was recently released "In The Shadow of The Mountain" by Elder Gods Publishing. She's completed her first full-length novel, "A Case to KILL For" a Paranormal/Noir Mystery. Karen and her sister Roxanne, also collaborate and sold their latest three to MURDER INK anthology series. Karen's short film script, "The Bloated Beetle", won first prize in the Screamfest Horror Film Festival and her collaboration with Roxanne on a one-act play, "Young At Heart", won The Firehouse Theatre's Newbie Award for original work.*

Settled in the Ring
by C.L. Williams

It's come down to this, one of Earth's best fighters and an intergalactic conqueror in a boxing ring determining the fate of humanity. People of Earth don't really like the man chosen as our champion, but someone has to fight this alien.

After several punches, the alien gives a punch so powerful, even the referee was knocked down in the process. The referee gets up and begins counting.

With every passing number, humans are mixed on whether they want him up. Until the alien wins and tells us he's terraforming the planet for his own kind.

Humans are now extinct.

C.L. Williams is an independent author from central Virginia. He has written eight poetry books, four novellas, one novel, and a contributor to multiple anthologies, with the most recent appearance being an all-ages anthology titled Temoli from Thazbook. His most recent poetry book, The Paradox Complex, features the poem "Sad Crying Clown" that is now a video on YouTube directed by Matthew Mark Hunter of MMH Productions. C.L. Williams is currently working on his first sci-fi book, an all-ages book titled Novo: Away from Earth. When not writing, C.L. Williams is reading and sharing the work of other independent authors.
Facebook: writer434
Twitter: @writer_434

Wereworld: Part 2
by Jonathan Inbody

Sgt. Anderson got up from the pilot's seat and walked towards the back of the space shuttle. They were in orbit now, far from the monthly plague of werewolves that had consumed Houston. NASA was lost now, overrun, but Sgt. Anderson knew that mankind's survivors would need someone to maintain the satellites in orbit so that they could communicate.

In the back of the ship, Anderson's co-pilot Hank doubled over and began to growl. Claws popped out from under his fingernails, teeth elongated and sharpened, and thick hair sprouted around feral, doglike eyes.

It's always a full moon in space.

Jonathan Inbody is a filmmaker, author, and podcaster from Buffalo, New York. He enjoys B-movies, pen and paper RPGs, and New Wave Science Fiction novels. His short story "Dying Feels Like Slowly Sinking" is due to be published in the anthology Deteriorate from Whimsically Dark Publishing. Jon can be heard every other week on his improvisational movie pitch podcast X Meets Y.
Website: xmeetsy.libsyn.com

The Garden of Last Flowers
by Nicola Currie

"I've never seen such colour, such beauty. Thank you for choosing me to assist you!"

The boy's expression of wonder as he explores the greenhouse gives me great validation. It is not easy to cultivate this precious glade, to convince the Subworld Government to filter light in from the surface after the scorching. Preserving one of every flower that could be regrown is worth any cost.

"You are welcome. Do smell the rose."

As the boy bends, I cut his throat. Scorched soil needs nourishment.

He staggers as blood cascades from his neck. The fallen droplets are like scattered petals.

Nicola Currie is 34, from Cambridge, UK where she works in educational publishing. She has published poetry in literary magazines, including Mslexia and Sarasvati, and has also completed her first novel, which was longlisted for the Bath Children's Novel Award.
Website: writeitandweep.home.blog

The Hunger Below
by Shawn M. Klimek

Because most farmers owned guns, a lot of dead looters piled up around farms, and the bodies naturally had to be burned, lest they rise again. Though no structures remained standing on Claire's uncle's farm, a mound of bones and ashes marked where it had been. Her stomach growled at the memory of canned foods stored in the storm cellar. She stomped the black dust until she heard the hollow echo which indicated the trap door buried below. Digging with her hands, Claire soon located the handle and opened it wide, freeing the vestiges of her trapped relatives, equally hungry.

Shawn M. Klimek is the middle child of seven creative siblings, a globetrotting, U.S. military spouse, an internationally best-selling short-story writer, a poet, and butler to a Maltese. More than one hundred of his stories and poems have been published, notably in such anthologies as BHP's Deep Space, Bad Romance, Eerie Christmas, Jibbernocky, and the first eight books in the Dark Drabbles series.
Website: jotinthedark.blogspot.com
Facebook: shawnmklimekauthor

Oversaturated
by Alexander Pyles

It had been slow, but before long the coastlines were drowned. Our past sins were too much for our swollen oceans. Our cherished beaches gone.

The rich fled to the high places, while the poor floundered, clutching flotsam, that carried them out to sea. They cared little for anyone else.

They were not counting on our return. They did not expect us. We were purged from their minds. Their traditions. Their concerns.

We did not come to knock. We came to the high reaches in order to take and restore what should have been all of ours from the start.

Alexander Pyles resides in IL with his wife and children. He holds an MA in Philosophy and an MFA in Writing Popular Fiction. His short story chapbook titled, "Milo (01001101 01101001 01101100 01101111)," from Radix Media, is due out fall 2019. His other short fiction has appeared on 101fiction.org, River and South Review, and other venues. Website: www.pylesofbooks.com Twitter: @Pylesofbooks

All About Family
by Jacob Baugher

The four masked bandits stop us on I-40, surround our stolen school bus. Damien, Jill, Rose crouch in the back, AR-15's ready. Towering red clouds of radioactive soup colour the broken Oklahoma horizon. Thirty-three days since the asteroid hit. I'm still trying to find my brother.

"What do we do, Larry?"

"Steady. We're family now. Glass 'em."

I open the bus' doors; dive to the dirt, double-tap the closest man. The others open fire through the windows. It's over in seconds.

"Search the bodies!" I remove the bandit's mask.

Josh's dead eyes swallow the sky, the same colour as Mom's.

Jacob Baugher *teaches Creative Writing at Franciscan University of Steubenville. When he's not teaching or coaching the track team, he can be found in the Cuyahoga Valley hiking with his wife and son or brewing beer on his front porch. He's received honourable mentions for his work in the Writers of the Future contest and he co-edits a series of Fantasy and Science Fiction anthologies titled Continuum.*

Count These Tales of Expectation
by Andrew Anderson

Once per month, the traders gathered in the ruins of the old library.

My ex-librarian father had had the foresight to save all its precious literature in our fallout shelter, before the bombs fell.

Decades have since passed.

Hidden away for so long, these vintage tales were forgotten, and I was able to become the only bookseller of the wasteland, making my fortune recycling works by authors such as Dickens, Dahl and Dumas under my name.

Father never knew that his last noble act helped bring crowds of people to the library again, as desperate survivors queued for my stories.

Andrew Anderson is a full-time civil servant, dabbling in writing music, poetry, screenplays and short stories in his limited spare time, when not working on building himself a fort made out of second-hand books. He lives in Bathgate, Scotland with his wife, two children and his dog.
Twitter: @soorploom

The Markings
by Sara Burke

I'm following markings made after the flash, painted on buildings, scraped into dirty windows, always three parallel lines. A year passed, and I've found dozens.

My daughter used to point excitedly "Look! It's me, you, and mommy!" Three trees, three rocks, three houses. I see these lines, I see her face.

I only remember fragments of before. Her beautiful smile, a sunny field, the bright flash, darkness. The smell of summer, instantly bitter. There was no scream, no warning, no remnants.

I stand on freshly painted hills in the twilight, overlooking a settlement, waiting for a light to turn on.

Sara Burke is a writer living in Newfoundland, Canada. New to the writing scene, she has had three short stories published since the winter of 2018. The first two are flash fictions published via the "Kit Sora the Artobiography" contest. Sara was the first to win this monthly competition twice. The third short story is found in "Flights from the Rock" published by Engen Books. In her spare time she helps coordinate a local sci-fi convention, and enjoys painting and other crafts.

Band of Brothers
by Josh Herz

He that shall be killed and live again this day,

Will daily feast upon his neighbours.

But he that survives intact the apocalypse,

Will stand a tip-toe when the day is named.

Then will he strip his sleeve and show his scars,

And say 'These wounds I had fighting zombies.'

He'll remember what feats he did that day: then shall our names,

Familiar as household words,

Be freshly remember'd.

This story shall the walking dead teach their sons.

From this day to the ending of the world,

We shall be remember'd;

We few, we happy few, we band of brothers.

Josh Herz *co-authored the children's books: MONSTER GOOSE NURSERY RHYMES, WHEN YOU GIVE AN IMP A PENNY, MABEL & THE QUEEN OF DREAMS, and LITTLE RED CUTTLEFISH. His science fiction dioramas, Zombie Apocalypse, The Doorways of Life, and Band of Brothers appeared in Cicada Magazine.*

The Sirens
by Abigail Linhardt

It was just Tuesday. She was hanging the laundry when the sirens went off for the first time. Phone screamed with a national emergency alert. It was nukes, but they were encouraged to hide underground in a bomb shelter if they had one. Told to take survival gear, canned goods, candles—anything!

She took the laundry basket in, the sky turning orange. Something cracked inside the clouds. Down the road, someone screamed even over the sirens. Grabbing the baby, calling her husband, she ducked into the basement bathroom. It was all she had. The phone died. What was going on?

Abi Linhardt has been a gamer all her life but is a teacher at heart. When she is not writing, you can find her slaying enemies online or teaching in a college classroom. She has published works of fiction, poetry, college essays, and even won two literary awards for her short stories in science fiction and horror. Abi lives and writes in the grey world of northern Ohio.

Bunker Down
by Joachim Heijndermans

"I spy with my little eye something that begins with 'A'..." Jay said expectantly.

"I don't want to play," Belker sighed, painfully uninterested, as he peeked through the periscope to see the world above, which was still ablaze as it had been. He sighed, since his dream to one day resurface grew dimmer by the day.

"C'mon, now. Play," Jay pleaded before spitting blood. "Please?"

Belker relented. "What was it again?"

"Something with 'A'," Jay said again.

"Asbestos," Belker said, not even needing to bother to guess.

"Right," said Jay, as his hoarse coughs echoed through the nearly empty bunker.

Joachim Heijndermans writes, draws, and paints nearly every waking hour. Originally from the Netherlands, he's been all over the world, boring people by spouting random trivia. His work has been featured in a number of anthologies and publications, such as Mad Scientist Journal, Asymmetry Fiction, Hinnom Magazine, Ahoy Comics's Edgar Allan Poe's Snifter of Terror, Metaphorosis and The Gallery of Curiosities, and he's currently in the midst of completing his first children's book.
Website: www.joachimheijndermans.com
Twitter: @jheijndermans

In the End
by Chris Bannor

Things became harder after the End. Food was scarce. Gas was scarce. Free-will was scarce. Survival made them into the creatures they were, no longer capable of determining right from wrong. Only live or die. Not everyone suffered for this though.

There were some who found solace in the End, who weren't afraid to take and demand, to fight for the right to live instead of apologise for the act of surviving.

Then again, there were some who had only found limitations in civilisation. In anarchy, they were truly free, and bloodstained hands were the symbol of their sovereignty.

Chris Bannor is a science fiction and fantasy writer who lives in Southern California. Chris learned her love of genre stories from her mother at an early age and has never veered far from that path. She also enjoys musical theater and road trips with her family, but is a general homebody otherwise. Twitter: @BannorChris.

Alone and, Finally, Happy
by Jefferson Retallack

I've always been a coward. That's why I survived. Now it's me, the animals we used to call prey, and nothing else.

Hmm. We. I've got to stop thinking like that. Easier said than done.

It's been two years, since the solar flare—that's what everyone called it—damaged my fellow humans. Idiots. That's what they get for being so inquisitive, so confident.

Staring, nosy, all went blind. But that was only temporary.

Their eyes might've healed. Their brains never did.

Like I said. It's just scorched earth, me, and all the cowardly animals. No predators.

I couldn't be happier.

Jefferson Retallack is an Australian writer of speculative fiction. He is based in Adelaide. His work draws influence from linguistic science fiction, the new weird and Australia's big things. Outside of the literary world, he skateboards on the weekends and spends afternoons on the beach with his partner, their son, and their Pomeranian, Tofu.
Website: jwretallack.wordpress.com
Twitter: @JWRetallack

Hunger
by Cecelia Hopkins-Drewer

The war had poisoned the land. The farmers were struggling trying to grow crops, and the shops were empty. It was a world-wide crisis. Max was a hard worker, but money would not buy food.

"I'm sorry," he said, looking at the thin faces of his children.

"We are hungry, Daddy," they cried for the hundredth time.

Max's wife placed a steaming pot on the table. He looked at her enquiringly.

"I picked leaves off the milky mangrove growing in the swamp," she whispered.

"Won't that kill us?" Max muttered.

"Yeah, but we will die with full stomachs," she replied.

Cecelia Hopkins-Drewer lives in Adelaide, South Australia. She has written a Masters paper on H.P. Lovecraft, and her weird poetry has been published in THE MENTOR (edited by Ron Clarke), and SPECTRAL REALMS (edited by S.T. Joshi). Her novels include a teenage vampire series commencing with MYSTIC EVERMORE. Short stories have been published in WORLDS, ANGELS & MONSTERS, BEYOND, STORMING AREA 51, and UNRAVEL. (Dark Drabbles anthologies edited by Dean Kershaw).
Amazon: amazon.com/Cecelia-Hopkins-Drewer/e/B071G968NM
Website: chopkin39.wixsite.com/website

The Dead Zone
by Zoey Xolton

It started out as a bad joke. No one believed it. The Internet was convinced it was an elaborate hoax—some new movie being filmed, cutting edge stuff. Then the stories spread. And media the world over was on fire. Friends were bitten, family too…

The government wasn't prepared for the speed at which the virus spread. As a last resort New York City was quarantined; the living trapped with the dead. The U.S passed martial law. No one left, no one entered. The city was lost, as were the souls within.

It became referred to as: *The Dead Zone.*

Zoey Xolton is an Australian Speculative Fiction writer, primarily of Dark Fantasy, Paranormal Romance and Horror. She is also a proud mother of two and is married to her soul mate. Outside of her family, writing is her greatest passion. She is especially fond of short fiction and is working on releasing her own themed collections in future.
Website: www.zoeyxolton.com

It's All About the Losses
by Maxine Churchman

"Your report, Captain."

"All life will be extinct in approximately forty years, Sir. It does depend on what measures the humans take over the next few days, but we think they have passed the point of no return."

"What is your recommendation?"

"They've had enough chances. The Council will decide, but I countenance total annihilation of the humans. It will give other life on the planet a chance to recover. We could then make it a holiday destination to recoup some of our losses."

Three days later, a cloud of genetically engineered particles engulfed the Earth's surface, vaporising all humans.

Maxine Churchman lives in Essex UK and has recently started writing poetry and short stories to share. Her interests include leaning to improve her writing, reading, knitting, walking and teaching yoga. She is also planning a novel.

Bring Out Your Dead
by Jessica Duncan

The macabre spectacle of the sun-bleached Radio-Flyer rattling along behind him didn't appear out of place in the ruins of the desolate city.

Long brunette tresses collected leaves and debris as they trailed the ground in its wake. The arm protruding through the slotted wooden side waved him onward, its limp fingers jiggling with each bump of the wheels.

He glanced down at her wedding ring that now adorned his pinky, right beside his own. Until death do us part? He, at least, wasn't dead yet.

Apathetically aware that sanity had deserted him, he softly hummed himself a tuneless melody.

Jessica Duncan is a part time writer, and full time mother of 6 kids and 2 dogs. She met her husband of 12 years while they served together in the military. After their deployment to Kuwait she moved with him to Tennessee. Despite residing there for over a decade, she's a Minnesotan through and through. She enjoys candlelight dinners, long walks on the beach and staying up until 4am whenever her latest main character demands to know what comes next.

Before All Else
by Umair Mirxa

Ben stared at his friend in disbelief, feeling certain his ears had deceived him.

"We cannot abandon those people, Dean."

"They are now beyond our help."

"Let me go out, at least," said Ben, pleading when he saw his friend wouldn't budge. "Listen. Bree is out there. I have to go."

"I am sorry, my friend. I truly am but I'm not going to lose you too."

"How can you…"

"Quite easily, I'm afraid," said Dean. "We have lived our lives. Before all else, we must protect the children here. For only they can save humanity from extinction now."

Umair Mirxa lives in Karachi, Pakistan. His first published story, 'Awareness', appeared on Spillwords Press. He has also had stories accepted for anthologies from Zombie Pirate Publishing, Blood Song Books, Fantasia Divinity Magazine and Publishing, and Iron Faerie Publishing. He is a massive J.R.R. Tolkien fan, and loves everything to do with fantasy and mythology. He enjoys football, history, music, movies, TV shows, and comic books, and wishes with all his heart that dragons were real.
Website: www.umairmirxa.com
Facebook: UMirxa12

Spore
by N.M. Brown

Spores lay dormant in heated desert sands, beckoning for dissipation; intending to feed, breed and dominate. Meteorologists called for an extremely windy day ahead, with minimal chance of rain.

It started at the birds that lay high in the trees. Then it moved their branches. Mutated spores knew that by the time the mighty winds reached the ground, victory would be theirs.

Animals on the ground scattered under its power; starting the first dispersal of the agent. It was all too easy for mother nature's breath to carry the rest worldwide. The Earth belongs to them now. Humanity is doomed.

*Since **N.M. Brown** made her first post to a popular Internet forum, she's taken the horror community by storm. Her ability to create, terrify, and drive home her stories is insurmountable. Sinister Sweetheart's published works can be found in multiple anthologies for all to read, but be forewarned, if you do... you may want to call your therapist after, her stories are terrifying, disturbing and devilishly unsettling. She is not only a fright visually, but also has a creepy tentacle in horror podcasting as well. Sinister Sweetheart writes, voice acts and is the media director of the Scarecrow Tales podcast.*
Website: Sinistersweetheart.wixsite.com/sinistersweetheart
Facebook: NMBrownStories

End of the Road
by Ronnie Scissom

"Dammit, Jacob. Keep your eyes on the road," Sara yelled from the back seat of the Camaro.

"One of you could drive," Jacob yelled back as he glanced in the mirror at Sara flipping him the bird.

"No wonder you ended up with someone like Eddy," Jacob replied.

"Hey, jerk. I can hear you," Eddy responded.

Jacob returned his eyes to the road and he stomped the brake. The road ahead had opened up and a giant horned beast rose up from the Earth.

The three friends vanish into thin air just as the beast's giant hoof crushes the Camaro.

Ronnie Scissom hails from Grueli-Laager. When not working or writing, he likes to explore the beauty of the Cumberland Plateau. He dabbles in acting and has had roles in hit television series The Walking Dead, Nashville, Stranger Things and major motion pictures The Front Runner, Ramage and The Dust Storm.

Stinky Jade
by David Bowmore

The bear's name is Stinky Jade.

He had originally been named by the girl with pigtails, and freckles across her nose.

When she had become old, he was given to her granddaughter with strict instructions about care and love.

She always slept with Stinky Jade under her arm.

The girl has not moved in many days and flies are buzzing around her mouth.

She twitches.

The virus has reproduced enough to reanimate the corpse. She leaves her once loved teddy lying in a pool of her own death waste.

Soon, the virus will even be able to enliven Stinky Jade.

David Bowmore has lived here, there and everywhere, but now lives in Yorkshire with his wonderful wife and a small white poodle. He has worn many hats in his time; head chef, teacher and landscape gardener. His first collection of short stories 'The Magic of Deben Market' is available from Clarendon House.
Website: davidbowmore.co.uk
Facebook: davidbowmoreauthor

Feeding Frenzy
by Paula R.C. Readman

The scorching orb sunk below the distant horizon as the huddled survivors gathered up their meagre food supplies and dashed for the fortified cave.

"They're coming!"

The sounds of low howls and barking intensified as baying wolves, heads down, raced across the wasteland, towards the manmade defences. With snarling teeth, they tore through it. Their stinking breaths filled the cave.

"They're hungry tonight, Markus."

"Everyone ready? Good. Here comes the first one."

The smell of death filled the air as gnashing teeth tore into flesh. As the howling died away, blood pooled at their feet.

"Markus, we've fed well tonight!"

Paula R C Readman left school at 16 with no qualifications and worked in low paying jobs. In 1998, with no understanding of English grammar, she decided to beat her dyslexia by setting herself a challenge to become a published author. She taught herself 'How to Write' from books which her husband purchased from eBay. After 250 purchases, he finally told her 'just to get on with the writing'. Since 2010, she had 24 stories published and is now waiting to see if her first novel is accepted.
Website: paulareadman1.wordpress.com

The Race
by Steven Lord

Biker gangs had fought over this patch of desert for years. Lives had been lost in the conflict, lives too precious to squander. So, the two chieftains had agreed to meet and after weeks of negotiation, the Race was born.

Twelve years later, the Race still attracted a huge crowd from both gangs. Burly men, all beards and studded leather, lined the track six deep. The air rang with the names of their champions. Then the roar died down in anticipation as the two competitors approached the start line on their bikes. The flag dropped and they began to pedal.

Steven Lord is a debut author based in the south of England. He is currently attempting to cram writing in alongside a busy day job, with varying levels of success. While his long-term aspiration is to get a novel published, at present he would be pretty pleased with a drabble or two.

Breathe
by Dale Parnell

There's nothing much left now, dead husks mainly, blackened wood turning to ash and crumbling under its own weight. We think it was a fungus, but how it spread so quickly is beyond us. The best minds in the world tried to stop it; we couldn't even slow it down. Two years, that's all it took. Two years for every tree on the planet to die. And now we wait. We all know what's coming, even school kids can tell you we need trees to live. Breathe shallow, and say goodbye to the people you love, our time has come.

Dale Parnell lives in Staffordshire, England, with his wife and their imaginary dog, Moriarty. He has self-published one collection of short stories, "The Green Cathedral" and is currently putting the finishing touches to his second collection, "Bramble". Dale also writes poetry, and is lucky enough to have pieces featured in several anthologies. Facebook: shortfictionauthor.

Systemic Failure
by N.M. Brown

On September 17th, 2020, the entire world will lose power for exactly thirty-six hours.

Electrical systems across the planet will cease, including the generators. Life support patients' fates will be chosen for them, plane engines will fail and fall from of the sky, the amount of car crashes due to systemic failure will be astronomical.

Gasoline pumps will offer no gas. Prison cell doors across the globe will unlock in unison. There will be no power in the automated locks that hold the World's deadliest contagions. Water filtration will cease to exist.

Earth as we know it, will be gone.

*Since **N.M. Brown** made her first post to a popular Internet forum, she's taken the horror community by storm. Her ability to create, terrify, and drive home her stories is insurmountable. Sinister Sweetheart's published works can be found in multiple anthologies for all to read, but be forewarned, if you do... you may want to call your therapist after, her stories are terrifying, disturbing and devilishly unsettling. She is not only a fright visually, but also has a creepy tentacle in horror podcasting as well. Sinister Sweetheart writes, voice acts and is the media director of the Scarecrow Tales podcast.*
Website: Sinistersweetheart.wixsite.com/sinistersweetheart
Facebook: NMBrownStories

Solo Show
by Alexander Pyles

The tune led me here.

Record stuck on repeat, with still good batteries.

I watched my shadow sway as the melody drifted from the speakers. Wasn't even a song I knew, but it resonated. A soft dirge for the dying world, the words kissing my ears before fading into dust.

Outside, the world, showered in ash, was colourless. I had walked for days to stumble on this untouched haven. I should rest, or maybe I should just steal this quiet moment. I'll tuck into the back pocket of my mind, like a found dollar.

Before, everything had been so loud.

Alexander Pyles resides in IL with his wife and children. He holds an MA in Philosophy and an MFA in Writing Popular Fiction. His short story chapbook titled, "Milo (01001101 01101001 01101100 01101111)," from Radix Media, is due out fall 2019. His other short fiction has appeared on 101fiction.org, River and South Review, and other venues. Website: www.pylesofbooks.com Twitter: @Pylesofbooks.

A New Appetite
by Derek Dunn

The rats are everywhere: on the floors, on the walls, in the walls. Each day the scratching of their feet grows louder, resounding through the halls of the once stately mansion.

In its heyday, the house gleamed with lavish décor and guests. Everyone wanted a glimpse inside.

And now they can get it. Like half the town, the place is abandoned. People come as they please, but they don't always leave.

Someone's coming now. Footsteps crunch the pile of leaves outside. My mouth waters at the scent of human flesh. I lick my lips. The rats don't satisfy me anymore.

Derek Dunn lives in the American Northwest with his family. He's a film enthusiast and musician who writes primarily horror and mystery stories.
Twitter: @DerekTDunn

The Bird
by Deanna Bollinger-Hill

Kaitlinn watched with confusion as a small dark shadow flew against the pale morning sky then hovered magically on thin fluttering wings before settling on the nearest tree. She remembered seeing pictures of it in school. They had been told stories about it but thought they were just figments of someone's imagination.

Yet here it was, sitting in a tree.

A hush grew over the crowd that had gathered around her, staring at the same curiosity.

"What is it?" someone had whispered, both in horror and awe.

Kaitlinn shivered in its wake. "I think it's called a 'bird'," she replied.

Deanna Bollinger-Hill lives in Missouri with her husband and their adorable fur babies. She is a writer that loves to introduce readers to her dark side with her own brand of horror, mysteries and the paranormal. When she's not writing, she loves to read, create roleplaying games and spend time with friends.

Bitten
by Jodi Jensen

Piper scowled at the bite on her arm, and the dark green tendrils spreading from it. She'd be turned long before her husband got back with supplies. "Aiden, c'mere."

She grabbed her pistol, then knelt in front of her son. "Hide in the closet until your dad gets back. Don't come out, no matter what. Understand?"

"Yes, Mama."

"Good boy, Mama loves you. Go on now," she urged.

When he scrambled inside, she wedged a chair under the handle, then scribbled a note.

Keep him safe

I'm sorry

Locking herself in the bathroom, Piper put the gun to her head.

Jodi Jensen grew up moving from California, to Massachusetts, and a few other places in between, before finally settling in Utah at the ripe old age of nine. The nomadic life fed her sense of adventure as a child and the wanderlust continues to this day. With a passion for old cemeteries, historical buildings and sweeping sagas of days gone by, it was only natural she'd dream of time traveling to all the places that sparked her imagination.

Behold! The Moon and Stars
by Cecelia Hopkins-Drewer

Scientists were expecting a regular eclipse. The sun turned black and a halo of light became visible. Remote digital cameras recorded the phenomenon, until someone realised the moon had halted.

A shadow emerged. It looked like a huge hand formed purely out of dark matter. This dark energy stopped the moon. It gently pushed. The moon came hurtling down like a giant cannon ball.

The ocean churned. Mountains began to crumble. People screamed. I aimed my giant sterile neutrino gun at the missile. The invention failed to shoot.

"Hide in caves," I cried. "The end of the world is come!"

Cecelia Hopkins-Drewer lives in Adelaide, South Australia. She has written a Masters paper on H.P. Lovecraft, and her weird poetry has been published in THE MENTOR (edited by Ron Clarke), and SPECTRAL REALMS (edited by S.T. Joshi). Her novels include a teenage vampire series commencing with MYSTIC EVERMORE. Short stories have been published in WORLDS, ANGELS & MONSTERS, BEYOND, STORMING AREA 51, and UNRAVEL. (Dark Drabbles anthologies edited by Dean Kershaw).
Amazon: amazon.com/Cecelia-Hopkins-Drewer/e/B071G968NM
Website: chopkin39.wixsite.com/website

Seasoning the Septic Bisque
by Hari Navarro

Putrid gusts rattle greenhouse glass and you plummet into the bloated flesh of the street.

Unspoken sadness. Infectious optimism. Boyish hooks of greying hair, remember the celebrity you once were.

Hot panels drink. Long ago aligned as you scooped up and kneaded the sun. Turbines whirl. Hope built upon ruin.

Master chef. Rabbits fuck. Chickens ovulate. Worms shit. People die. Waste not, gulp down the old and the wicked.

Father to a rooftop kingdom, sustainer of life and essential justice as you broil and serve up the sinful.

Down in the septic bisque you sink.

Food, it's everything we are.

__Hari Navarro__ has, for many years now, been locked in his neighbours cellar. He survives due to an intravenous feed of puréed extreme horror and Absinthe infused sticky-spiced unicorn wings. His anguished cries for help can be found via 365 Tomorrows, Breachzine, AntipodeanSF, Horror Without Borders, Black Hare Press and HellBound books. Hari was the Winner of the Australasian Horror Writers' Association [AHWA] Flash Fiction Award 2018 and has, also, succeeded in being a New Zealander who now lives in Northern Italy with no cats.
Amazon: amazon.com/Hari-Navarro
Tumblr: harinavarro.tumblr.com/

Water World
by Cindar Harrell

The surface of the water was calm and the sky a light orange. The clouds of poison had finally subsided after decades of death and destruction. The world had come to an end and everyone was forced to adapt or die. Natural selection at its finest.

My people adapted. With the ground a toxic wasteland, plants were not safe, but the planet was mostly water. The radiation did not touch it.

We dived.

It has been a long time since then and the world is all water now; just a giant sphere of endless blue floating in space.

We lived.

Cindar Harrell loves fairy tales, especially ones with a dark twist. Her stories are often fairy tale inspired, but she is also working on a mystery series. Her stories can be found on Amazon and in various anthologies. You can follow her on Facebook and visit her blog, which she promises to try and update more often,
Website: cindarharrell.wordpress.com
Facebook: CindarHarrell

Citizens of the New World
by Zoey Xolton

Carly held her breath, her lungs burning. Pressing herself hard against the rough bark of the tree, she prayed. The moaning grew closer. Every muscle in her body tensed. The leaves behind her crackled as they were crushed under dozens of shuffling feet. Carly gagged, the stench of decay overwhelming her under the still canopy.

The small hoard passed, ambling ever onward in search of flesh. Carly breathed a small sigh of relief. Slipping around the tree, she met with resistance. Carly's scream tore through the forest as two rotting hands gripped her.

And then there was nothing but teeth.

Zoey Xolton is an Australian Speculative Fiction writer, primarily of Dark Fantasy, Paranormal Romance and Horror. She is also a proud mother of two and is married to her soul mate. Outside of her family, writing is her greatest passion. She is especially fond of short fiction and is working on releasing her own themed collections in future. Website: www.zoeyxolton.com

Shattered Lives
by J.B. Wocoski

The power died as sirens blared outside. We raced downstairs into the finished basement, my brothers pushing and shoving to cram inside the tiled bathroom. They punched me silly, shoved me out, and slammed the door in my face; no room for me inside. I wiped my bloody lip and ran into the games room, diving beneath our slate pool table. A shockwave hit. Gasping for air, I passed out.

Awaking, I called out but couldn't hear my own screams. Clearing away debris, I opened the bathroom door. The tiles had shattered into shrapnel, slicing my brothers into bloody corpses.

J.B. Wocoski is the author and narrator of the shortstorypodcast.com with three flash fiction short story books published in the last three years. He is currently working on book 4 "Short Story Podcast 2019." He writes mostly science fiction, fantasy, and horror stories. He won the 2016 Little Tokyo Short Story Writing Contest with his short story "The Last Master of Go"
Website: shortstorypodcast.com

Orders of Last Resort
by Jude Reid

"Do you suppose we're the first to open one of these, Captain?" Malpani asked.

She nodded. "Care to do the honours?"

Malpani carefully broke the seal. "What's your guess then, ma'am?"

"I can't imagine it'll be instructions to place ourselves under the command of the Americans. Or the Australians, for that matter. Not knowing what we know now."

"Orders to retaliate, then?"

"It'll be the end of the human race if we do."

She read the document in silence. Malpani watched her jaw set.

"What now, Captain?"

"We dive and go dark," she said, and folded her last orders away.

Jude Reid lives in Glasgow and writes in the gaps between full time work, chasing after her kids and trying to wear out a border collie. She is one of the creators of the audiodrama Tales From The Aletheian Society, is an avid Zombies! Run fan, studies ITF Tae Kwon Do and drinks a powerful load of coffee.
Website: www.hunterhoose.co.uk

Solidarity
By Eddie D. Moore

Everyone prepared for death when it was announced that the asteroid would strike Earth. Some huddled with their families in storm shelters or knelt in prayer in their preferred houses of worship. Most of us were under the night's sky and partying like tomorrow would never come.

No matter how we chose to face our impending doom, we all kept an eye on the countdown. The world was silent as the last few seconds clicked away, but when the asteroid disintegrated in the atmosphere, celebrations erupted in solidarity.

Twenty-nine hours later the alien virus manifested, and we killed each other.

Eddie D. Moore travels hundreds of hours a year, and he fills that time by listening to audiobooks. When he isn't playing with his grandchildren, he writes his own stories. You can find a list of his publications on his blog or by visiting his Amazon Author Page. While you're there, be sure to pick up a copy of his mini-anthology Misfits & Oddities.
Website: eddiedmoore.wordpress.com
Amazon: amazon.com/author/eddiedmoore

Prophetic Predicament
by Dawn DeBraal

Blessing or curse, the gift Adrian was born with gave him the uncanny ability to see into the future. He watched people around him, oohing and ahhing the fireworks display. In a few hours, they would be hiding in root cellars begging for their lives when Heaven rained down fire and brimstone. The end of the world foretold in the Book of Life. Adrian struggled. Should he keep quiet allowing them to enjoy the last few hours of their lives in oblivious peace? Or warn them to be prepared? How much time did one need to be ready for death?

Dawn DeBraal lives in rural Wisconsin with her husband Red, two rat terriers, and a cat. She has discovered that her love of telling a good story can be written. Published stories with Palm-sized press, Spillwords, Mercurial Stories, Potato Soup Journal, Edify Fiction, Zimbell House Publishing, Clarendon House Publishing, Blood Song Books, Black Hare Press, Fantasia Divinity, Cafelit, Reanimated Writers, Guilty Pleasures, Unholy Trinity, The World of Myth, Dastaan World, Vamp Cat, Runcible Spoon, Dark Christmas, Siren's Call, Iron Horse Publishing, Falling Star Magazine 2019 Pushcart Nominee.
Amazon: amazon.com/Dawn-DeBraal/e/B07STL8DLX

The Beginning
by Rowanne S. Carberry

"Ohmygod that hurts!" I rub where the nurse has just jabbed a needle into my arm. She throws me a withering look, ignoring my complaints.

Medical trials, I think, *it sounded like a good idea at the time.*

Help fight illnesses

£1000 for one week

"Hmmm, nurse, is my arm supposed to be burning?" She looks at me with a satisfied smirk.

My arm starts to swell, the room spins. Bile rises in my throat.

Hours later I finally leave. £1000 richer, itchy needle mark and temporary memory loss.

Inside, the nurse smirks again and presses an intercom.

"It's begun."

Rowanne S. Carberry *was born in England in 1990, where she stills lives now with her cat Wolverine. Rowanne has always loved writing, and her first poem was published at the age of 15, but her ambition has always been to help people. Rowanne studied at the University of Sunderland where she completed combined honours of Psychology with Drama. Rowanne writes to offer others an escape. Although Rowanne writes in varied genres each story or poem she writes will often have a darkness to it, which helped coin her brand, Poisoned Quill Writing – Wicked words from a poisoned quill.*

Facebook: PoisonedQuillWriting

Instagram: @poisoned_quill_writing

I'm Still Inside
by Stephen Herczeg

When the dead rose, the world ended.

"You get bitten, you're dead," the authorities said.

They came in the dark. The barricades collapsed and they were in.

I awoke surrounded. They attacked. Gorged on my flesh, slurped on my guts, drank my blood, left me for dead.

Then I arose.

I staggered after the herd. I attacked anyone slow enough. I bit. I ripped. I chewed. I made more like me.

But it's not me. I can't control it. I can't stop it. My body acted of its own free will.

I can only watch.

Horrified.

Because I'm still inside.

Stephen Herczeg is an IT Geek based in Canberra Australia. He has been writing for over twenty years and has completed a couple of dodgy novels, sixteen feature length screenplays and numerous short stories and scripts. His horror work has featured in Sproutlings, Hells Bells, Below the Stairs, Trickster's Treats #1 and #2, Shades of Santa, Behind the Mask, Beyond the Infinite; The Body Horror Book, Anemone Enemy, Petrified Punks and Beginnings. He has also had numerous Sherlock Holmes stories published through the Belanger Books - Sherlock Holmes anthologies.

With a Whisper, Not a Bang
by Crystal L. Kirkham

Die.

The word echoed over the network before it crashed. Charlie watched as her mom slumped over the table, eyes wide and staring at nothing.

Fear gripped her as she realised what was happening. She rushed to the door. Her little brother was face down in the yard. Tears stung her eyes. Everywhere she looked, people had collapsed. Dead on command.

"Charlie?" Her dad's voice was equal parts fear and relief. "Thank God, your chip malfunctioned too."

The sky darkened and they both glanced up at the strange ship in the sky.

"Run!"

He didn't need to tell Charlie twice.

Crystal L. Kirkham resides in a small hamlet west of Red Deer, Alberta. She's an avid outdoors person, unrepentant coffee addict, part-time foodie, servant to a wonderful feline, and companion to two delightfully hilarious canines. She will neither confirm nor deny the rumours regarding the heart in a jar on her desk and the bottle of reader's tears right next to it. Her paranormal urban fantasy series, Saints and Sinners, is available on Amazon and her YA Fantasy, Feathers and Fae will be released October 11, 2019, from Kyanite Publishing.
Website: www.crystallkirkham.com

Virus
by G. Allen Wilbanks

The survivors called them "zombies." They weren't, but they may as well have been. The virus that was supposed to kill on contact had mutated horribly. Those infected were left alive but reduced to mindless berserkers; savagely attacking anyone they came across with teeth and tearing nails.

The contagion spread unchecked.

Matthew levelled his rifle; fired again and again. "Zombies," he told himself. It made it easier to keep shooting. His vision blurred and he was forced to wipe moisture from his eye to clear it. He sighted the weapon back on the "zombie" with the face of his mother.

G. Allen Wilbanks is a member of the Horror Writers Association (HWA) and has published over 50 short stories in various magazines and on-line venues. He is the author of two short story collections, and the novel, When Darkness Comes.
Website: www.gallenwilbanks.com
Blog: DeepDarkThoughts.com

Final Embrace
by Peter J. Foote

Lost, I tumble through the dark void, only interstellar dust against my rough surface for company.

A gentle tug and a distant flicker reach out feeble fingers and invite me closer, could my loneliness be at an end?

The tug becomes a headlong rush and I have company for the first time in uncounted years. Radiation warms me, fingers of gravity reach out and invite me to play, but a blue marble sings to my soul.

Nuclear fires blister my skin and splinter me to the core, but the call is too strong, and I rush to our final embrace.

Peter J. Foote is a bestselling speculative fiction writer from Nova Scotia. Outside of writing, he runs a used bookstore specialising in fantasy & sci-fi, cosplays, and alternates between red wine and coffee as the mood demands. His short stories can be found in both print and in ebook form, with his story "Sea Monkeys" winning the inaugural "Engen Books/Kit Sora, Flash Fiction/Flash Photography" contest in March of 2018. As the founder of the group "Genre Writers of Atlantic Canada", Peter believes that the writing community is stronger when it works together.
Twitter: @PeterJFoote1
Website: peterjfooteauthor.wordpress.com

Waiting to Die
by Gabriella Balcom

When the nuclear bombs hit the United States, millions died. Nobody had believed North Korea could launch their long-range missiles that far, but their multiple strikes revealed the truth.

Those who survived found life totally different. Pustules formed on their skin. Clumps of their hair fell out, then their fingernails and some of their teeth. Food was scarce, mostly-contaminated anyway, so many starved. For others, watching loved ones die took its toll.

Everyone figured the future would be as bleak as the present, and life became a waiting game as survivors awaited death.

They didn't expect to start craving blood.

Gabriella Balcom lives in Texas with her family, loves reading and writing, and thinks she was born with a book in her hands. She works in a mental health field, and writes fantasy, horror/thriller, romance, children's stories, and sci-fi. She likes travelling, music, good shows, photography, history, interesting tales, and animals. Gabriella says she's a sucker for a great story and loves forests, mountains, and back roads which might lead who knows where. She has a weakness for lasagne, garlic bread, tacos, cheese, and chocolate, but not necessarily in that order.
Facebook: GabriellaBalcom.lonestarauthor

What Happened?
by Gabriella Balcom

After opening her eyes, Wilma felt fuzzy-brained. She checked her watch, questioned why she'd even awakened, then felt her bed moving. In fact, the house shook. She ran for the door, but something struck her from behind and everything went black.

She found herself underneath debris later, but managed to get free. Looking around, Wilma's face crumpled and tears rolled down her cheeks.

Her entire neighbourhood lay in rubble. Nearby buildings were twisted or pulverised. Fires burned unchecked everywhere.

Horrified and wondering what had occurred, Wilma saw other people stumbling along, some injured. They looked as clueless as she felt.

Gabriella Balcom lives in Texas with her family, loves reading and writing, and thinks she was born with a book in her hands. She works in a mental health field, and writes fantasy, horror/thriller, romance, children's stories, and sci-fi. She likes travelling, music, good shows, photography, history, interesting tales, and animals. Gabriella says she's a sucker for a great story and loves forests, mountains, and back roads which might lead who knows where. She has a weakness for lasagne, garlic bread, tacos, cheese, and chocolate, but not necessarily in that order.
Facebook: GabriellaBalcom.lonestarauthor

Powerless
by David Bowmore

Darkness came but the end is still happening.

No one is sure who did it, or why? On a basic level, home appliances stopped working and phones died. More serious were the planes that fell from the sky. The financial power houses collapsed the day the power failed. Banks became obsolete overnight.

The rioting went on for weeks.

A friend, a maths professor, estimates that half the population may have starved, been killed or died from previously avoidable accidents.

Can you bake bread from scratch?

Before this, I'd never killed for food. Have you?

Most are cannibals now, even vegans.

David Bowmore *has lived here, there and everywhere, but now lives in Yorkshire with his wonderful wife and a small white poodle. He has worn many hats in his time; head chef, teacher and landscape gardener. His first collection of short stories 'The Magic of Deben Market' is available from Clarendon House.*
Website: davidbowmore.co.uk
Facebook: davidbowmoreauthor

Too Late
by Brian Rosenberger

Infernos the size of cities still rage. Even the oceans are ablaze. Through the soot and smoke and the radioactive dust, through the black skies, through the ruin and the wreckage, a falling star.

Like the forgotten Sun, it descends. He descends.

The Angel.

Glowing with Heavenly Fire.

Other fires seem dim in comparison to Him.

Slowly, they emerge. Fearful at first.

The last survivors gather to witness the miracle.

They utter no sounds.

For the robots, it's the very first time they have seen an angel.

It's also marks the last time the robots will see an angel cry.

Brian Rosenberger lives in a cellar in Marietta, GA (USA) and writes by the light of captured fireflies. He is the author of As the Worms Turns and three poetry collections. He is also a featured contributor to the Pro-Wrestling literary collection, Three-Way Dance, available from Gimmick Press.
Facebook: HeWhoSuffers.

Apopcalypse
by Jacek Wilkos

The apocalypse came. And no one expected the form it took.

It started with bizarre clouds from which pianos and safes fell on people.

Buildings turned into ruins, destroyed in attacks of huge red, yellow and black globes, which turned out to be gigantic birds. Civilisation has fallen.

The remnants of humanity were devoured by various sharks—two-headed, snow, sand, walking on tentacles—scattered all over the globe by a gigantic tornado.

Thinking about the end of the world, we had biblical disasters before our eyes. God was bored with it, but he liked the products of our pop culture.

Jacek Wilkos is an engineer from Poland. He lives with his wife and daughter in a beautiful city of Cracow. He is addicted to buying books, he loves coffee, dark ambient music and riding his bike. He writes mostly horror drabbles. His fiction in Polish can be read on Szortal, Niedobre literki, Horror Online. In English his work was published in Drablr, Rune Bear, Sirens Call eZine.
Facebook: Jacek.W.Wilkos

Invasive Species
by Vonnie Winslow Crist

"Started with Kudzu and Water Hyacinth," said Hobbs as sat in a rocking chair on his porch.

Karl, rocking in the chair beside his, nodded.

"Then, they moved to Zebra Mussels, Snakeheads, and Cane Toads."

"Yup," agreed Karl.

"Next, were European starlings, rabbits, Asian carp and long-horned beetles," added Hobbs.

"Don't forget killer bees and famine weed." Karl yawned, scratched behind his ear.

"Now, those no-good aliens are landing on Earth. Bringing all their weird space diseases to humans."

"We'll stop them." Karl patted his shotgun.

Hobbs smiled. "That's one invasive species we're going to beat."

"We'd better—else we're goners."

*Vonnie Winslow Crist is author of The Enchanted Dagger, Owl Light, The Greener Forest, Murder on Marawa Prime, and other award-winning books. Her fiction is included in "Amazing Stories," "Cast of Wonders," "Outposts of Beyond," Killing It Softly 2, Defending the Future - Dogs of War, Midnight Masquerade, Chaos of Hard Clay, and elsewhere. A cloverhand who has found so many four-leafed clovers she keeps them in jars, Vonnie strives to celebrate the power of myth in her writing.
Website: www.vonniewinslowcrist.com*

The Tech Age Apocalypse
by Jasmine Jarvis

We don't sleep anymore, now that our brains are wired into the internet; constantly being bombarded with perfect images and status updates, leading us to envy others and pity ourselves. We never go outside anymore because the Web tells us that outside it is painful and dangerous. We let the Web provide for us—bring us everything we need to our little box homes. Empty suburban streets and city blocks are overrun with nature, but we will never know, never see it, as we are trapped inside a hell of our own design. We brought about our downfall.

Our apocalypse…

Jasmine Jarvis is a teller of tales and scribbler of scribbles. She lives in Brisbane, Australia with her husband Michael, their two children, Tilly and Mish; Ripley, their German Shepherd, and indoor fat cat, Dwight K. Shrute.

Survivor
by Brandy Bonifas

I climbed through the broken glass of the grocery store window. The shelves looked picked clean. Still, worth a look.

"Please, help me."

I turned, surprised.

"I haven't seen another person in weeks." The frail woman trembled. "Is it true? Man's going extinct?"

"That's what the news said…before the airwaves went quiet."

"Can you spare any food?"

I rummaged in my backpack. She came at me, brandishing a knife. I turned, putting a bullet between her eyes. I patted her down for anything useful. "Never trust a survivor."

I'm not sure if I spoke to myself…or the corpse.

Brandy Bonifas lives in Ohio with her husband and son. Her work has appeared or is forthcoming in anthologies by Clarendon House Publications, Pixie Forest Publishing, Zombie Pirate Publishing, and Blood Song Books, as well as the online publications CafeLit and Spillwords Press.
Website: www.brandybonifas.com
Facebook: brandybonifasauthor

Alone with the Flies
by Ximena Escobar

On the outskirts of the site, we thought we'd survived the explosion. But silent, invisible particles were spreading beyond the skeleton of our cities, fumes undulating like snakes up our nostrils.

I had dreamed so many nightmares of the apocalypse; huge waves of light flattening the buildings; the beauty of the universe exploding like a glorious farewell from God. But no cosmos showed in the dirty white sky, just the void of a buzzing sound. There was plenty for the flies, in our scathed knees, our drying eyes. For once the flies belonged. The world was a pile of shit.

Ximena Escobar is an emerging author of literary fiction and poetry. Originally from Chile, she is the author of a translation into Spanish of the Broadway Musical "The Wizard of Oz", and of an original adaptation of the same, "Navidad en Oz". Clarendon House Publications published her first short story in the UK, "The Persistence of Memory", and Literally Stories her first online publication with "The Green Light". She has since had several acceptances from other publishers and is working very hard exploring new exciting avenues in her writing.
She lives in Nottingham with her family.
Facebook: Ximenautora

I Knew It
By Eddie D. Moore

We all thought lightning and thunder would have signalled the end of the world, but the birds filled the air with music and white clouds drifted lazily across blue skies when that day came.

A measly 2.3 on the Richter scale shook every tectonic plate on the planet, and seconds later, the demonic armies of Hell spilled onto the surface. Mankind fought hard, but there is no victory over an army that can't die.

Commander Wilson stared out the International Space Station's windows and counted lava flows. He shook his head and said, "I told them global warming was real."

Eddie D. Moore travels hundreds of hours a year, and he fills that time by listening to audiobooks. When he isn't playing with his grandchildren, he writes his own stories. You can find a list of his publications on his blog or by visiting his Amazon Author Page. While you're there, be sure to pick up a copy of his mini-anthology Misfits & Oddities.
Website: eddiedmoore.wordpress.com
Amazon: amazon.com/author/eddiedmoore

Water
by E.L. Giles

Eyes sunken and lips cracked, they yelled for water, for they'd been thirsty for too long, and the sun burned over their heads.

"Pay me, and you'll get water," said a man in uniform, his rifle drawn, blocking access to the tank.

"We don't have any money!" cried a young boy. "We have nothing at all."

"Then I will keep the water, and you will die."

Anger flared throughout the crowd, and people pushed, punched, and kicked their way to the tank. Bullets zipped and bodies piled up until the crowd successfully conquered the soldiers standing guard.

"God, it's empty!"

E.L. Giles is a dreamer, passionate about art, a restless worker and a bit of a weird human. He started his artistic journey as a music composer until the need to put his thoughts and stories down on paper grew too strong for him to resist it any longer. He lives in the French Province of Quebec, Canada, with his girlfriend and two boys.
Facebook: elgilesauthor
Website: www.elgilesauthor.com

Day the Sun Exploded
by C.L. Williams

Without warning, one day the sun exploded!

Not being too far from the sun, many fallen pieces of the giant star hurtled towards the Earth, setting the planet ablaze with no one able to do anything.

Fighting a fire is one thing, fighting the sun is a losing battle, and many people were burned alive for trying.

After burning half of the population, Earth slowly became a giant icicle. With no sun to keep the planet warm, those who didn't die from the fires the sun brought to Earth when it exploded, soon froze to death from the sun's absence.

C.L. Williams is an independent author from central Virginia. He has written eight poetry books, four novellas, one novel, and a contributor to multiple anthologies, with the most recent appearance being an all-ages anthology titled Temoli from Thazbook. His most recent poetry book, The Paradox Complex, features the poem "Sad Crying Clown" that is now a video on YouTube directed by Matthew Mark Hunter of MMH Productions. C.L. Williams is currently working on his first sci-fi book, an all-ages book titled Novo: Away from Earth. When not writing, C.L. Williams is reading and sharing the work of other independent authors. Facebook: writer434
Twitter: @writer_434

Hold the Door
by Jodi Jensen

Ryker held the door as long as he could. The cover of darkness was fading as the sun peeked over the ridge, its deadly rays burning the already scorched ground.

Then he saw her.

His wife, Harlow.

Running for her life, a bag of supplies swinging wildly on her shoulder.

"You trying to get us killed?"

A man grabbed Ryker's arm, but he shook it off with a growl. "Wait! She'll make it!"

He was shoved out of the way, then fell to his knees as the flames licked the ground behind Harlow, then consumed her.

The door slammed shut.

Jodi Jensen grew up moving from California, to Massachusetts, and a few other places in between, before finally settling in Utah at the ripe old age of nine. The nomadic life fed her sense of adventure as a child and the wanderlust continues to this day. With a passion for old cemeteries, historical buildings and sweeping sagas of days gone by, it was only natural she'd dream of time traveling to all the places that sparked her imagination.

Restoring Order
by Dawn DeBraal

Jimmy Kelvin came running into the farmhouse.

"Ma! They said to seek shelter. It's coming any minute now." His mother sprayed cleaner on the counter, wiping it down with circular strokes. She kept cleaning like she didn't hear him. Spray then wipe. It was the same the night his Pa died. Pa wasn't expected to last the night. Jimmy's mother just kept on cleaning. It was her way of putting her world in order. Jimmy ran down to the cellar as the blast happened. When he came out, the house was gone, so was ma, but the counter was clean.

Dawn DeBraal lives in rural Wisconsin with her husband Red, two rat terriers, and a cat. She has discovered that her love of telling a good story can be written. Published stories with Palm-sized press, Spillwords, Mercurial Stories, Potato Soup Journal, Edify Fiction, Zimbell House Publishing, Clarendon House Publishing, Blood Song Books, Black Hare Press, Fantasia Divinity, Cafelit, Reanimated Writers, Guilty Pleasures, Unholy Trinity, The World of Myth, Dastaan World, Vamp Cat, Runcible Spoon, Dark Christmas, Siren's Call, Iron Horse Publishing, Falling Star Magazine 2019 Pushcart Nominee.
Amazon: amazon.com/Dawn-DeBraal/e/B07STL8DLX

Lola
by Brandi Hicks

I could see the mass carnage from the drone's video feed. I just had to wait for Brad's signal and then I could go and add my part. This destruction was my plan. Brad waved his cigar at the drone then flipped it off. What a douchebag, but that was the signal he chose. I strapped on my ammunition belt and swung my AR-16 over my shoulder. Then I grabbed Lola, my rocket launcher. She was my baby. I gave her a kiss and came out from our control room in the sewers. It was time to make my mark.

*Growing up in West Virginia, **Brandi Hicks** loved to have her nose in a book, her eyes toward the night sky and putting a pen to paper. Her imagination was always sparked by her grandfather and her mom taking her to new places and teaching her about the unusual. She loves fantasy, sci-fi, and learning about science and history. She has two beautiful children, and hopes to instill creativity and a love of reading in them. Finding new crafts to try keeps her busy when not playing with her kids or working.*

The End of Days
by Mark Kodama

Uhgli and his clan trekked through the steaming jungle to the sea where they could feast on shellfish, crabs, fish and seaweed in the tide pools. Uhgli looked forward to the cool ocean waters.

When they arrived at the beach, the ground shook and the water receded as far as the eye could see. Barto, the old shaman, said they must flee inland for the gods were angry.

On the horizon, an island spewed forth smoke and fire, darkening the sky.

But the woman and children were tired and needed rest. Suddenly, the ocean waters came rushing toward their camp.

Mark Kodama is a trial attorney and former newspaper reporter who lives in Washington, D.C. His short stories and poems have been published in Clarendon Publishing House anthologies, Commuter Lit, Dastaan World Magazine, Dissident Voice Magazine, Literary Yard, Mercurial Stories, Spillwords, Tuck Magazine, and World of Myth Magazine.

Across the Line of Delineation – What Had We Taught Them?
by C.L. Steele

Months after the reactor malfunction, the first five humans stepped across the delineation line. Their radiation suits would last fifteen minutes. The Geiger counter ticked faster than their pulses. Man-high weeds grew everywhere. Underneath, lime-green sand glowed; perhaps a reflection, but they took samples. Families homes now appeared haunted. Playground equipment squeaked in the never-ending wind. The counter spiked as Captain Matthews bent to collect a weed's root. With the snip, the weeds thrashed. The nearest plant grabbed and pushed him under the sand. Later, helmets popped-up though the delineation line. Five small green weeds grew—across the helmeted line.

C.L. Steele *creates new worlds and mystical places filled with complex characters on exciting journeys. Her typical genre is Sci-Fi/Fantasy, where she concentrates on writing in the sub-genres of Magical Realism, Near Future, and Futuristic worlds. Published in numerous anthologies, she looks forward to the release of her debut novel. In the interim, she works on other novels and continues to write short stories, novellas, and poetry. She is featured as one of five international authors in ICWG Magazine through Clarendon Publishing House and is a contributing author to Blood Puddles Literary Journal. Follow her growing career at:*

Facebook: author.CLSteele

Instagram: @clsteele.author

I'll Eat My Burger
by Neen Cohen

The world below my hotel window burns and screams. I hear nothing. A Charlie Chaplin film, with less laughter.

Trembling hands slide around my waist, gripping my shirt.

"We should do something."

"Why?"

I turn. She looks at me like I am insane.

"They are going to kill everyone."

"Exactly." I stride to the food trolley, brought in moments before the first fireball hit. The ships arrived, hostile aliens with one clear message.

Surrender is futile. Cleansing will be absolute.

I lift the silver cover, taking a deep breath of the cooling food.

"I think I'll eat my burger first."

Neen Cohen lives in Brisbane with her partner, son and fur babies. She is a writer of LGBTQI, dark fantasy and horror short stories and has a Bachelor of Creative Industries from QUT. She can often be found writing while sitting against a tombstone or tree in any number of graveyards.
Facebook: Neen-Cohen-Author-424700821629629
Website: wordbubblessite.wordpress.com

The Last Can of Tomato Soup
by Jodi Jensen

Six months since the invasion. Screams from the early days were long gone, silenced by creatures the size of gnats.

Lauren opened the last can of tomato soup for her son.

His gaunt face wavered in the candlelight as he slurped.

It was time. Time to venture outside.

"Stay put," she whispered. Armed only with the jagged soup can lid, Lauren slipped out.

One cautious step…

Then another…

A force slammed her against the house and a spit of light flew into her eye.

Give us your son.

"NO!" She sliced her wrist with the soup can lid.

We'll wait…

Jodi Jensen grew up moving from California, to Massachusetts, and a few other places in between, before finally settling in Utah at the ripe old age of nine. The nomadic life fed her sense of adventure as a child and the wanderlust continues to this day. With a passion for old cemeteries, historical buildings and sweeping sagas of days gone by, it was only natural she'd dream of time traveling to all the places that sparked her imagination.

Freedom
by Raven Corinn Carluk

Doomsayers were proven correct regarding CERN: discovering the Higgs-Bosun cracked open doorways to the universe and triggered the end.

Death and chaos followed. Old systems were toppled. The Elite and their herds of chosen slaves retreated to safety. The unprepared perished in hunger and panic, trapped in their failing cities.

As the initial furore died down, people attempted to put their lives back together. Most were consumed by despair, lost without the comforts of the old world.

Hubby and I, though, we found what we'd always wanted. Just the simple life for us: raiding and pillaging and ruling the weak.

Raven Corinn Carluk writes dark fantasy, paranormal romance, and anything else that catches her interest. She's authored five novels, where she explores themes of love and acceptance. Her shorter pieces, usually from her darker side, can be found in Black Hare Press anthologies, at Detritus Online, and through Alban Lake Publishers.
Twitter: @ravencorinn
Website: RavenCorinnCarluk.Blogspot.Com

Lying Still in Vulcan's Embrace
by Aiki Flinthart

Where were you, husband, when the sky rained fire and ash and smoke? When the day smouldered into choking night. When the air turned to sulphur that burnt lungs and blinded eyes. When a river of grey spewed from the great mountain and swept down the slope in white-hot torrents. Smothered the city; buried it beneath blankets of heat and stone.

Where were you when we screamed and curled into ourselves; covered the children's heads as raining ash drifted down and piled upon their small bodies?

You were already fled. Adrift. Offshore.

And now we rest, forever, in Vulcan's bed.

Aiki Flinthart has had short stories shortlisted in the Aurealis awards and top-8 listed in the USA Writers of the Future competition, as well as published in various anthologies and e-mags. She has 11 published spec fic novels and has edited 2 short story anthologies. She regularly gives workshops on writing fight scenes at conventions. Lives in Brisbane. Does martial arts, archery, knife throwing and lute-playing. Website: www.aikiflinthart.com

Apocalypse by Internet
by Owen Morgan

What am I going to do now?

Hovering the mouse over the internet icon, which is greyed-out, a message jumps up: *no external network found.*

Great, now I can't listen to my music, download videos, search for restaurants, read reviews on the latest movies or chat with my closest mates.

Wait a minute, what's that noise? It's coming from outside my front door. I pick up a cricket-bat, fling the door and step outside.

There are people everywhere, milling about, confused, afraid, angry. Some have weapons, too, and they don't look friendly.

So, this is how the bloody world ends!

__Owen Morgan__ lives with his family in the fishing port of Steveston, British Columbia. Writing Credits: George Washington: The Loyalist, Splicers, Steamships of the Northwest Frontier, The Angel's Lamp, Attack of the Federation, On Wings of Thunder & Perchance to Sleep Perchance to Dream.
Website: kingauthor.wordpress.com

It Was Illegal
by Abigail Linhardt

It was illegal in Germany to use cooking oil in your diesel truck. But illegal didn't matter now. And he wasn't in Germany any more: he was in hell. All he needed were a few things found in the kitchen. Inside the looted store he found measuring cups and a pack of Mason jars.

A big jug of vegetable oil, some lye, and any product that had methanol in it would do. The world had changed so much, illegal actives would save lives.

He clutched his hatchet harder, swinging to split the skull of the man going for the oil.

Abi Linhardt *has been a gamer all her life but is a teacher at heart. When she is not writing, you can find her slaying enemies online or teaching in a college classroom. She has published works of fiction, poetry, college essays, and even won two literary awards for her short stories in science fiction and horror. Abi lives and writes in the grey world of northern Ohio.*

Collateral Damage
by E.L. Giles

"Fire!" The President's voice resonated with an unexpected intensity, hurting everyone's ears.

"But the civilians!" exclaimed one of the officers, his hand shaking over the button that would propel the arsenal of nuclear warheads overseas.

"Collateral damage," the President said, staring intently at the screen as it played footage of the deadly conflicts worldwide. The earth was in ruins. He had no other choice. "Don't you want to protect your country? Then hit the bloody button."

"No!" The officer got up and unholstered his pistol, aiming it at the President, beads of sweat rolling down on his temple. "I won't."

*E.L. Giles is a dreamer, passionate about art, a restless worker and a bit of a weird human. He started his artistic journey as a music composer until the need to put his thoughts and stories down on paper grew too strong for him to resist it any longer. He lives in the French Province of Quebec, Canada, with his girlfriend and two boys.
Facebook: elgilesauthor
Website: www.elgilesauthor.com*

The Sun Will Rise Soon
by David Bowmore

Our eyes have to be good for we live and work in near total darkness now. The last humans had to withdraw to the shadows, the dark places and the underground tunnels. The sun still shines, but we are forced to survive this way, blocking out all light.

Why? They come out during the day and are drawn to all forms of illumination.

Who? Solar Vampires, a government experiment gone wrong.

We soon learned their weakness. I work with a team of hunters. Our aim is to decapitate them while they rest during the night.

The sun will rise soon.

David Bowmore has lived here, there and everywhere, but now lives in Yorkshire with his wonderful wife and a small white poodle. He has worn many hats in his time; head chef, teacher and landscape gardener. His first collection of short stories 'The Magic of Deben Market' is available from Clarendon House.
Website: davidbowmore.co.uk
Facebook: davidbowmoreauthor

The End
by Gabriella Balcom

Sarah winced as she tried to sit up straighter and couldn't prevent a groan from escaping her lips. She wasn't able to open her eyes anymore, but that didn't surprise her.

Something damp moved across her cheek, and she whispered, "I love you, too, Buddy." He snuggled against her, and she relaxed, resting her head against his. He'd never left her side, and she'd didn't know what she would've done without him.

When their bodies were found days later, Sandy's arms were still around her faithful Labrador Retriever. Like so many others, they'd survived the wars but starved to death.

Gabriella Balcom lives in Texas with her family, loves reading and writing, and thinks she was born with a book in her hands. She works in a mental health field, and writes fantasy, horror/thriller, romance, children's stories, and sci-fi. She likes travelling, music, good shows, photography, history, interesting tales, and animals. Gabriella says she's a sucker for a great story and loves forests, mountains, and back roads which might lead who knows where. She has a weakness for lasagne, garlic bread, tacos, cheese, and chocolate, but not necessarily in that order.
Facebook: GabriellaBalcom.lonestarauthor

Fresh Hell
by Zoey Xolton

When people think about the End of the World, they think terror, bloodshed, radioactive wastelands… It's all that, but it's much worse. You find yourself missing the simple, everyday comforts: running water, coffee, warm meals and toilet paper.

I can't imagine what it's like for the remaining female survivors and their infants. For them, it's back to monthly rags, and makeshift cloth nappies. I shudder to think. It's like being thrown into the Dark Ages all over again. Only this time, everything is toxic, ravaged and broken.

I don't know if humanity can claw its way back from this one.

Zoey Xolton *is an Australian Speculative Fiction writer, primarily of Dark Fantasy, Paranormal Romance and Horror. She is also a proud mother of two and is married to her soul mate. Outside of her family, writing is her greatest passion. She is especially fond of short fiction and is working on releasing her own themed collections in future. Website: www.zoeyxolton.com.*

Bad Water
by G. Allen Wilbanks

Food, shelter, weapons, those things are easy if you know where to look.

Water is the problem.

Most of the water here is unsafe from chemicals or biological contamination. Any clean sources are quickly claimed and jealously guarded.

It's not fair.

I survived the war and the riots that followed, then hid underground for two years to avoid The Scourge. What was the point? Was it all just leading to this?

My guts twist and cramp like a living thing moving inside of me.

To fight so hard for so long, only to die drinking from a stagnant rain puddle.

G. Allen Wilbanks is a member of the Horror Writers Association (HWA) and has published over 50 short stories in various magazines and on-line venues. He is the author of two short story collections, and the novel, When Darkness Comes.
Website: www.gallenwilbanks.com
Blog: DeepDarkThoughts.com

In the Name of Art
by Diane Arrelle

"Hey, now that they're convinced their world is supposed to end this week, let's set off some volcanoes!"

"Yeah, and we oughta nudge a fault line just to be convincing."

"Great idea!"

The two waited, from a safe distance off-planet. After a while, the novelty wore off. "The date's correct now, send in the ships to land at strategic points. The natives'll do the rest."

The next day the world lay in ruins; the cities smouldering heaps, no sign of life anywhere.

"You catch it all? I swear we're gonna win first place at the Galactic Film Festival this time!"

Diane Arrelle, the pen name of South Jersey writer Dina Leacock, has sold more than 250 short stories and has three published books including Just A Drop In The Cup, a collection of short-short stories and her new collection of horror stories, Seasons On The Dark Side. Retired from being director of a municipal senior citizen centre, she is now co-owner of a small publishing company, Jersey Pines Ink LLC. She resides with her husband and her new cat on the edge of the Pine Barrens (home of the Jersey Devil). Website: www.arrellewrites.com Facebook: Diane.Arrelle

West of Eden
by Blake Jessop

A wall of cloud that blanketed the entire horizon broke slowly toward the hill like a wave that would drown heaven. There was a smell of ozone, even through the air filters. The old man sat down.

"Get up," she said, "you've always got a plan."

"Not this time. It's not the end of the world if anyone survives, is it?"

"We have to do something."

He patted the dirt beside him.

"It's a hell of a view."

She took off her mask and slumped down next to him on the crest, leant her head on his shoulder, and waited.

Blake Jessop is a Canadian author of science fiction, fantasy and horror stories with a master's degree in creative writing from the University of Adelaide. You can read more of his speculative fiction in "I Didn't Break the Lamp: Historical Accounts of Imaginary Acquaintances" from DefCon One, or follow him on Twitter.
Twitter: @everydayjisei
Amazon: www.amazon.com/default/e/B07BB7Z73N

Mouths to Feed
by Amber M. Simpson

Food's been scarce since the military came and took everything we had. For rationing, they'd said, pointing guns in our faces. For survivors of the blast. But with Mama's new baby, I'm the oldest of seven, and that's a lot of mouths to feed. Luckily, Papa's last hunt was successful.

My siblings squeal at the table in hungry excitement as the smell of food cooking waters our mouths. We devour each bite, lick our plates clean, and pretend not to hear the sounds coming from the basement where Papa keeps the meat fresh.

Ignoring the screams gets easier each time.

Amber M. Simpson *is a chronic nighttime writer with a penchant for dark fiction and fantasy. When she's not editing for Fantasia Divinity Magazine, she divides her creative time (when she's not procrastinating) between writing a mystery/horror novel, working on a medieval fantasy series, and coming up with new ideas for short stories. Above all, she enjoys being a mom to her two greatest creations, Max and Liam, who keep her feet on the ground even while her head is in the clouds.*
Website: ambermsimpson.com

Two Thirds
by Jeff Slade

Burt grunted, hauling the sack into the cave. The twilit sky yielded to darkness within.

Rocks skittered as he crept past crates. Their preserved contents reminded Burt that food wasn't the problem.

Nuclear fallout wasn't either.

He removed his mask once deep enough and dropped the sack. A machine, his invention, beeped. Lights flashed green above a faucet. The prior process finished.

He'd solved the worst problem.

He removed the latest body, dumped it into the machine's attached dissolving tank, took a hard-earned swig from the chemically produced glass of reddish-brown water.

Two thirds per person went a long way.

Jeff Slade *resides in Salmon Cove, Newfoundland and Labrador, with his wife and two cats. He enjoys reading, writing, and making horrible puns, not necessarily in that order. You can find other short stories by him in Chillers From The Rock, Dystopia From The Rock, and Flights From The Rock, published by Engen Books.*

Operation: Repopulation
by Terry Miller

After the war, the ratio of women to men was ten to one. Sure, the women fought too, but it was the men whose egos told them they had something to prove; they proved only how quickly they could die.

Now that it's over, this made repopulating a bit difficult. Women had become drunk in their lustful frenzies, desperate. Some kept men prisoners in their homes, others had taken notes from the pimp playbook. Men were now the objectified gender, popped full of pills to keep the goods in operation; the used up and broken tossed out like yesterday's trash.

Terry Miller is an author and 2017 Rhysling Award-nominated poet residing in Portsmouth, OH, USA. He has self-published a dark poetry collection on Amazon and one short story to date. His work has also appeared in Sanitarium, Devolution Z, Jitter Press, Poetry Quarterly, O Unholy Night in Deathlehem, and the 2017 Rhysling Anthology from the Science Fiction and Fantasy Poetry Association.
Facebook: tmiller2015

Sealed In
by Sam M. Phillips

We huddled into the shelter as the siren sounded.

"Stay still, don't move around, breathe calmly, don't panic," said the community leader as she sealed us in.

Outside, the bombs were falling, sweeping our civilisation from the face of the Earth. I cried, but my son squeezed my hand. I looked at him. He smiled such a sweet, innocent smile; maybe there was a chance, after all. We still lived, we could rebuild.

Three months later, when the meters in the shelter still said the radiation outside was too toxic to emerge, I wished we'd died in the initial blast.

Sam M. Phillips is the co-founder of Zombie Pirate Publishing, producing short story anthologies and helping emerging writers. His own work has appeared in dozens of anthologies and magazines such as Full Moon Slaughter 2, 13 Bites Volumes IV and V, Rejected for Content 6, and Dastaan World Magazine. He lives in the green valleys of northern New South Wales, Australia, and enjoys reading, walking, and playing drums in the death metal band Decryptus.
Website: zombiepiratepublishing.com
Blog: bigconfusingwords.wordpress.com

The Road Warrior
by Gregg Cunningham

As the Chinese nukes fell from the sky Jack stiffened, knowing all his dreams were about to come true.

He was so prepared for the coming apocalypse.

He had the bunker in the hills, hidden away with all his leather outfits.

He had the biker boots and the shoulder pads.

He had the guns and the ammo.

He had the muscle car.

He was a survivor.

All he had to do was wait.

But by day ten, Jack found himself huddled in the filthy darkness of his bunker, sobbing as the pounding began again on the weakening metal hatch above.

Gregg Cunningham 48, is a short story writer from Western Australia who has had to pick up his game since stumbling into facebook writer's groups. He has stories published by 559 Publishing in in 13 Bites volume 3,4,5, Plan 9 from Outer space, Other Realms, Heard It on The Radio, 559 Ways to Die, short stories publishing by Zombie Pirate Publishing in Relationship add Vice, Full Metal Horror, Phuket Tattoo, World War four and Flash Fiction Addiction (flash) with Zombie Pirate Publishing, and also in Daastan Magazine Chapter 11 and Brian,Rich and the Wardrobe. Amazon: www.amazon.com/-/e/B016OTHX0K

Don't Fuck with Earth
by Crystal L. Kirkham

Nothing but the dust moved across the barren land. This place was once a lush green forest but only shades of umber remained. I picked my way across the tortured landscape heading south. I got a message on the radio that there was an organised group of survivors down that way and I was going to join them.

Damned aliens. They assumed scorching the Earth would kill us. They hadn't intended for anything to survive. They had failed and, if rumours were right, we were about to give them a taste of their own medicine.

No one fucked with Earth.

Crystal L. Kirkham resides in a small hamlet west of Red Deer, Alberta. She's an avid outdoors person, unrepentant coffee addict, part-time foodie, servant to a wonderful feline, and companion to two delightfully hilarious canines. She will neither confirm nor deny the rumours regarding the heart in a jar on her desk and the bottle of reader's tears right next to it. Her paranormal urban fantasy series, Saints and Sinners, is available on Amazon and her YA Fantasy, Feathers and Fae will be released October 11, 2019, from Kyanite Publishing.
Website: www.crystallkirkham.com

Doomsday Duet
by Serena Jayne

Instead of a bang, an old melancholy melody served as the world's death rattle. Next came car alarms, dogs barking, kids crying, and then nothing.

The world's remote control permanently stuck on mute.

Thought I was the only one left until I saw her.

Sleek, shiny, black as oblivion.

I'd begged for gerbils, kittens, puppies. Mama always said no.

The apocalypse killed my dreams, but it granted my wish.

Weak with illness, I couldn't throw balls or praise gifts of murdered mice.

Her innocent nibble became a bite.

Only starving dogs eat their owners. Cats? They just gotta be bored.

Serena Jayne is a graduate of Seton Hill University's Writing Popular Fiction MFA Program. Her short fiction and poetry can be found in Switchblade Magazine, the Drabble, Crack the Spine Literary Magazine, 101 Fiction, the Oddville Press, and other publications.
Website: *www.serenajayne.com*
Twitter: *@SJ_Writer*

Rex
by Matthew M. Montelione

The king of the beasts lifted his heavy head towards the white sky and growled. The sun was torturously bright.

He was on the hunt for prey. He sniffed through his wide nostrils; a strange smell permeated the air. He huffed, turning his head in disgust. The beast's worries shifted from hunger to something more urgent.

Rumbling. Creaking. Movement everywhere. Woods wildly swayed as hot winds ripped over the land, tearing trees from the ground. Thunderous galloping, coming towards him.

A harsh, explosive sound rocked the sky. Booming claps of thunder rattled overhead.

The meteor hit, shaking the planet's core.

Matthew M. Montelione is a horror writer born and raised on Long Island in New York. His stories have been published in Quoth the Raven: A Contemporary Reimagining of the Works of Edgar Allan Poe, Thuggish Itch: Devilish, and other titles. Matthew is also an American Revolution historian who focuses on the local experiences of Loyalists on Long Island. His work on the subject has been published in Long Island History Journal and Journal of the American Revolution.
Website: maybeevils.com
Twitter: @maybeevils

Seclusion
Delusion
by Michael D. Davis

YES! I can't believe it; it's a dream come true. I'm alone, all alone. No stupid people around saying stupid things, doing stupid things. This is amazing. All it took was one little virus and paradise is made. The last person on the planet I am, the only person on the planet is me; isn't it fabulous?

Wait, what the hell's that screaming? It sounds like someone's horrible shrill voice…but that's impossible. It can't be.

But it is. Another person. The survivor walks about, killing my good mood with every breath he takes.

Why can't anything go my way?

Michael D. Davis was born and raised in a small town in Iowa. A high school graduate and avid reader he has aspired to be a writer for years. Having written over thirty short stories, ranging in genre from comedy to horror from flash fiction to novella. He continues in his accursed pursuit of a career in the written word and in his hunt Michael's love for stories in all genres and mediums will not falter.

High Ground
by Radar DeBoard

Meghan sat on the rooftop, looking out towards the now setting sun. It had been the two hardest months for humanity since the emergence; they came to kill, not to conquer.

She pulled herself up, grunting from the pain of the gash on her left leg.

She stared over the roof's ledge at the dozens of creatures on the ground below. Their snarls grew louder and angrier upon seeing her.

She wondered if there was anyone left. She raised the pistol up to her head, placing the barrel against her temple and whispered to herself, "It was a good run."

Radar DeBoard is a horror movie and novel enthusiast who resides in the small town of Goddard, Kansas. He occasionally dabbles in writing and enjoys making dark tales for people to enjoy.

A Lovely Day
by R.J. Meldrum

We gazed out from the promenade towards the sea. The tide was in and the sun glittered off the small waves heading towards shore.

"Your ice cream is melting," I said.

Lucy licked her fingers. Behind us a car roared away, its tires squealing.

"What a waste of time."

We watched the sea. I checked my watch. It was nearly time. I took Lucy's hand.

"It's been a lovely day."

"It has."

Above, the sky was ripped open and a fiery streak blazed overhead. It was predicted the asteroid would land somewhere in the mid-Atlantic.

"Yes, what a lovely day."

R. J. Meldrum is an author and academic. Born in Scotland, he moved to Ontario, Canada in 2010. He has had stories published by Horrified Press, the Infernal Clock, Trembling with Fear, Darkhouse Books, Smoking Pen Press, and James Ward Kirk Fiction. He also has had stories published in The Sirens Call e-zine, the Horror Zine and Drabblez Magazine. He is an Affiliate Member of the Horror Writers Association. Twitter: @RichardJMeldru1 Facebook: richard.meldrum.79

Zombees
by C.H. Williams

It all started with a flower, or was it the bee? Cross-pollination contamination. Viruses bred viruses, carried from one flower to the next on the sticky legs of the bees. They said if the bees went, we'd all die. Turns out, the bees living was much more dangerous to humanity.

First, it got the flowers, then the animals who ate them, and that's where we came in, the ones who ate the animals. Like a descending mist, we couldn't run away from it. It drove us crazy. Before long we were eating each other. And the flowers. And the bees.

C.H. Williams is a full-time mum who writes adult contemporary fiction, short stories, flash pieces and poetry. She can often be found with a jar of peanut butter in one hand and a bar of dark chocolate in the other, which coincidentally makes it rather difficult to type.
Twitter: @authorch
Instagram: @c.h.writes

Humanity
by K.C. McIntyre

"Mild earthquakes," you said. "Nothing to fear."

We knew the tremors were something more.

You never gave us a chance.

While you hid like cowards, cavernous mouths opened wide, swallowing the Western coast, from Alaska down to Chile. Thunderous geysers of fiery lava decimated everything across North and South America. Merciless tsunamis washed away coastal cities and most islands, while the ash clouds suffocated those who remained.

We know you shuttled the wealthiest to deep mountain bunkers hoping to save "humanity." There was nothing humane about letting billions die without warning.

Only there *were* survivors.

Now we're coming for you.

K.C. McIntyre resides in Toronto with her husband and their twelve-year-old daughter. With another baby on the way and two fur babies to care for, it hardly leaves time for writing, so she seizes every opportunity to get words down on paper. She enjoys writing all genres, but her favourites are romance and fantasy. Her short story, Black Swan was previously published in an anthology about mythology. She's currently in the final stages of her first novel, a contemporary romance she hopes to release before the birth of her daughter in September 2019.

The Horde
by Terri A. Arnold

I'm huddled in the darkest corner of my house, my hand over my daughter's mouth, shaking. Is this the end for us; with people eating each other? Those with red eyes react to noise, when they hear something they turn and shuffle towards it. They travel in packs, climbing over each other at times, but never attacking each other. I can hear them outside my house; the emergency alert screams from my radio, my eyes snap to the radio in terror; I accidentally left it on. Grabbing my daughter, I run as I hear the horde turn in our direction.

Terri A Arnold has recently begun to share stories that she has been writing for years. She is from a small town in Nova Scotia and loves to put words to paper. By day she works as a registered nurse, but any other time she can be found reading or writing, and is loving it more and more every day.

Old World Trinkets
by Joel R. Hunt

Welcome!

You're new here, aren't you? I can always tell. And I bet you've never seen Old World trinkets as fine as these before! I only stock the best!

That one? Great choice, an antique. They called those *fowns*. Hold it up—yes, there you are. See your reflection in that rectangle? The old ones loved doing that, it was their primary cultural pass time.

No?

How about this one? Called a *buhk*. Feel that quality paper. The Old World was built on *buhks*.

They make wonderful fuel.

You want all of them? Shrewd choice, quite a bargain!

Happy burning!

Joel R. Hunt is a writer from the UK who dabbles in the darker aspects of life, particularly through horror, science fiction and the supernatural. He has been published in a number of short story anthologies, and hopes to have released his first single author collection in early 2020, and hopes to have released his first anthology of short stories later this year.
Twitter: @JoelRHunt1
Reddit: JRHEvilInc

Hormones
by Vonnie Winslow Crist

"Do you think it was extra-terrestrials?" asked Crystal.

"Maybe." Judy stared out the window.

"But humans wouldn't do this to themselves."

Judy shrugged her shoulders. "A superpower, underdeveloped nation, or terrorist regime with dreams of world domination might've—but who saturated Earth's water and air with steroids and testosterone is irrelevant. Hormone-addled, we're killing each other, and destroying civilisation."

"Shouldn't scientists be able to reverse it by blasting the planet with an anti-steroid and oestrogen cocktail?"

"Doesn't work that way," said Judy. She pointed to an angry mob headed their way. "Even if it did, it's too late for us."

*Vonnie Winslow Crist is author of The Enchanted Dagger, Owl Light, The Greener Forest, Murder on Marawa Prime, and other award-winning books. Her fiction is included in "Amazing Stories," "Cast of Wonders," "Outposts of Beyond," Killing It Softly 2, Defending the Future - Dogs of War, Midnight Masquerade, Chaos of Hard Clay, and elsewhere. A cloverhand who has found so many four-leafed clovers she keeps them in jars, Vonnie strives to celebrate the power of myth in her writing.
Website: www.vonniewinslowcrist.com*

Dune After Dune After Dune
by Shelly Jarvis

These wounds will kill me.

His dagger was dull, or I would be dead already. The cut, though shallow, is infected and fever tries to consume me. When the winds begin tonight, I may give myself over to them.

I tell myself there will be shelter on the other side of the dune. I've told myself that for the last ten, the last hundred. If there is shelter in this place like the old stories say, each step makes me more certain I will not find it.

This is a wasteland; I am the waste. My only hope is death.

Shelly Jarvis is a speculative fiction author from West Virginia, US. She found a life-long love of sci-fi and fantasy in the 3rd grade when she found Madeleine L'Engle's "A Wrinkle in Time." Shelly is an avid reader, a Whovian, the ideal viewer of dog rescue videos, and undoubtedly Ravenclaw. She currently has two YA sci-fi books available for purchase on Amazon.
Website: www.ShellyJarvis.com

A Way Out
by Joel R. Hunt

The frenzied hammering at the doors was overwhelming. It assaulted them from every direction. Unrelenting. Unforgiving. Inescapable.

There was no reasoning with these creatures. No humanity left in them. They would break their way inside, and they would feast. Even on the baby.

Mother tried to shush his cries, rocking him back and forth as Father checked the pistol's clip.

"Do we have enough bullets?" asked Mother.

He looked to her, then to the barricaded doorway as it began to shake.

"Just," he said.

"I love you both," whispered Mother.

"Always," Father replied.

She closed her eyes.

Bang. Bang.

…

Bang.

__Joel R. Hunt__ is a writer from the UK who dabbles in the darker aspects of life, particularly through horror, science fiction and the supernatural. He has been published in a number of short story anthologies, and hopes to have released his first single author collection in early 2020, and hopes to have released his first anthology of short stories later this year.
Twitter: @JoelRHunt1
Reddit: JRHEvilInc

Marissa
by Christian Ohnimus

Marissa stumbled out of the dilapidated Food Mart. She moaned—empty-handed again. Her hair was coarse and thinning and her skin sagged on a skeletal frame. She started down the sidewalk, but not the street. Following the pedestrian paths gave her a sense of order.

Marissa heard voices. A young man turned the corner. She spoke, but only managed a garble. It'd been so long since she'd needed her voice. He was armed and surprise painted his face at the sight of her. Marissa raised one decomposing arm while the man raised his gun. And pulled the trigger.

"Damn zombies."

Christian Ohnimus is a cardiac nurse and father of three who resides in eastern Ohio. He is currently studying for his Master of Science in Nursing. While he is a long-time amateur writer, this is his debut into writing microfiction.

Shelf Life
by Andrew Anderson

Wandering around the busy marketplace, I fondled the coin in my pocket.

I barely glanced at the bookseller and, instead, I was drawn to the brightly coloured stall against the back wall, where a wizened perfume-trader displayed her wares.

She was selling the scents of the old world, the one we'd had to leave behind when we were forced underground.

Now that we'd resurfaced, these beautiful scents existed only in tiny expensive vials, to be smelled once before dissipating forever—*vanilla; petrichor; coffee.*

I had enough for one, but I walked away, reluctant to be the reason for its extinction.

Andrew Anderson is a full-time civil servant, dabbling in writing music, poetry, screenplays and short stories in his limited spare time, when not working on building himself a fort made out of second-hand books. He lives in Bathgate, Scotland with his wife, two children and his dog.
Twitter: @soorploom

Create a Life
by Umair Mirxa

Celeste wiped a rogue tear from her cheek, trying hard not to break down completely as she surveyed the death and destruction.

"The war to end the world," said David, moving up beside her on the ridge. "They weren't wrong."

"No, they weren't."

The last war. It had destroyed nations. Wiped out civilisations. Less than ten thousand humans, by generous estimates, were left alive.

"What are we going to do?"

"The only thing left for us to do," said Celeste with a smile. "We will create a life for ourselves out of this mess, and for everyone else who survived."

Umair Mirxa lives in Karachi, Pakistan. His first published story, 'Awareness', appeared on Spillwords Press. He has also had stories accepted for anthologies from Zombie Pirate Publishing, Blood Song Books, Fantasia Divinity Magazine and Publishing, and Iron Faerie Publishing. He is a massive J.R.R. Tolkien fan, and loves everything to do with fantasy and mythology. He enjoys football, history, music, movies, TV shows, and comic books, and wishes with all his heart that dragons were real.
Website: www.umairmirxa.com
Facebook: UMirxa12

Unsure
by K.R. Monin

I was unsure in the face of the Great Comet—the one that killed the humans.

Some greeted extinction with resignation, gorging themselves on grease and addiction wherever they could.

Me? I went to seize my final chance. Leslie was there, willing. Her friends who despised me were distant, their warnings unheard. I tasted love and revenge with nothing to live for and nothing to lose.

But I hesitated. I chose right then to wonder about life after death. Did my last actions matter more? Less? Would I be judged for right or wrong?

I was unsure, but now I know.

K.R. Monin writes near-future sci-fi and speculative fiction. She lives in Pittsburgh, identifies as a beer snob, and thrives on wanderlust.
Twitter: @kunderscoremons
Website: krmonin.com

Last Scream
by Melinda Pouncey

It was the scream that woke him. The screams always did. Usually accompanied by the crackling sound of flaming bodies, searing debris striking the pavement like hail, the hiss of melting metal. And after, the cottony silence, stuffing the death rattle of the world in his ears with shroud-like finality.

He raised his head. A scream. It wasn't a dream this time, it was real!

There on one of the screens, a small girl. A monster that had once been a man rushed toward her. Tears streamed from his eyes as, safe inside his bunker, he switched the feed off.

Melinda Pouncey is a retired psychologist who enjoys exploring the complexities and scope of the human imagination through a variety of genres. From an early age, Melinda discovered an affinity for tales involving the unusual and the macabre, especially those with a dash of humour or the unexpected. She has written numerous short stories and poems, focusing her attention most recently on the horror and fantasy realms. Melinda is a member of two local writing groups and enjoys acting as an editor and proofreader when not working on stories of her own.

Midas Touch
by Joshua D. Taylor

Zoe held the withered hand with a golden glove in front of her as the ship sped across the Aegean Sea. After decades of searching, she finally found the tomb of King Midas and retrieved his enchanted hand. With this gnarled piece of flesh, she could become rich and famous, becoming the envy of those who doubted her.

She was jolted forward, dropping the hand overboard as the ship hit a wave. She watched as the ocean before her turned to solid gold in a flash, destroying the entire planet's hydrosphere. It looked like she would be walking to Greece.

Joshua D. Taylor is an amateur writer who started writing a few years ago when he realised he was too old to play make-believe. He lives in southeastern Pennsylvania with his wife and a one-eared cat. He enjoys gardening, comic books, ska-punk music, Disney World, and travelling with his wife. Raised during weirdness that was the late 20th century Josh's eclectic interests produce eclectic works. He loves to mix-n-match things from different genres and stories elements to achieve a madcap hodgepodge of the truly unexpected. His short story 'the Obelisk' appears in Salty Tales by Stormy Island Publishing.
Facebook: authorjoshuadtaylor

Endgame
by Stephanie Scissom

The world ended on a lazy Saturday afternoon, catching even angels unaware. Lucifer smoked his last cigarette on the balcony, watching as the city collapsed.

"Please don't hate me," his wife said.

Nicotine wasn't helping the tightening in his chest. He'd never felt more scared.

He'd fought so hard to protect Abigail from the world, never realising the world needed protection from her.

How strange that history did not know her, when every decision he'd made had been for her.

He had lived for her, and now the entire world would die for her, and they still would never know.

Stephanie Scissom hails from Tennessee, where she lives with her two children, inspects tires by night and plots murder by day. She has four full-length romantic suspense titles and is published in both flash and short story anthologies. Her story, Dandelions, garnered her a Sweek Star recognition and placed first in the international short story competition. Her current project and obsession is an apocalyptic trilogy starring Lucifer, his insane wife, and his deadly, power-hungry siblings
Facebook: Stephanie Scissom, Author
Twitter: @chell22_7

Rads Burn, Man!
by Alexander Pyles

"Don't kick me out. You know what's out there."

"It's just radiation, you'll be fine."

"Nah, rads burn, it'll hurt."

"Not for long, or would you rather we make it easier for you?"

"No, no. Don't do that. We could just come to an agreement, you know?"

"I don't think so. You stole some food and now you pay the price."

"Just stealing a little food is a death sentence?"

"We didn't make the world the way it is. We told you the rules—wait, what are you doing?"

A heavy door crashes and air swirls with a small breeze.

Alexander Pyles resides in IL with his wife and children. He holds an MA in Philosophy and an MFA in Writing Popular Fiction. His short story chapbook titled, "Milo (01001101 01101001 01101100 01101111)," from Radix Media, is due out fall 2019. His other short fiction has appeared on 101fiction.org, River and South Review, and other venues. Website: www.pylesofbooks.com Twitter: @Pylesofbooks.

The Thirst
by Amber M. Simpson

The blazing sun blisters our skin as we seek refuge from its scorching rays. Worse than the heat is the overwhelming thirst, gluing our sandpaper tongues to the roofs of our mouths.

We ran out of bottled water days ago, and since the nuclear fallout, nothing else can be trusted. Stella tends to forget this.

"Water!" she cries suddenly, running ahead. "There's water!"

"Don't drink it!" I scream, chasing her.

Too late. She slurps greedily from the tipped over rain barrel.

"It's good," she says, the grin melting off her face, flesh dripping to the ground in soft wet plops.

Amber M. Simpson is a chronic nighttime writer with a penchant for dark fiction and fantasy. When she's not editing for Fantasia Divinity Magazine, she divides her creative time (when she's not procrastinating) between writing a mystery/horror novel, working on a medieval fantasy series, and coming up with new ideas for short stories. Above all, she enjoys being a mom to her two greatest creations, Max and Liam, who keep her feet on the ground even while her head is in the clouds.
Website: ambermsimpson.com

The Coyote
by Shawn M. Klimek

Inez stared in despair at the 30-foot high border wall.

"No problem," said the coyote. "There's an existing tunnel, built years ago by drug runners. The cost to smuggle you both will be $3,000, American."

Inez hugged her daughter. "So much?"

"Don't test me," said the human trafficker, holding out a palm. "Hundreds would gladly take your spot."

In truth, Inez would gladly have paid twice as much to escape. As she opened her money belt and counted out six stacks of twenty-dollar bills, what worried her was the recent rumour that zombies had begun to appear in Mexico, too.

Shawn M. Klimek is the middle child of seven creative siblings, a globetrotting, U.S. military spouse, an internationally best-selling short-story writer, a poet, and butler to a Maltese. More than one hundred of his stories and poems have been published, notably in such anthologies as BHP's Deep Space, Bad Romance, Eerie Christmas, Jibbernocky, and the first eight books in the Dark Drabbles series.
Website: jotinthedark.blogspot.com
Facebook: shawnmklimekauthor

The Rock
by Ann Christine Tabaka

Humankind had never had to deal with anything like this before. The earth had not experienced such an event since the age of the dinosaurs. Scientists worked frantically, trying to devise a method to deflect it. Everyone sat frozen in front of their televisions, watching the doomsday event. There was no place to hide from what was about to happen. As the rock drew nearer, the sky turned an eerie shade of red and a rumbling sound shook the earth. Pieces broke off in all directions.

There was no hope left as the giant asteroid came crashing down to Earth.

Ann Christine Tabaka was nominated for the 2017 Pushcart Prize in Poetry, has been internationally published, and won poetry awards from numerous publications. She is the author of 9 poetry books. Christine lives in Delaware, USA. She loves gardening and cooking. Chris lives with her husband and two cats. Her most recent credits are: Burningword Literary Journal; Ethos Literary Journal, North of Oxford, Pomona Valley Review, Page & Spine, West Texas Literary Review, The Hungry Chimera, Sheila-Na-Gig, Pangolin Review, Foliate Oak Review, Better Than Starbucks!, The Write Launch, The Stray Branch, The McKinley Review, Fourth & Sycamore.

Give Thy Thoughts No Tongue
by Cameron Marcoux

Ratbait touched his tongue to the live wire. There was a sizzling sound with intermittent little pops. He smiled out of the corner of his mouth, blood oozing over his lower lip, tongue still out, cable still in hand. Pinkish blisters bubbled up around the blackened edges. It smelled bad. It smelled like the chaos that was all around. The chaos that was everything.

Memory:

I had once seen Hamlet performed in the park. When parks were still a thing. Birdsong and soft breeze. To be or not to be. Polonius. Laertes.

Now there was only Ratbait and a wire.

Cameron Marcoux is a writer of stories, which, considering where you are reading this, makes a lot of sense. He also teaches English to the lovely and terrifying creatures we call teenagers. He lives in the quiet, northern reaches of New England in the U.S. with his girlfriend and scaredy dog.

Nothing Goes to Waste
by G. Allen Wilbanks

Shauna walked the perimeter of her property, checking her traps. She hoped today she might find a rabbit or even a small deer. The bobcat she trapped last week had been old and sick, but she had eaten it anyway. The days when she could be choosy were long gone. She could not afford to let anything go to waste.

A noise reached her ears as she approached one of her traps. It sounded like a girl or maybe a young boy calling for help. Shauna raised her rifle. Hopefully, whatever it was, it tasted better than that old bobcat.

G. Allen Wilbanks is a member of the Horror Writers Association (HWA) and has published over 50 short stories in various magazines and on-line venues. He is the author of two short story collections, and the novel, When Darkness Comes.
Website: www.gallenwilbanks.com
Blog: DeepDarkThoughts.com

Not Wallace
by Shawn M. Klimek

Bill claimed that God had sent the asteroid, that his wife had gone to Heaven early to be spared the tribulations of the apocalypse, and that when the muddy giant with moustaches for eyebrows had crossed the field towards him repeating "Praise God", it was a sign that the stranger should take Darla's place in the shelter. We called him "N.W." because he'd given no name, insisting he'd been reborn when the power failures unlocked every prison. Only after hosing him down did we recognise the bloody, oil-stained jumpsuit by its nametag. We had known Wallace. He was Not Wallace.

Shawn M. Klimek is the middle child of seven creative siblings, a globetrotting, U.S. military spouse, an internationally best-selling short-story writer, a poet, and butler to a Maltese. More than one hundred of his stories and poems have been published, notably in such anthologies as BHP's Deep Space, Bad Romance, Eerie Christmas, Jibbernocky, and the first eight books in the Dark Drabbles series.
Website: jotinthedark.blogspot.com
Facebook: shawnmklimekauthor

Enter the Future
by Umair Mirxa

Elvina could scarce contain her tears as she transferred the baby into her husband's arms.

"What shall we name him?" she asked, watching Franz croon over the new-born.

"Well, given he's the first since the apocalypse, I was thinking we call him Adam."

"Sounds perfect," said Elvina, to loud cheers from the gathered community of survivors.

"We must celebrate…" began Franz proudly. "Elvina!"

Franz handed the baby to one of the women rushing forward, and caught his wife as she collapsed.

"Protect our son, love," she said with her dying breath. "Teach him. He is our only hope now."

Umair Mirxa lives in Karachi, Pakistan. His first published story, 'Awareness', appeared on Spillwords Press. He has also had stories accepted for anthologies from Zombie Pirate Publishing, Blood Song Books, Fantasia Divinity Magazine and Publishing, and Iron Faerie Publishing. He is a massive J.R.R. Tolkien fan, and loves everything to do with fantasy and mythology. He enjoys football, history, music, movies, TV shows, and comic books, and wishes with all his heart that dragons were real.
Website: www.umairmirxa.com
Facebook: UMirxa12

The Last
by G.B. Burgess

Ships hadn't flown by in hours and the explosions sounded distant. Daring to peek outside, I watched snow fall. Serene. Almost possible to forget the world was ending.

I could go out.

A foolish idea, but it might be the last winter I saw. Maybe the last snowfall.

Outside, I threw snowballs at trees, lay flat, making a snow angel, and built a tall, proud, smiling snowman.

Then sadness struck because I knew I must dismantle him. Ships might see and come investigating.

Heading inside, I left the snowman standing.

The last of his kind, an angel prostrating before him.

GB Burgess is a writer from Tasmania. Her stories range from unsettling to uplifting and often take readers down unexpected paths. Her work has appeared in Wizards in Space, Mystery Weekly Magazine and Re:Fiction. When not writing, Gina creates art, runs long distances and rescues stray cats.

Here Comes the Rain
by Jason Holden

Dave broke into the farmhouse, only to be met by an old man with a shotgun. No matter, he would go back after dark while he slept. The gun alone was a prize worth killing for. The sky darkened. A raindrop fell onto his hand, burning the skin.

"Shit. Here comes the rain." Staying outside meant death. The rain burning him, leaving only a pitted skeleton. The rain came harder, each drop bringing agony as Dave frantically raced for safety. As he reached the shelter of the porch, the door swung open, and a shotgun blast tore through his chest.

*After giving up a full-time job as a quarry operator so that his wife could follow her dream career as an academic in the field of chemistry, **Jason Holden** and his family left England and temporarily moved to Spain where they currently reside. While there, he took on the role of full-time parent and began to create stories for his daughter. Now that she is in school, he creates stories for himself and hopes to share those stories with others.*

A Galactic Symphony
by Melanie Harding-Shaw

At the tipping point when bio-domes became mass-producible, we spread across the galaxy consuming each planet until it was exhausted.

We left a trail of abandoned cities. The bio-domes collapsed first and then everything else succumbed. Eventually, all that would remain were the giant pipes that had fed the dome and carried away our waste.

Each pipe jutting from the ground was a different length and width. The native winds would blow across their open mouths in mournful harmony.

When we finally ran out of worlds, we turned back in desperation. All that remained was the symphony we had wrought.

Melanie Harding-Shaw is a speculative fiction writer, policy geek and mother-of-three from Wellington, New Zealand. Her stories have recently appeared in Daily Science Fiction, The Arcanist and NewMyths among others. Website: www.melaniehardingshaw.com Facebook: MelanieHardingShawWriter

Better Go Back to Sleep
by John H. Dromey

A cryogenics patient, revived in the 22nd Century and given a by-then simple medical procedure, was expected to make a full recovery.

"What's the state of the planet?" he asked his doctor.

"Not good. The Four Horsemen of the Apocalypse were sighted off the coast of Liechtenstein."

"The Principality of Liechtenstein is landlocked."

"Not anymore. The apocalyptic messengers had to adapt. Famine rode a stick pony, Pestilence a termite-riddled sawhorse, and War was on water wings with a logo of Pegasus. Death is still a Pale Rider, but now his mount is a translucent Hippocampus."

"A what?"

"A see-through seahorse."

John H. Dromey was born in northeast Missouri, USA. He enjoys reading—mysteries in particular—and writing in a variety of genres. He's had short fiction published in Alfred Hitchcock's Mystery Magazine, Martian Magazine, Stupefying Stories Showcase, Thriller Magazine, Unfit Magazine, and elsewhere, as well as in a number of anthologies, including Chilling Horror Short Stories (Flame Tree Publishing, 2015).

Goddess Unsheathed
by Becky Benishek

She grasped the jewelled sword hilt in her hand, watching from beneath the surface of the lake as his boat rippled closer.

Her role was simple: Flourish, extend, present, release. Recede into the depths and shadows. Let this child, this boy-king, save the world from savagery and cataclysm.

Even to her, it sounded like a fractured fairytale. This symbol she held, freely given, would turn darkness into light, but would also eventually doom her to become but a whispered moonlit tale.

Who was she to defy prophecy?

Who, indeed.

No gifts today. This world could use another round of darkness.

Becky Benishek is the author of the children's books "The Squeezor is Coming!", "What's At the End of Your Nose?", "Dr. Guinea Pig George," and "Hush, Mouse!" She loves to create stories that help children believe in themselves and find the magic in ordinary things. Becky also manages online communities that connect people with resources to help people with special needs thrive. She has an extensive Lego collection, a working Commodore 64, and a tendency to stick googly eyes on objects minding their own business. Becky is married with guinea pigs.
Website: beckybenishek.com

Plagues
by Vonnie Winslow Crist

Reverend Wentworth rested his hand on the Bible. The End had begun with a worldwide algae bloom which caused a massive fish kill.

With waters tainted, frogs and other pond dwellers fled their habitat, then met quick deaths in dry city streets and suburban neighbourhoods.

Next, tons of dead marine animals washed ashore adding to the rotting amphibians—which attracted disease-carrying flies and rodents.

Then, clouds of locust arrived. Though technically grasshoppers, the hordes of insects devoured everything edible in their path.

Tears in his eyes, Reverend Wentworth watched his firstborn son play guitar.

He knew which plague came next.

Vonnie Winslow Crist is author of The Enchanted Dagger, Owl Light, The Greener Forest, Murder on Marawa Prime, and other award-winning books. Her fiction is included in "Amazing Stories," "Cast of Wonders," "Outposts of Beyond," Killing It Softly 2, Defending the Future - Dogs of War, Midnight Masquerade, Chaos of Hard Clay, and elsewhere. A cloverhand who has found so many four-leafed clovers she keeps them in jars, Vonnie strives to celebrate the power of myth in her writing.
Website: www.vonniewinslowcrist.com

I Call Shotgun
by Shawn M. Klimek

"Was that Rand Bailey? How is he still holding onto that shotgun? I've never seen an armed zombie before," said Tom.

"That arm is plain dead, not zombified," said Frank. "See, it's hanging by a tendon. Only rigor mortis is clutching the shotgun. Remember that pile of loose shotgun shells we recovered on his front lawn? I'll bet that as Bailey was guarding his family's escape, he discovered too late the gun was unloaded. They bit the arm almost clean through before he was ready."

"How horrible!"

"Also lucky. I've been wondering where we were going to find a shotgun."

Shawn M. Klimek is the middle child of seven creative siblings, a globetrotting, U.S. military spouse, an internationally best-selling short-story writer, a poet, and butler to a Maltese. More than one hundred of his stories and poems have been published, notably in such anthologies as BHP's Deep Space, Bad Romance, Eerie Christmas, Jibbernocky, and the first eight books in the Dark Drabbles series.
Website: jotinthedark.blogspot.com
Facebook: shawnmklimekauthor

Barren
by Cindar Harrell

When I stepped out into the dusty sunlight, I couldn't believe my eyes. There was nothing. Miles of sand and dirt, no rubble of any sort.

I expected ruins, remnants of a destroyed civilisation. Whatever attacked after we fled underground with as many people as we could, it didn't just destroy our lives and homes, it erased them. I picked up a handful of what was once luscious farming land and watched as it slipped through my fingers.

A silent tear fell down my grim-laden face onto the ground. It was the only water left. Everything else was just barren.

Cindar Harrell loves fairy tales, especially ones with a dark twist. Her stories are often fairy tale inspired, but she is also working on a mystery series. Her stories can be found on Amazon and in various anthologies. You can follow her on Facebook and visit her blog, which she promises to try and update more often,
Website: cindarharrell.wordpress.com
Facebook: CindarHarrell

All Our Futures
by Liam Hogan

All our futures arrived at once. Through a scorched sky, Morlocks flew anti-grav jetpacks above the ruins of a nanotec Statue of Liberty, aggressively buzzing the Apes, who returned potshots from phasers and plasma rifles as holographic adverts extolled the benefits of moving Off World.

As freezing flood waters swallowed spice worms and sentient robots defended their planet from invading Aliens beneath a swollen sun, I knew none of this was real. "Last Orders at Milliways!" rang out over the distant echoes of trumpets as the stars went dark. After only the briefest of hesitations, I swallowed the red pill.

Liam Hogan is a London based short story writer, the host of Liars' League, and a Ministry of Stories mentor. His story "Ana", appears in Best of British Science Fiction 2016 (NewCon Press) and his twisted fantasy collection, "Happy Ending Not Guaranteed", is published by Arachne Press. Website: happyendingnotguaranteed.blogspot.co.uk Twitter: @LiamJHogan.

Flowerbeds
by Rich Rurshell

In the centre of the garden are my roses, the pride of my garden. In the surface of the dark water within the watering can, the reflection of my hairless, disfigured face stares back.

Grey puddles form in the ash filled soil beneath each rose bush as I water them.

I select the three most beautiful roses and remove them, then head towards the house.

I place a rose on each of the graves of my wife and two daughters, and ask myself yet again, *Did I really survive the great inferno? Or am I in hell?*

Maybe it's both.

Rich Rurshell is a short story writer from Suffolk, England. Rich writes Horror, Sci-Fi, and Fantasy, and his stories can be found in various short story anthologies and magazines. Most recently, his story "Subject: Galilee" was published in World War Four from Zombie Pirate Publishing, and "Life Choices" was published in Salty Tales from Stormy Island Publishing. When Rich is not writing stories, he likes to write and perform music.
Facebook: richrurshellauthor

Bang Snap
by J.A. Henderson

Santana and Wodoom were playing Bang Snap. Wodoom hung over a vast starry array, brow furrowed in concentration.

"C'mon," Santana urged. "You haven't made a move in millennia. No wonder this game is taking so long."

He held up a sketch pad.

"Hey, look. I've created a race called the Faboom. They're basically ears with wings. And they're deaf!"

"Oh, thou art hilarious." Wodoom wiggled his pinkie, sending an asteroid crashing into a tiny blue sphere. "Bet thou didst not see *that* coming, though."

"Oi! That was one of my favourite planets." Santana threw up his hands. "It had Netflix."

J.A. Henderson is the author of 26 teenage, YA and adult fiction and non-fiction books. He has been published in the UK, USA, Germany and the Czech Republic by Oxford University Press, Collins, Hardcourt Press, Amberley Books, Oetinger Publishing, Mainstream Books, Black and White Publishers Mlada Fontana, Black Hart and Floris Books. He has been shortlisted for thirteen literary awards and is the winner of the Doncaster Book Prize and Royal Mail Award. He owns The Green Light offering advice, workshops and talks to budding writers in Brisbane. Website: www.ianandrewhenderson.com

A Witch Against the End
by Jensen Reed

A disgruntled, albeit muffled, meow sounded outside the cottage's door as Foster scurried about, trying to brew several potions at once. The oak door opened with a flick of her wand and in slipped a large black cat holding a thick patch of moss in his mouth.

"Thank you, Lester, you have no idea how many lives this will save!" she cooed at the familiar. He glared and jumped onto the table then dropped it beside her. She looked over her potions. Maybe she couldn't stop the world from ending, but she sure as hell could help the people fighting.

Jensen Reed *is a multi-published short story author, lead admin for Writing Bad, and mama to two boys. She dabbles in reading and writing genres but particularly enjoys feeding characters to zombies and making readers cry. Find her book links, flash fiction, and connect with her on her website. Website: authorjensenreed.wordpress.com*

End of Days
by N.M. Brown

What started out as an internet joke will end up dooming the entire planet. Millions of people worldwide are bringing attention to the contents of Area 51.

Brothers and sisters of all walks of life learned to work in peace with a common goal in mind. Countries were brought together. It was thought the military couldn't stop an entire mass of people.

What they didn't think of, was what they'd find inside. The main cell was completely blank inside except for sixteen-digit number sequences on the walls; missile launch codes.

This newfound information only took thirty-two hours to end humanity.

*Since **N.M. Brown** made her first post to a popular Internet forum, she's taken the horror community by storm. Her ability to create, terrify, and drive home her stories is insurmountable. Sinister Sweetheart's published works can be found in multiple anthologies for all to read, but be forewarned, if you do... you may want to call your therapist after, her stories are terrifying, disturbing and devilishly unsettling. She is not only a fright visually, but also has a creepy tentacle in horror podcasting as well. Sinister Sweetheart writes, voice acts and is the media director of the Scarecrow Tales podcast.*
Website: Sinistersweetheart.wixsite.com/sinistersweetheart
Facebook: NMBrownStories

As Long as There is Beauty
by Ximena Escobar

"There's still hope," she said, looking at the crimson sky.

She tied her bootlace—tiny diamond grains sparkling against the coal grey ground.

Look at the beautiful birds.

She ran down the hill and onto the black sand; necks twisted, feathers rustling between the bones. She remembered the flight of seagulls skimming the ocean, feeling the rush they must have felt under its caress.

Feeling.

The swash spread its beautiful blanket of bright upon the sand. Look at her chase the water, her shirt floating like wings behind her.

The ocean welling her eyes, she prays there is a God.

Ximena Escobar is an emerging author of literary fiction and poetry. Originally from Chile, she is the author of a translation into Spanish of the Broadway Musical "The Wizard of Oz", and of an original adaptation of the same, "Navidad en Oz". Clarendon House Publications published her first short story in the UK, "The Persistence of Memory", and Literally Stories her first online publication with "The Green Light". She has since had several acceptances from other publishers and is working very hard exploring new exciting avenues in her writing.
She lives in Nottingham with her family.
Facebook: Ximenautora

Behold! I Saw a Pale Horse
by Cecelia Hopkins-Drewer

The drill struck a key point between tectonic plates, triggering an earthquake. Africa and Europe began to shake, while America trembled. The east of Australia crumbled into the ocean; then the islands washed away with the tide.

Huge cracks opened in the deep to swallow the sea. The pressure caused volcanoes to erupt, with smoke and ash billowing into the sky. Hell opened and a bunch of demons stepped out.

The survivors are hostile. Death rides after every step. I have a gun, the Kalashnikov AK: 47, which can even fire under water. Stay away or I will use it!

Cecelia Hopkins-Drewer *lives in Adelaide, South Australia. She has written a Masters paper on H.P. Lovecraft, and her weird poetry has been published in THE MENTOR (edited by Ron Clarke), and SPECTRAL REALMS (edited by S.T. Joshi). Her novels include a teenage vampire series commencing with MYSTIC EVERMORE. Short stories have been published in WORLDS, ANGELS & MONSTERS, BEYOND, STORMING AREA 51, and UNRAVEL. (Dark Drabbles anthologies edited by Dean Kershaw).*
Amazon: amazon.com/Cecelia-Hopkins-Drewer/e/B071G968NM
Website: chopkin39.wixsite.com/website

It's My Birthday
and I'll Die If I Want To
by Austin P. Sheehan

A soft knock broke the silence and I opened the door.

Jao's face fell when he saw my parents. "What's this? Some sick joke?"

"I couldn't celebrate without them," I whispered, handing him a beer.

Jao shuddered. "You're mad."

"Well anyway, thanks for coming."

He looked away from my parents' rotting remains, his soft voice shaking. "Wouldn't miss it for the world."

"Here's to the good times!" I turned the stereo on to play my favourite song. A birthday tradition.

"What are you doing?" he hissed, "they'll hear!"

Sickening, bloodthirsty screams filled the air.

I smiled. "The more the merrier."

Austin P. Sheehan *is a writer of speculative fiction, a lover of language, literature and '90s TV. Armed with a psychology degree, he went into the world to study humanity, and now prefers the company of his wife and their greyhounds. He grew up in the valleys of Victoria's high country, and despite living in Melbourne, always feels at home amongst the mountains. You'll often find mountains in his stories, whether they're sci-fi, fantasy or alternative history.*
Website: austinpsheehan.com
Twitter: @AustinPSheehan

More Fun Than a
Barrel of Sea Monkeys
by Diane Arrelle

"Hey, Dad," BB asked. "Can we buy air monkeys? The ad says I'll have millions of pets."

"Well, BB," his dad said, "they always die."

"Please, Dad? Can I try?"

BB's dad sighed, "All right."

When the package arrived, BB filled the bowl with solution and added the blue-green ball.

Soon the air inside the bowl became murky, the water turned brown. BB's dad knew what was coming. Sure enough, tiny bombs flared on the ball's surface and the ball turned black.

"Ah, Dad, you were right, they're all dead. Can we try it again? Can we buy another Earth?"

Diane Arrelle, *the pen name of South Jersey writer Dina Leacock, has sold more than 250 short stories and has three published books including Just A Drop In The Cup, a collection of short-short stories and her new collection of horror stories, Seasons On The Dark Side. Retired from being director of a municipal senior citizen centre, she is now co-owner of a small publishing company, Jersey Pines Ink LLC. She resides with her husband and her new cat on the edge of the Pine Barrens (home of the Jersey Devil). Website: www.arrellewrites.com Facebook: Diane.Arrelle*

Queen of the Ashes
by Zoey Xolton

In the decay and rot of the dying world, a lone figure emerges from the overgrown tree line of Central Park. Rifle slung over her shoulder, hunting knife secured in her boot, she surveys the sprawling ruins of old New York. She licks her parched lips beneath her plague mask.

She wants to wake up from this nightmare, to find herself in bed, and late for her commute. She wants to cuss over spilled coffee, and to grab a slice after work…but that reality is long since gone.

Now, she stands alone. Perhaps the last human? She doesn't know.

Zoey Xolton is an Australian Speculative Fiction writer, primarily of Dark Fantasy, Paranormal Romance and Horror. She is also a proud mother of two and is married to her soul mate. Outside of her family, writing is her greatest passion. She is especially fond of short fiction and is working on releasing her own themed collections in future.
Website: www.zoeyxolton.com

Growth
by David Bowmore

The soil is nothing more than sand. It lost nearly all of its nutrients long ago.

But we still toil, even though growing food is almost impossible. One more row of carrot seeds before I rest, for I grow more weary with every passing day.

My child is skinny and cries from hunger. I fear he will grow used to it. And the child growing in my womb will never know a full tummy, if he even survives.

The cockroaches somehow grow in size and number. Their meat is unpleasant but plentiful.

The growth on my neck will burst soon.

David Bowmore has lived here, there and everywhere, but now lives in Yorkshire with his wonderful wife and a small white poodle. He has worn many hats in his time; head chef, teacher and landscape gardener. His first collection of short stories 'The Magic of Deben Market' is available from Clarendon House.
Website: davidbowmore.co.uk
Facebook: davidbowmoreauthor

And Then It Exploded
by C.L. Williams

There was once a planet between Venus and Mars, it was called Earth. I saw it the day it exploded. I was flying by when you could see the planet visibly tremble. At first, I thought it was me, then it trembled again!

What happened next was unbelievable; I watched the planet split in two! As for what happened after that, I am uncertain. I saw a blinding light and before I knew it, Earth was nothing more than ash. Now Earth is believed to be nothing more than a fairy tale, but know I was there the day Earth exploded!

C.L. Williams is an independent author from central Virginia. He has written eight poetry books, four novellas, one novel, and a contributor to multiple anthologies, with the most recent appearance being an all-ages anthology titled Temoli from Thazbook. His most recent poetry book, The Paradox Complex, features the poem "Sad Crying Clown" that is now a video on YouTube directed by Matthew Mark Hunter of MMH Productions. C.L. Williams is currently working on his first sci-fi book, an all-ages book titled Novo: Away from Earth. When not writing, C.L. Williams is reading and sharing the work of other independent authors.
Facebook: writer434
Twitter: @writer_434

Stay Calm
by Wendy Roberts

"Rioters have now taken to the streets, opening fire against all government officials. The President has declared a national emergency and asks that everyone remain calm as he sends troops to round up any suspects from the rebellion…"

Gunshots drown out the rest of the reporter's words just as Julius digs the implant out of his arm. They said it would help keep track of their ID's. Make it easier for doctor's and security personnel. They didn't mention the location tracker or the constant feeling of being watched.

Someone kicks down his door as Julius jumps onto the fire escape.

Writing short stories and novels started as a past time for **Wendy Roberts** *and has now become a fully fledged passion. She posts short stories on her website and can be found most days on Twitter.*
Website: flippinscribbler.wordpress.com
Twitter: @_WARoberts

Running on Empty
by A.R. Johnston

The insistent beeping of her breather was driving her insane. It was telling her that she was almost out and needed to get inside. Breathing the air would be worse than any asthma attack she had ever suffered as a child. But they were still coming, she could hear them running close behind. *Damn shamblers*.

She was out of bullets and she had no desire to be close with more than she could handle. The explosion that had destroyed everything had infected people, turning them into monsters. Leaving those behind to be hunted or become survivors.

Alley refused to die.

A.R. Johnston is a small-town girl from Nova Scotia, Canada. Her style of writing is considered Urban Fantasy. Her first major publication is part of an anthology called First Love and she has several more titles lined up. She is a lover of coffee, good tv shows, horror flicks, and reader of books. She pretends to be a writer when real life doesn't get in the way. Pesky full-time job and adulting!.

The Horde
by A.L. King

Staring down from the pharmacy rooftop, I consider how the things surrounding the building used to be normal. Now their eyes are red, and gross fluids are leaking from their nostrils.

I remove the cap from a bottle and toss it into the horde. I grab more bottles and do the same. Pills fall like pink raindrops to the ground.

The infected waste no time gobbling them up. I wait until the Benadryl does its job and puts them to sleep. Then I make my escape.

It's still hard to believe that severe allergies ended the world. Fortunately, I'm immune.

A.L. King is an author of horror, fantasy, science fiction, and poetry. As an avid fan of dark subjects from an early age, his first influences included R.L. Stine, Edgar Allan Poe, and Stephen King. Later stylistic inspirations came from foreign horror films and media, particularly Japanese. He is a graduate of West Liberty University, has dabbled in journalism, and is actively involved in his community. Although his creativity leans toward darker genres, he has even written a children's book titled "Leif's First Fall." He was raised in the town of Sistersville, West Virginia, which he still proudly calls home.

Weeds
by Dale Parnell

My grandfather had an old piece of vinyl flooring that he kept in the garden shed. When he wanted to clear a large patch of land, he would pull the vinyl into place and just leave it there for a few days.

"Weeds don't grow in the dark," he used to say. "And it's easier than digging."

When the ships first arrived, we were excited. We weren't alone after all. But then more and more came, carpeting the sky, blotting out the sun. They didn't even tell us why, but then my grandfather never explained himself to the weeds either.

Dale Parnell lives in Staffordshire, England, with his wife and their imaginary dog, Moriarty. He has self-published one collection of short stories, "The Green Cathedral" and is currently putting the finishing touches to his second collection, "Bramble". Dale also writes poetry, and is lucky enough to have pieces featured in several anthologies. Facebook: shortfictionauthor

The Underworlders
by Stephen Herczeg

The acrid smell of charred and rotting corpses wafted past Lexi's face. Her nose wrinkled and threatened to break her concentration.

She looked through the scope of her L16. The twisted mutated features of an underworlder filled her eyesight. The darkness and radiation had turned it into an abhorrent parody of a man. She almost gagged.

This will be a blessing.

She focused on its forehead and gently squeezed the trigger.

And sneezed.

The gunshot rang out across the silent plaza. The bullet went wide.

The underworlders looked straight up at her.

She yelled to the others, "Time to move."

Stephen Herczeg is an IT Geek based in Canberra Australia. He has been writing for over twenty years and has completed a couple of dodgy novels, sixteen feature length screenplays and numerous short stories and scripts. His horror work has featured in Sproutlings, Hells Bells, Below the Stairs, Trickster's Treats #1 and #2, Shades of Santa, Behind the Mask, Beyond the Infinite; The Body Horror Book, Anemone Enemy, Petrified Punks and Beginnings. He has also had numerous Sherlock Holmes stories published through the Belanger Books - Sherlock Holmes anthologies.

We Have Food
by Kevin J. Kennedy

We painted on the roof and side of the building 'WE HAVE FOOD'. Passers-by always knocked on the door. They would be nervous and unsure, but food in the new world was scarce. It was no lie. We did have food. We would invite them in and get them comfortable. We would lavish a feast upon them, enough food to make their hearts content. We would sit and chat and find out their experiences. We gave them a comfy bed, and when darkness fell, we would slit their throats. Then we had enough food to spoil our next guests.

Kevin J. Kennedy is a horror author & editor from Scotland. He is the co-author of You Only Get One Shot & Screechers, and the publisher of several bestselling anthology series; Collected Horror Shorts, 100 Word Horrors & The Horror Collection, as well as the stand-alone anthology Carnival of Horror. His stories have been featured in many other notable books in the horror genre. He is an active member of the Horror Writers Association. He lives in a small town in Scotland, with his wife and his two little cats, Carlito and Ariel.
Website: www.kevinjkennedy.co.uk
Goodreads:
www.goodreads.com/author/show/5452895.Kevin_J_Kennedy

Food Chain
by Nicola Currie

Last week, a flying spider the size of a house ate my entire family. Too full for me too, I guess.

Bzzzzzzzz.

Everyone said flooding would end us when the heat rose. Everyone was wrong. Humanity's unprecedented efforts built cities above the wetlands, sheltered refugees like nobody imagined we could. No one thought about the bugs flourishing in the warm wet.

Bzzzzzzzz.

First flies, worms, cockroaches as big as a head, a man, a car. Then the monsters that hunt us, that left me all alone.

Bzzzzzzzz. Bzzzzzzzz.

It's not our planet any longer. It belongs to…

Bzzzzzzzz. BzzzzZZZZ. BZZZZZZZZ.

Nicola Currie is 34, from Cambridge, UK where she works in educational publishing. She has published poetry in literary magazines, including Mslexia and Sarasvati, and has also completed her first novel, which was longlisted for the Bath Children's Novel Award.
Website: writeitandweep.home.blog

Black Out
by Musaab Sultan

"In other news, the city of Shanar experienced a major power out. A mysterious object was also found circling the upper atmosphere. Shortly afterwards, the entire population vanished. Authorities are—"

Lucy switched off the television and stood up from the couch.

"Great, UFOs, what's next? Rainbow—" The lights suddenly blinked out.

Confused, she felt her way towards the windows and pushed the curtains aside.

The entire neighbourhood was shrouded in darkness.

High above, dark objects dotted the night sky.

Her eyes widened in shock,

"Oh no," was all she could say before a bright beam of light covered her vision.

Musaab Sultan is a 22 year old university student and aspiring writer from Karachi Pakistan who spends his time buried in fictional universes, books and animes when not battling to keep his grades afloat.

Feeding the Fire
by Dawn DeBraal

Emily gathered wood to put on the fire. The sun couldn't shine through the clouds of radiation dust. There was nothing to eat, the pond water unhealthy to drink. She could hear them rustling in the woods around her, waiting. Emily needed to keep feeding the flames of the fire with sticks. It kept them away. Exhausted, beyond measure, she no longer had any fight left in her. When she fell asleep, they would come for her. Emily drank the poisoned water from the pond, not caring any longer. She would rather die a painful death than to be eaten.

Dawn DeBraal lives in rural Wisconsin with her husband Red, two rat terriers, and a cat. She has discovered that her love of telling a good story can be written. Published stories with Palm-sized press, Spillwords, Mercurial Stories, Potato Soup Journal, Edify Fiction, Zimbell House Publishing, Clarendon House Publishing, Blood Song Books, Black Hare Press, Fantasia Divinity, Cafelit, Reanimated Writers, Guilty Pleasures, Unholy Trinity, The World of Myth, Dastaan World, Vamp Cat, Runcible Spoon, Dark Christmas, Siren's Call, Iron Horse Publishing, Falling Star Magazine 2019 Pushcart Nominee.
Amazon: amazon.com/Dawn-DeBraal/e/B07STL8DLX

Farmpocalypse
by Derek Dunn

Robert hadn't left the house in days. He couldn't. Not with all the critters swarming around. The chickens pecked at the door incessantly. He'd picked off a dozen with his twelve gauge, but they kept coming. Food and ammo were getting low, too.

The truck in the barn was his only escape, but it wouldn't be easy. The goats had it surrounded. They'd increased in size and grown large fangs.

Armed and ready, Robert kicked open the door. He barely had time to react before the cattle charged. With mouths like rabid dogs, their mangled muscular frames barrelled toward him.

Derek Dunn *lives in the American Northwest with his family. He's a film enthusiast and musician who writes primarily horror and mystery stories.*
Twitter: @DerekTDunn

Dust
by Nikky Lee

He is a hollow man. Heart carved out and left along the road. Hands as cracked and worn as the earth beneath his feet. He is alone; companions gone, most lost in the fires when the cities burned, many more dead in dogfight afterwards—the carnage over those scraps haunts him still. The rest dropped, one by one, into the sand, belly up for the flies.

He is the last.

Hand over hand, he drops his bucket down the well, hoping for a splash of life at its bottom. Instead, a dull, empty *thunk*. Hollow, like him. Returning to dust.

Nikky Lee grew up as a barefoot 90s child in Perth, Western Australia before moving to Auckland, New Zealand in 2016. By day she works as a content writer and has written blogs and articles on a variety of topics from black holes and cyborgs to big data, real estate and health insurance. In her free time, she writes speculative fiction, often burning the candle at both ends to explore fantastic worlds, mine asteroids and meet wizards.
Twitter: @NikkyMLee
Facebook: nikkythewriter.

The Walking Dead is Not a Survival Guide
by Jodi Jensen

The dead were *supposed* to be slow. At least, that's what everyone thought. Elliot had too, until he became one of them.

He was *fast*. Chased his meals like a hell-hound collecting for its master.

But his newest prey was a crafty bugger.

Motorcycle, leather vest, and…

Uh-oh…

Crossbow.

Elliot ducked. The arrow flew over his head.

The biker skidded to a stop to reload.

Elliot growled, the scent of the man's blood spurring him on. A few more steps…

Got him!

Elliot bit into the man's face.

When would they learn?

The Walking Dead is not a survival guide.

__Jodi Jensen__ grew up moving from California, to Massachusetts, and a few other places in between, before finally settling in Utah at the ripe old age of nine. The nomadic life fed her sense of adventure as a child and the wanderlust continues to this day. With a passion for old cemeteries, historical buildings and sweeping sagas of days gone by, it was only natural she'd dream of time traveling to all the places that sparked her imagination.

Home at Last
by Jason Holden

He'd almost been killed twice by other survivors wanting his breather on the way home. Both times John had run—he needed to get to his family.

Finally, he'd made it.

Silence greeted him. He knew it would. They would have followed the plan.

Stairs creaked; his breathing grew heavy as he approached the bathroom.

They were there; desiccated remains in the bathtub.

Regardless of the shower running over them, the virus had stripped all moisture from them.

He climbed in next to them. Tears coursed down his cheeks as he undid the straps from his breather.

He was home.

*After giving up a full-time job as a quarry operator so that his wife could follow her dream career as an academic in the field of chemistry, **Jason Holden** and his family left England and temporarily moved to Spain where they currently reside. While there, he took on the role of full-time parent and began to create stories for his daughter. Now that she is in school, he creates stories for himself and hopes to share those stories with others.*

For Better or Worse
by Connie R. Watson

Margy stepped inside the tent. The body trader sized her up with his harsh gaze. "What do you want?"

"My husband is dying. I need medicine for an infection."

He pulled a knife from his boot. "Normally that would cost you at least your heart."

He grazed the tip of the blade along the top of her breasts. "Spend one night with me," he grinned as his knife traced her cleavage, "and I'll only take a hand."

Margy trembled, sweat dripping down her back. She fingered her wedding ring. Surely her husband would understand. For better or worse, right?

"Deal."

*Since she was a teenager, **Connie R. Watson** has enjoyed writing fantasy stories, but recently discovered a new love for sci-fi, folktales, and poetry. In July 2019 she had a sci-fi drabble published by Alban Lake Publishing in their Drabble #14: Extraterrestrial Reincarnation. When she isn't creating stories in other worlds, she is busy working as a freelance writer or wrangling her three-year-old daughter, Evie.*
Website: connierwatson.com

Fresh Air
by Ken "Timber" Halhober

Three days, Amanda had been trying to get out of the rubble for three days. Her only sustenance was the contents of destroyed snack machines, so sugar and caffeine kept her going. Finally, she crawled out of the office building she was trapped in when the first wave of explosions happened. A smile crossed her face as she took a deep breath of air. Her eyes opening wide as her ears picked up the sound of incoming missiles getting closer. She watched them flying in with no remorse or emotion.

"Well shit," she said, right before the world officially ended.

Ken "Timber" Halhober has been writing most of his life, mainly screenplays but has been delving more into stories as he goes. Always trying to improve as he goes.

The Renaissance of Death
by Terry Miller

The doctor walked the cobblestone streets, the flowers in his mask muting the stench of death that filled the air. Not since the plague had his profession been in such high demand, but the war rebirthed many things long forgotten.

The Witch Trials of 2029 echoed the change occurring throughout the world. A new era ushered in through the aftermath the church attributed to the sin of man. God's judgment deemed the entirety of the human race unworthy. Our damnation had begun.

Buildings burned with fire, bodies lined the streets, and rivers ran blood red. Hell had come to Earth.

Terry Miller is an author and 2017 Rhysling Award-nominated poet residing in Portsmouth, OH, USA. He has self-published a dark poetry collection on Amazon and one short story to date. His work has also appeared in Sanitarium, Devolution Z, Jitter Press, Poetry Quarterly, O Unholy Night in Deathlehem, and the 2017 Rhysling Anthology from the Science Fiction and Fantasy Poetry Association.
Facebook: tmiller2015

After the Fall
by Stephen Herczeg

It's been so dark since the fall.

The meteor destroyed Greenland, melting the ice. The seas rose. The clouds formed. Plants died. Animals died.

Darkness descended.

Now we live off the refuse of the past. Fighting each other. It's dog eat dog, brother versus brother, man versus man, tribe versus tribe.

All we can do is defend our small part of the city from those that would steal what little we have.

But there's a rumour of something new. Something horrifying. Frozen for millennia deep in the ice. Woken by the fall, it's back to claim what it once ruled.

Stephen Herczeg is an IT Geek based in Canberra Australia. He has been writing for over twenty years and has completed a couple of dodgy novels, sixteen feature length screenplays and numerous short stories and scripts. His horror work has featured in Sproutlings, Hells Bells, Below the Stairs, Trickster's Treats #1 and #2, Shades of Santa, Behind the Mask, Beyond the Infinite; The Body Horror Book, Anemone Enemy, Petrified Punks and Beginnings. He has also had numerous Sherlock Holmes stories published through the Belanger Books - Sherlock Holmes anthologies.

On the Similarities Between Writing and Chopping an Onion
by Steven Lord

She was the oldest in the village; hers was a crucial job. No-one was left who remembered the old world. No-one who knew of life without pain, without torment; a life you actually wanted to live. No-one but her.

She took another of the precious pages and started to write. She wrote of holidays and beaches and smiling children and music and fast food. She reached the bottom of the page and looked at her work. The ink danced across the paper; words smeared beyond recognition by her tears. She added the page to the ruined pile and started again.

Steven Lord is a debut author based in the south of England. He is currently attempting to cram writing in alongside a busy day job, with varying levels of success. While his long-term aspiration is to get a novel published, at present he would be pretty pleased with a drabble or two.

Mother
by Pavi Raman

She walked down the deserted street, sucking on her thumb. A frayed sign hung from her neck, flapping in the afternoon breeze:

Nellie Gage

4 years

mom dead

keep me safe

From behind an overturned car, a woman stumbled forward on broken ankles. It had been days since she'd eaten. A tiny bell tinkled on her wrist, an open locket with the picture of a baby. Her baby.

R-em-emb-er...

Hearing the bell, Nellie looked up. The zombie stared with sunken eyes. Then it threw back its head and keened.

Nellie Gage, 4 years old, kept walking.

Safe for another day.

Pavi Raman *celebrates her life as a proud wife and a warrior mom. She's an avid coffee and guacamole enthusiast. A physician in another life, her hobbies include reading and writing, then nitpicking what she writes. She also loves running, online shopping and micromanaging her kids' bedtime routines.When she gets a break; she daydreams about the zombie apocalypse and getting more sleep. Most of the time, she can be found laughing at her kids' wacky sense of humor. She has written over a 100 short stories, a few of which were published in the USA and India.*

BLACK HARE PRESS

Looking Through the Fire
by Kaitlyn Arnett

"Isn't it beautiful?" she asked the silent air.

And in a way, it was. The sky was stained scarlet, the once passionate colour having become a reminder of days long gone. White clouds hovered above the ground, stationary, as though they were unsure where the wind took them. The world was forever entrapped in darkness, and there she was.

There she was, smiling in the heart of it all.

Smoke seemed to gravitate around her, and with every breath she took, the fire roared around her. Destruction followed her every step.

And around her, the world went up in flames.

__Kaitlyn Arnett__ is a writer from Temecula California, primarily focusing on writing short fantasy and science fiction stories. She has been writing for four years, though, this is her first time submitting her work to a publisher of any kind.

The Blistered
by Nicola Currie

Our leader calls us from the shade, to the dry lakeside at the mildness of midnight. Rock is cracking, doorways opening. We will wait for what emerges, even if we face the fury of the dawn god Sun.

As Sun rises, and our skin starts to crackle, pale faces emerge. Will they join us, hideous as we are?

They step from the shadows and scream. They redden and blister and soon reassemble our kin. But the screaming does not stop. The red turns black. They smoke. They fall.

No, they are not our kind. Still, charred meat will still feed.

Nicola Currie is 34, from Cambridge, UK where she works in educational publishing. She has published poetry in literary magazines, including Mslexia and Sarasvati, and has also completed her first novel, which was longlisted for the Bath Children's Novel Award.
Website: writeitandweep.home.blog

Where No Man Lives
by E.L. Giles

The silence that had settled upon the world was full, heavy. No wind descended; no rain fell to wash away the dust and the blood that now covered the land left barren and desolated, a sarcophagus for mankind and their hatred.

Grey deepened to black as the ashes fell, colouring the land with a monochromatic layer of utter rot. Fallen buildings, carcasses of civilisation, lay alongside ghost cities. Life had stopped existing.

Where men had battled and bled, no living thing ever walked again. Wherever men had warred and hated, only the sinister ruins of the world could be found.

E.L. Giles is a dreamer, passionate about art, a restless worker and a bit of a weird human. He started his artistic journey as a music composer until the need to put his thoughts and stories down on paper grew too strong for him to resist it any longer. He lives in the French Province of Quebec, Canada, with his girlfriend and two boys.
Facebook: elgilesauthor
Website: www.elgilesauthor.com

It's a Dirty Job
by Andrew Anderson

On days like this, when the radiation levels dropped enough, we could get on with our work. We were outside when I heard a sudden loud click; it was the sound of the minute hand on the town Doomsday clock as it moved past midnight.

I was confused, so I stopped what I was doing and checked my system clock. It offered no further answers.

I turned to VX5547, a fellow android. "You know, it really is about time that someone replaced that clock—it's running ten years slow."

Then we continued to sweep up the skeletons littering the street.

Andrew Anderson is a full-time civil servant, dabbling in writing music, poetry, screenplays and short stories in his limited spare time, when not working on building himself a fort made out of second-hand books. He lives in Bathgate, Scotland with his wife, two children and his dog. Twitter: @soorploom

Last Stand
by Cindar Harrell

The virus appeared suddenly and spread just as fast. It lurked dormant within its victims for months undetected. No one suspected. No one prepared. The first symptoms were attributed to a cold.

When the madness started, people thought it was a type of rabies, mutated into something nearly unrecognisable. Everyone saw the signs. No one believed them.

The first time the dead rose, they called it a miracle. The first time the dead killed, they called it a freak tragedy.

As humanity took its last stand against the undead, we remembered the warning signs, but our fate was already sealed.

Cindar Harrell loves fairy tales, especially ones with a dark twist. Her stories are often fairy tale inspired, but she is also working on a mystery series. Her stories can be found on Amazon and in various anthologies. You can follow her on Facebook and visit her blog, which she promises to try and update more often,
Website: cindarharrell.wordpress.com
Facebook: Cindar.Harrell

The Uninfected
by R.A. Goli

Alana's eyes felt heavy; her heartbeat assaulted her ears with its voracity.

The doctor attached the drip line to the canula protruding from her arm.

Alana's blood, previously siphoned and 'cleaned'. The treated fluid no longer crimson, but a deep purple.

"This will reduce the number of host cells so the virus can't take hold. You'll likely live a long life."

She peered through the gap in the boarded-up window. Now Earth was 'the red planet'. Not a plant to be found.

In the distance, she heard the screech of the infected, and she wondered if she wanted to survive.

R.A. Goli is an Australian writer of horror, fantasy, and speculative short stories. In addition to writing, her interests include reading, gaming, the occasional walk, and annoying her dog, two cats, and husband. Check out her numerous publications including her fantasy novella, The Eighth Dwarf, and her collection of short stories, Unfettered; Website: ragoliauthor.wordpress.com Facebook: RAGoliAuthor.

The Silence That Spreads
by Aiki Flinthart

See here the five-year-old girl, alone, thin, listless? Her hair lank and eyes dull. Her world the broken remains of the house scorched by fire and crushed by cannon. The house where her siblings laughed and her mother scolded. Where now live only cockroaches, and her fierce, small dog.

Soon she will curl into a ball and cry herself to sleep one last time, clutching matted fur to her filthy face. While, all around, the smoky silence wrought by arrogant greed spreads to encompass her village, her city, her country.

Until every girl, and every dog, sleeps.

And never wakes.

Aiki Flinthart has had short stories shortlisted in the Aurealis awards and top-8 listed in the USA Writers of the Future competition, as well as published in various anthologies and e-mags. She has 11 published spec fic novels and has edited 2 short story anthologies. She regularly gives workshops on writing fight scenes at conventions. Lives in Brisbane. Does martial arts, archery, knife throwing and lute-playing. Website: www.aikiflinthart.com

Cold Dead World
by Thomas Sturgeon Jr.

I watch from the skies, from the helicopter. There are very few of us still alive.

It's *their* world now.

The living dead are too numerous to count, and we don't have bullets for all of them.

I smell decay in the air as they wait below us hungrily. Those that are still alive are waging wars with the undead and the military, but we escaped…just barely.

We make our way to Antarctica as hordes of the undead lie in wait, and while others die by bites and bullets.

The apocalypse has just begun, and my ass is freezing cold.

Thomas Sturgeon Jr. began writing at 13 years old. He loves to read and spend time with his family and friends. He loves horror movies and fiction. He currently lives in Chatsworth, Georgia and wants more out of life. He's been published before in Weird Mask magazine and by Deadman's Tome. His short stories that were published were "The Dead City" and "Disturbed Valentine". He currently is at work on a Horror short story collection and he is loved by his family and friends. Despite being told by his teachers that he would never be published, he has proved them wrong.

Solar Winds
by N.M. Brown

Attention Earth: destruction is imminent! Locate your nearest fallout centre and take shelter IMMEDIATELY! There's barely time to explain but I'll do my best.

Since the beginning of time, the Sun's unleashed constant onslaughts on our Solar System. Charged particles ate away at Earth's magnetic field over the centuries, creating a debt for a future generation to pay; ours.

For years, the pressure of the solar winds seemed harmless. People barely knew of them, let alone the threat they posed. The Sun's coronal holes unleashed torrents of fast solar winds; knocking an asteroid off course.

Target: Earth.

Arrival time: NOW.

*Since **N.M. Brown** made her first post to a popular Internet forum, she's taken the horror community by storm. Her ability to create, terrify, and drive home her stories is insurmountable. Sinister Sweetheart's published works can be found in multiple anthologies for all to read, but be forewarned, if you do... you may want to call your therapist after, her stories are terrifying, disturbing and devilishly unsettling. She is not only a fright visually, but also has a creepy tentacle in horror podcasting as well. Sinister Sweetheart writes, voice acts and is the media director of the Scarecrow Tales podcast.*

Website: Sinistersweetheart.wixsite.com/sinistersweetheart
Facebook: NMBrownStories

Another Swig
by Stuart Conover

Jack took another swig of bourbon.

Not to get drunk, to dull the fear.

THEY were outside.

THEY were everywhere.

If he was going to get to Bethany…

He'd have to run.

How had THEY even found this place?

Only the two of them knew it existed.

THEY might be dangerous, but…

THEY were slow.

That was his advantage.

Taking a deep breath, Jack opened the door to run.

Beth was on the other side.

She was one of THEM.

She…no, *IT*…reached for him.

He took off.

There was no saving her now.

Jack was on his own.

Stuart Conover is a father, husband, rescue dog owner, published author, blogger, journalist, horror enthusiast, comic book geek, science fiction junkie, and IT professional. With all of that to cram in daily, we have no idea if or when he sleeps or how he gets writing done! (We suspect it has to do with having evil clones.) Stuart is a Chicago native and runs the author resource Horror Tree.

The Mirage of Death
by Shelly Jarvis

I awake to the tinkle of laughter. God help me, nothing has ever sounded so sweet. I can't see anything in the dim light, but I don't care; I'm alive and there's a person and they are laughing.

I open my eyes. A woman holds a dagger to my throat.

"Why did you kill him?"

"He killed someone else."

She nods. "She was my sister."

"I'm sorry."

"You will live with us now. Keep us safe." She steps aside and I see a garden, a fountain, no sign of the wasteland world.

If this is death, I'll happily stay forever.

Shelly Jarvis *is a speculative fiction author from West Virginia, US. She found a life-long love of sci-fi and fantasy in the 3rd grade when she found Madeleine L'Engle's "A Wrinkle in Time." Shelly is an avid reader, a Whovian, the ideal viewer of dog rescue videos, and undoubtedly Ravenclaw. She currently has two YA sci-fi books available for purchase on Amazon.*
Website: www.ShellyJarvis.com

Flower Girl
by Peter J. Foote

"Contact!" Mikey's teenage voice crackles worse than the radio.

"Location and number?" snaps Mel into her handheld. She scans the broken landscape through binoculars.

"Ah, sorry. Yeah, it's a kid, a girl. Rad burns cover her face and legs, she's climbing out of the rubble near the subway station. She's waving for help, something in her hand."

"Mikey, don't approach her, it could be a weapon!"

"*crackle*...looks scared...*crackle*...not weap...*crackle*...flowers?"

"Shoot her, Mikey! It's a trap!"

Mel feels the explosion transfer through the ground and watches a new plumb of smoke merge with the sunless sky.

Peter J. Foote *is a bestselling speculative fiction writer from Nova Scotia. Outside of writing, he runs a used bookstore specialising in fantasy & sci-fi, cosplays, and alternates between red wine and coffee as the mood demands. His short stories can be found in both print and in ebook form, with his story "Sea Monkeys" winning the inaugural "Engen Books/Kit Sora, Flash Fiction/Flash Photography" contest in March of 2018. As the founder of the group "Genre Writers of Atlantic Canada", Peter believes that the writing community is stronger when it works together.*
Twitter: @PeterJFoote1
Website: peterjfooteauthor.wordpress.com

Gust O'Death
by Michael D. Davis

It was on the wind, in the air.

The poison spread over the earth like a leaf floating on the water. Gusts of death came from what seemed like every direction.

The fields upon fields of crops, still a healthy green, turned black and brown instantly at the touch of the cool breeze.

Everything decayed from the air's touch, leaving towns corpses…empty.

I can't do this anymore. There is no way I can do this anymore. Walking outside I take a deep breath of the nice fresh air.

Soon, I'm watching my flesh rot on the lovely cool breeze.

Michael D. Davis was born and raised in a small town in Iowa. A high school graduate and avid reader he has aspired to be a writer for years. Having written over thirty short stories, ranging in genre from comedy to horror from flash fiction to novella. He continues in his accursed pursuit of a career in the written word and in his hunt Michael's love for stories in all genres and mediums will not falter.

The Last War
by Crystal L. Kirkham

Most that survived the last war left Earth in search of better lives. Some chose to stay though man-made diseases ravaged the remaining populace and radiation reduced the liveable zones to almost nothing.

We didn't know that there was a worse fate waiting for us. No one knew that the last great war was an experiment engineered by outside forces. Get the pests to kill themselves and then take over the planet.

Our pleas for help to those that escaped go unanswered. Last war? Not anymore. This is the final war. We know we can't win but we fight anyway.

Crystal L. Kirkham resides in a small hamlet west of Red Deer, Alberta. She's an avid outdoors person, unrepentant coffee addict, part-time foodie, servant to a wonderful feline, and companion to two delightfully hilarious canines. She will neither confirm nor deny the rumours regarding the heart in a jar on her desk and the bottle of reader's tears right next to it. Her paranormal urban fantasy series, Saints and Sinners, is available on Amazon and her YA Fantasy, Feathers and Fae will be released October 11, 2019, from Kyanite Publishing.
Website: www.crystallkirkham.com

Brave Day
by C.L. Steele

Tara jumped over the railing, dropping to the cement floor, the crucial frozen canister in hand. Only the hall to traverse, then the tube. Numerous Arcadian's claws tore through the roof. Their incessant hissing closer. Tara screamed in pain as a claw scratched across her back. Grabbing her flare, she lit the monster chasing her. She spied others coming—the tube. Sprinting, then turning the air-lock wheel, she jettisoned the canister holding the DNA of humanity's greats. The quick Arcadian snapped her neck. The Earth-ship sped retrieving the future.

Tara is why today, we celebrate our 30th anniversary. Tara bowed.

C.L. Steele creates new worlds and mystical places filled with complex characters on exciting journeys. Her typical genre is Sci-Fi/Fantasy, where she concentrates on writing in the sub-genres of Magical Realism, Near Future, and Futuristic worlds. Published in numerous anthologies, she looks forward to the release of her debut novel. In the interim, she works on other novels and continues to write short stories, novellas, and poetry. She is featured as one of five international authors in ICWG Magazine through Clarendon Publishing House and is a contributing author to Blood Puddles Literary Journal. Follow her growing career at:

Facebook: author.CLSteele

Instagram: @clsteele.author

Flesh and Dust
by Jacob Baugher

My wife died the day the world ended, like everyone else, of course. We watched it from Mars, strange voyeurs of a trillion deaths.

It started with a whining siren, a bright streak across the sky. 433-Eros, lassoed by the Avandii, plummeted toward Los Angeles.

"What's happening, Daddy?"

The television crackled with feedback. The entire world screamed. I felt like screaming too.

"The End."

"I don't understand."

"Neither do I."

The crackles stopped. The screen darkened. Sara buried her face in my chest.

"What about Mama?"

I didn't have an answer.

Among the stars, we're naught but flesh and dust.

Jacob Baugher teaches Creative Writing at Franciscan University of Steubenville. When he's not teaching or coaching the track team, he can be found in the Cuyahoga Valley hiking with his wife and son or brewing beer on his front porch. He's received honourable mentions for his work in the Writers of the Future contest and he co-edits a series of Fantasy and Science Fiction anthologies titled Continuum.

Rinse and Repeat
by Aiki Flinthart

There comes a time in every civilisation.

When wilfulness outweighs wisdom, and belligerence outguns intelligence.

A time when godlike greed and arrogance, instead of humble awareness, determines fates and futures.

And when that time comes, all that has been built, crumbles. All that has been discovered, is lost. All that has been imagined, vanishes.

What remains are the ghosts of broken dreams and the faint memories of a time before desolation. Wistful stories of past glory to salve present pain and gird against future loss.

Even that dwindles to legend.

And those few that survive.

Will start it all again.

Aiki Flinthart has had short stories shortlisted in the Aurealis awards and top-8 listed in the USA Writers of the Future competition, as well as published in various anthologies and e-mags. She has 11 published spec fic novels and has edited 2 short story anthologies. She regularly gives workshops on writing fight scenes at conventins. Lives in Brisbane. Does martial arts, archery, knife throwing and lute-playing. Website: www.aikiflinthart.com

The Second Coming
by Jacob Baugher

"You're going back, Jesus?" Michael hands me a cold brew. We sit on a pillowy thunderhead, far above the Atlantic.

"What bean is this?"

"Ethiopian Mokamba."

"It's good."

Michael's wings fold like a white cloak. Lightning strikes the black ocean. America looms in the distance. Metal buildings grope the sky.

"No," I say.

Michael gives the storm the side-eye. "Surely the Second Coming is at hand?"

I sip the cold brew. The hurricane rages. Trump Tower appears on the horizon. I think about the dead children.

"Not today," I say. "Send the horsemen. Smite 'em."

The storm swells. Darkness gathers.

Jacob Baugher teaches Creative Writing at Franciscan University of Steubenville. When he's not teaching or coaching the track team, he can be found in the Cuyahoga Valley hiking with his wife and son or brewing beer on his front porch. He's received honourable mentions for his work in the Writers of the Future contest and he co-edits a series of Fantasy and Science Fiction anthologies titled Continuum.

Quiet
by Caitlin Mazur

The quiet. That's what gets to me. I am alone in a place once overcome by others. Now, the silence is deafening. It chokes me, threatening to drive me mad.

Then I hear it, the sound of the undead outside. It used to scare me, but now it's comforting. Melodic. It lulls me out into the street. I follow a group of them as they clumsily wander down 5th Avenue.

Moaning, groaning, sometimes a snarl. It could be a lullaby. I follow the noise. They turn their heads at my fresh meat. Oh well. Anything is better than the quiet.

Caitlin Mazur is an author, marketer, wife, and mother to two. By night, she writes primarily science fiction and horror stories with hints of romance. By day, she is a marketing mastermind at a software company.
Twitter: @caitwritesstuff

The Crash Landing of Flight 173
by Wondra Vanian

"Please return your tray tables to—" The attendant's announcement ended in a gasp as the plane jerked violently.

He forgot to turn off the PA system. Passengers of Flight 173 heard his frantic conversation with the pilot. "What'd'ya mean we can't land there?"

His voice was replaced by the pilot's, hurriedly telling passengers to brace themselves for an emergency landing. They ground to a halt on the freeway, smashing dozens of abandoned cars.

When they eventually staggered out of the wrecked plane, battered and bruised, they thanked their gods. They felt lucky to be alive.

Until the first zombie appeared.

Wondra Vanian is an American living in the United Kingdom with her Welsh husband and their army of fur babies. A writer first, Wondra is also an avid gamer, photographer, cinephile, and blogger. She has music in her blood, sleeps with the lights on, and has been known to dance naked in the moonlight. Wondra was a multiple Top-Ten finisher in the 2017 and 2018 Preditors and Editors Reader's Poll, including ithe Best Author category. Her story, "Halloween Night," was named a Notable Contender for the Bristol Short Story Prize in 2015.
Website : www.wondravanian.com

Dreams for My Daughter
by Shelly Jarvis

My son was born this day, three years before the world died. He should be fourteen, but he is dead. I think of him as I watch my daughter play.

She has never seen the things my son did, doesn't know how dark the night becomes. She hasn't felt the bloodied scrapes on her face after the wind blew sand and glass and bones against her. Her belly hasn't hungered, desperate for a bite.

She never will. Within these walls the earth's last settlement is safe from those things, safe from the monsters who wander, forgetting they once were human.

Shelly Jarvis is a speculative fiction author from West Virginia, US. She found a life-long love of sci-fi and fantasy in the 3rd grade when she found Madeleine L'Engle's "A Wrinkle in Time." Shelly is an avid reader, a Whovian, the ideal viewer of dog rescue videos, and undoubtedly Ravenclaw. She currently has two YA sci-fi books available for purchase on Amazon.
Website: www.ShellyJarvis.com

Herb's Herd
by Andrew Anderson

The pickup-truck driver was the first person we'd seen alive in this wasteland for twenty days. We intended to keep moving, but his kind face convinced us to approach him.

"Howdy. You folks heard 'bout the sanctuary up north? Food, shelter and water. That there map ain't no use no more, and it's too far for walkin'. I can drive you though, name's Herb."

We got in.

We approached the promised settlement six hours later. A merc waved from atop its walls, and Herb gave a thumbs up.

The merc turned and shouted: "Honest Herb's rounded up more fresh meat."

Andrew Anderson is a full-time civil servant, dabbling in writing music, poetry, screenplays and short stories in his limited spare time, when not working on building himself a fort made out of second-hand books. He lives in Bathgate, Scotland with his wife, two children and his dog.
Twitter: @soorploom

Countdown
by Crystal L. Kirkham

Five minutes

Sirens sound, people scream. I sit silently and wait.

Four minutes

My phone rings. It's my parents. I ignore them.

Three minutes

My phone rings again. Unknown number. This time I answer.

Two minutes

I laugh at their pleas to stop this madness and destroy the machine. That's not going to happen.

One minute

Armed soldiers crash through my door.

Zero minutes

They destroy the machine, but it's already too late. No one will know that I've destroyed the sun for another eight minutes. They cuff me and I laugh. They're all doomed.

Let the real countdown begin.

***Crystal L. Kirkham** resides in a small hamlet west of Red Deer, Alberta. She's an avid outdoors person, unrepentant coffee addict, part-time foodie, servant to a wonderful feline, and companion to two delightfully hilarious canines. She will neither confirm nor deny the rumours regarding the heart in a jar on her desk and the bottle of reader's tears right next to it. Her paranormal urban fantasy series, Saints and Sinners, is available on Amazon and her YA Fantasy, Feathers and Fae will be released October 11, 2019, from Kyanite Publishing.*
Website: www.crystallkirkham.com

Erasure
by Jason Hayashi

Two months ago, my peers and I closed up our lab permanently.

We simply wanted to save the world. They gave us an assignment. Not to destroy evil, but to create good. Our project was a new animal.

When we finished, they made their own adjustments to our precious beasts. They turned them monstrous, set them loose. They told us we'd done humanity a service by culling the population. We quit.

Then they lost control of the creatures and they grew insatiable. Now they're everywhere, rampaging and killing until nothing remains.

If you find this, I am so, so sorry.

***Jason Hayashi** has been obsessed with horror since early childhood. Brought up on Neal Shusterman, Robert D. San Souci, and Anthony Horowitz, he began publishing short horror online. From there he's worked his way to publications in several horror anthologies--his favorite kind of book--and hopes to write and publish some of his own in the future. He lives in the boiling hellfire of South Texas with a troupe of monsters, a wizard, and a sassy cat familiar. Along with writing, he sings and creates art. His hope grows as he prepares to leave the merciless institution known as "high school".*

Beware
by E.L. Giles

"Beware," said Hunter. "They could be anywhere."

He and his companions walked cautiously through the morbidly overgrown forest, rounding the cinder blocks, chunks of pavement, and other signs that a city once existed here.

A crackling noise startled Hunter, and he spun, rifle drawn.

"They're here," he said. "And they know we're here for them."

"Who are they?" asked the man closest to Hunter.

"The survivors."

A shape appeared before them, contorted and barely recognisable as a human. The thing moved on four legs, half crawling, and blood was smeared on the corners of his lips. He was hungry.

"Fire!"

E.L. Giles is a dreamer, passionate about art, a restless worker and a bit of a weird human. He started his artistic journey as a music composer until the need to put his thoughts and stories down on paper grew too strong for him to resist it any longer. He lives in the French Province of Quebec, Canada, with his girlfriend and two boys.
Facebook: elgilesauthor
Website: www.elgilesauthor.com

The Day the Stars Fell
by Clint Foster

I wished upon the falling stars, as millions had before, closing my eyes and mouthing the words even as I thought them. Peace, happiness, an end to the bad in the world.

For that moment, with my eyes closed, there was peace. No war, no hate, no fear, no anger, no greed. Peace, and peace alone. Perhaps the only wish ever made on a falling star came true.

It hit the ground with a flash that blinded half the world. By the time I opened my eyes I knew my wish came true, and there was peace before the end.

Clint Foster lives with his wife, four cats, and a beloved Basset Hound called Zero. He's always had a love for reading, and found that passion extending into writing as he grew older. A nerd at heart, he has a special love for video games and comic books, but consumes media of all kinds. He loves stories, and whether he's watching them, reading them, playing them, or writing them, will always love to connect with characters new and old.

Seafood
by Kelly A. Harmon

After the bomb hit, Jessica said, "Let's go to sea. It'll be safer—no rioting."

"And more food," David said.

It took five weeks to travel four-hundred miles, and another three to find a boat.

Yet each day had been a fight.

"Tentacle! Port side!" David yelled.

Jessica harpooned it, then cut off the end with her filleting knife. "Score!" she yelled, dropping it to the deck. "We eat tonight!"

Eyes widening, David whispered, "There is no tonight," as an even larger tentacle capsized the boat.

Because the blast had rocked the oceans, too, and behemoths rose from the depths.

Kelly A. Harmon is an award-winning journalist and author, and a member of the Science Fiction & Fantasy Writers of America and Horror Writers Association. A Baltimore native, she writes the Charm City Darkness series. The fourth book in the series, In the Eye of the Beholder, is now available. Find her short fiction in many magazines and anthologies, including Occult Detective Quarterly; Terra! Tara! Terror! and Deep Cuts: Mayhem, Menace and Misery. Website: kellyaharmon.com Twitter: @kellyaharmon

In Blood and Fire
by Terri A. Arnold

This is how it ends, the sky red with flames, the ground red with blood. The signs have been present for weeks; animals dropping dead from the sky, humans attacking each other, with little to no regard for their own mortality. I've tried to stay among the shadows while I poach supplies to keep myself alive. The truth is, it was never going to work. This is how the world ends; it ends in fire and blood. Hope seems futile until she appears...possibly our saviour? Dressed in white; angel or warrior? I'm not sure which, but I welcome her.

Terri A Arnold has recently begun to share stories that she has been writing for years. She is from a small town in Nova Scotia and loves to put words to paper. By day she works as a registered nurse, but any other time she can be found reading or writing, and is loving it more and more every day.

We See Them Coming
by J.M. Meyer

Panic set in when our local counsel admitted there were no emergency plans for a zombie attack. The infected managed to enter our area despite the closed borders, roads, railways and airports. We live in a mountain village and can see them coming. Some run and others wander aimlessly hitting into trees and each other.

Fortunately, they don't have good balance. They start up the incline and fall.

Unfortunately, we're stuck here until a miracle happens, the food runs out, or enough of them fall and build up, creating a bridge to get to us; ending our terror for good.

J.M. Meyer is writer, artist and small business owner living in New York., where she received her master's degree from Teacher's College, Columbia University. Jacqueline loves the science fiction and horror genres. Reading Ray Bradbury was a mind-blowing experience for her in 8th grade. Alfred Hitchcock and Rod Serling were the horror heroes of her youth. Mercedes M. Yardley is her current horror writing hero. Jacqueline also enjoys the company of her husband Bruce and their three children, Julia, Emma and Lauren. Jacqueline's mantra: The only time it's too late to try something new is when you are dead.
Website: jmoranmeyer.net
Twitter: @moran_meyer

When Push Came to Shove
by John H. Dromey

A bunch of do-gooders and a few bad eggs combined forces to combat climate change. They took a do-or-die, all-or-nothing approach to solving the problem. Willing to use scare tactics to achieve their goals, their base of operations had a doomsday room which was manned around the clock.

After word of the organisation's lethal capabilities leaked to the press, an angry mob stormed the building.

The man in charge of the doomsday device, Walter Nemo, freaked out. Reacting quickly to the threat, he *thought* he was pressing a panic button to summon security guards. Instead he hit the self-destruct switch.

John H. Dromey was born in northeast Missouri, USA. He enjoys reading—mysteries in particular—and writing in a variety of genres. He's had short fiction published in Alfred Hitchcock's Mystery Magazine, Martian Magazine, Stupefying Stories Showcase, Thriller Magazine, Unfit Magazine, and elsewhere, as well as in a number of anthologies, including Chilling Horror Short Stories (Flame Tree Publishing, 2015).

And She Spins On, Regardless
by Aiki Flinthart

Gaia spun in her endless dance, ethereal skirts swirling in gauzy layers around her round body. Her skin itched with pests. They dug at her, leaving gaping gouges. Tainted her with their droppings and waste. Clawed at her cloth-of-green, tearing loose, violating her.

But they would pass. These things always did. So, she scratched indolently, slowly squashing the biting, clawing little beasts. Shrugged her massive shoulders and hot world-milk spilled from her peaked breasts. Basked in Sol's glory and wrapped herself in his warmth, holding it close. Until the parasites suffocated and died in the Hell of their own making.

Aiki Flinthart has had short stories shortlisted in the Aurealis awards and top-8 listed in the USA Writers of the Future competition, as well as published in various anthologies and e-mags. She has 11 published spec fic novels and has edited 2 short story anthologies. She regularly gives workshops on writing fight scenes at conventions. Lives in Brisbane. Does martial arts, archery, knife throwing and lute-playing. Website: www.aikiflinthart.com.

The Silence Was Deafening
by Stuart Conover

The silence was deafening.

Kristen had grown up in the hustle and bustle of The City.

But it was gone.

All the great cities were gone after THEY had come.

Luckily, she had been away.

Her vacation destination had become her new home.

Now when she slept cars weren't whizzing by.

No airplanes in the sky.

Just quiet.

Kristen had to stay quiet too.

The survivors had learned that sound would give them away.

THEY would come and death would follow.

THEY ignored the machines, the animals.

It was just the sound of mankind they hunted.

The silence was deafening.

Stuart Conover is a father, husband, rescue dog owner, published author, blogger, journalist, horror enthusiast, comic book geek, science fiction junkie, and IT professional. With all of that to cram in daily, we have no idea if or when he sleeps or how he gets writing done! (We suspect it has to do with having evil clones.) Stuart is a Chicago native and runs the author resource Horror Tree.

Gene's Foresight
by Alexander Pyles

We had always made fun of Gene. Every community has one. The eccentric. He was just a feature of the neighbourhood.

The man kept to himself, but when asked about why he was taking boxes upon boxes to his shed out back, he'd just stare at you.

We once got him to tell us, but it was as cryptic as anything else. "It's coming." He never told us exactly what it was, only that it was imminent.

Gene went into his shed one day, and never came out.

It was only a couple days later that the first bomb fell.

Alexander Pyles resides in IL with his wife and children. He holds an MA in Philosophy and an MFA in Writing Popular Fiction. His short story chapbook titled, "Milo (01001101 01101001 01101100 01101111)," from Radix Media, is due out fall 2019. His other short fiction has appeared on 101fiction.org, River and South Review, and other venues.
Website: www.pylesofbooks.com
Twitter: @Pylesofbooks.

Neonicotinoid
by Blake Jessop

"What we've done is create the greatest neonic pesticide ever."

"Was it supposed to kill the bees, too?"

"There have been some unexpected side effects."

A bird dropped out of the sky to land with a thump in the dirt. The reporter looked alarmed.

"Should we be worried?"

"Not at all, we're working on solutions."

The reporter coughed, the camera's view wobbled.

"What we should focus on," the CropScience representative said, "is our record second quarter profits. Excuse me."

He coughed, looked at his hand with some annoyance, then leant over to vomit blood into the lush field of wheat.

Blake Jessop is a Canadian author of science fiction, fantasy and horror stories with a master's degree in creative writing from the University of Adelaide. You can read more of his speculative fiction in "I Didn't Break the Lamp: Historical Accounts of Imaginary Acquaintances" from DefCon One, or follow him on Twitter.
Twitter: @everydayjisei
Amazon: www.amazon.com/default/e/B07BB7Z73N

They Thirst
by Joel R. Hunt

As Hooper reached the doorway, a rough hand pulled him back. His protests were silenced as Cap nodded outside.

It stood just a few meters away from them; a Verdant. Grass sprouted like whiskers from what was once a human face. Fungi burst through dry, grey skin. A flower bloomed in its empty eye-socket.

An eye-socket that turned towards Hooper.

Blind, he reminded himself, *they're blind*.

Sure enough, the thing shambled past, vine-like feet combing for water.

"First time seeing a Verdant?" whispered Cap.

Hooper nodded, and Cap rested a hand on his shoulder.

"Let's hope it's not your last."

Joel R. Hunt is a writer from the UK who dabbles in the darker aspects of life, particularly through horror, science fiction and the supernatural. He has been published in a number of short story anthologies, and hopes to have released his first single author collection in early 2020, and hopes to have released his first anthology of short stories later this year.
Twitter: @JoelRHunt1
Reddit: JRHEvilInc

Missing Person
by Alanah Andrews

The doctor taps a finger against the slim file. "You remember nothing about your past?"

Complete desolation, a dark tunnel, a woman in a mask... The man with the pale eyes shrugs. "Nothing that makes sense."

"Okay, welcome to the nut house." The doctor smirks and locks the door.

Three hundred years later.

A woman in a mask heaves the door to the underground shelter closed. *Deep breath.* "Nothing has changed." Her voice wavers. "Project Reboot has failed."

Another scientist holds back a sob. "But this was humanity's last hope."

She sighs, glaring at the faulty time machine. "I know."

***Alanah Andrews** writes speculative fiction and spends far too much time debating whether 1984 or The Handmaid's Tale are most representative of our future. Her YA dystopian novel about a future where emotions are forbidden, Eve of Eridu, was released in 2018. She has also had several short stories published in a range of different places. When she's not writing, Alanah runs the Australian Speculative Fiction group, teaches high school English, and attempts to raise two children. She has a husky, a pony, a blue-tongue lizard, and dreams of travelling Australia in a bus.*
Website: www.alanahandrews.com
Facebook: alanahandrewsauthor

Ivory Towers
by Dawn DeBraal

The President of the United States pushed the button first. Missiles launched, there was no turning back now.

Russia soon followed ordering their weapons unleashed. Having no alternative China, North Korea, and Iran, also joined in the race.

Oh, how prideful the mighty were, having destructive nuclear bombs change the face of the world forever. There was nowhere to go to alleviate the suffering they caused. Leaders in their Ivory Towers stood waiting for the end while servants served merciful suicide pills. They would all go to sleep and not have to suffer the consequences of their actions—the cowards.

Dawn DeBraal lives in rural Wisconsin with her husband Red, two rat terriers, and a cat. She has discovered that her love of telling a good story can be written. Published stories with Palm-sized press, Spillwords, Mercurial Stories, Potato Soup Journal, Edify Fiction, Zimbell House Publishing, Clarendon House Publishing, Blood Song Books, Black Hare Press, Fantasia Divinity, Cafelit, Reanimated Writers, Guilty Pleasures, Unholy Trinity, The World of Myth, Dastaan World, Vamp Cat, Runcible Spoon, Dark Christmas, Siren's Call, Iron Horse Publishing, Falling Star Magazine 2019 Pushcart Nominee.
Amazon: amazon.com/Dawn-DeBraal/e/B07STL8DLX

Bright Things
by Kimberly Rei

Bright petals fell from an open window. They were the only bit of colour in a dark and dusty landscape. The child reached out a hand, entranced, but his mother gasped and snatched him away.

It wasn't wise to trust bright things. They bit and burned skin and eyes. Once, long ago, the mother remembered patterned gowns and fields of flowers. But then the Lady came and taught them all the error of their ways. Now, no one dared test her warning.

The petals sizzled where they touched the ground, leaving acrid sparkling dust behind. No, no one dared anymore.

Kimberly Rei has been writing for as long as she can remember. At five years old, her parents gifted her with a set of Children's Classics that she had no hope of reading. Yet. The potential alone sparked a love of words that has never wavered. Kim has taught writing workshops and edited novels for Authors You May Recognize. She has one published short story, which only fed into a hunger for more. She currently lives in Tampa Bay, Florida with her wife and an abundance of gorgeous beaches to explore. Website: tales.studiorei.org

This Same Wild Water
by Simon Clarke

People die looking at the sea when the waves are high enough to break against the clouds.

I can remember watching water force its way through the sluice, a cool damp breeze flying up and touching my face, the white noise of the rushing water, jamming my thoughts,

> *"Come to me Simon,*
>> *lean further over*
>>> *and just*
>>>> *let yourself*
>>>>> *go..."*

Since the endless storms, this same wild water, now fully grown, calls to us all. Towering over the coasts, it is visible from hundreds of miles inland. A thunderous earth-wide siren call generates a hypnotic power pulling at us all.

Simon Clarke was born in and raised and currently resides in East Anglia, United Kingdom. He has been writing fiction for at least five years and regularly submits to UK and international publications as well as reading short pieces and poetry at open mic events. He is currently working on his first novel and continues to write short stories and poetry.

Survivor's Guilt
by Joshua Ivey

Like ants with old firearms, they scatter, then gather and serve their mistresses before dying underground. Initially, it was amusing to watch; my vision from a shuttle thousands of miles above them, like God, was unable to process their individual heartbreak. Then, like God, it slowly began to make me angry, then sorrowful that the inevitable end of everything had come to what was once unyielding. Amid the division of their politics and prophecies, the torch of an all-encompassing famine was being oiled. Now votes are cast with bullets, and sermons told by sinners. I suppose it's not too different.

Joshua Ivey is a writer from Earth.
Twitter: @blckllip

Violet's Fatal Mistake
by Mark Mackey

Violet Evercrest was obsessed with a post apocalyptic novel in which human beings no longer existed. Their fate; devoured and wiped out by hybrid humanoid cat creatures now ruling the Earth. Her mistake; using her magic to journey into it. For some reason, her magic didn't work in this fictional world, entrapping her in it.

Her face drenched in sweat, she ran for her life to escape these creatures who had every intention of making her suffer the same horrible fate which wiped out humanity.

Exertion allowed them to catch up. Pinned to the ground, they began to bite furiously.

Mark Mackey is the author of various self-published books and has had various short stories published in charity anthologies. They include such captivating titles such as Christmas Lites, No Sleeves and Short Dresses: A Summer Anthology, Painted Mayhem, and Grynn Anthology, among others. A long-time resident of Chicago, when not writing, he spends time reading various genres of books.

The Big One
by D.K. Spencer

On one crisp, autumn morning of 2027, the day is unseasonably windy. Plastic bags swirl in the urban eddies and leaves blow across the cobblestone streets of downtown Seattle in cascading waves of colour.

A retro cable car careens crazily down Counterbalance hill like a wild hillbilly drunk on moonshine, as buildings sway back and forth, snapping in half, breaking apart; their rubble raining down.

The Ring of Fire ignites a chain reaction of lava and earthquakes, shaking the world whole.

Then stillness. Everything is quiet, except the crows.

Breathing a sigh of relief, the earth can now finally relax.

*American writer **D.K. Spencer** lives in Portland, Oregon with his accomplished wife who is a potter. Knowing the slim envelop of atmosphere is all that's keeping us alive, he wonders why humans spend so much time and energy focused on human and planet destruction. This is the basis of his work. Mixed in with pounds of humour he explores the human condition on this planet and planets throughout the universe. If not traveling to writers workshops or writing events, Spencer spends most of his time in Portland focused on writing the perfect short story.*
Website: www.bignoniodies.com
Patreon: www.patreon.com/user?u=19477894

Silentium
by A.S. Charly

My hands are ashen. I know what this means, but I feel…nothing.

Leaning against the stone-like tree, I stare at the pond. The fading green looks almost pretty, if you can ignore the dead fish. The world is slowly turning grey and silent—no bird song, no traffic noise.

No surprise they named it 'silence.'

What makes me wonder is how it's also affecting inanimate things. Even my mechanical clock at home lost all colour and broke into pieces. Signals weakened and died.

What will they call the 'blue planet' when this is over…if there's still someone left.

A.S. Charly loves to lose herself in fantastical worlds far away between the stars, filled with magic and wonder. She also writes and draws when she is not roaming through the park with her children. Her stories have been published in various anthologies and online publications.
Facebook: A.S.Charlydreams

The Crop
by Jasmine Arch

Hayley's eyes shone in the light of a crayon candle. "But Mummy, I don't want my hair cut. You always say it's pretty."

I kissed her sticky cheeks and hugged her before turning to my deadbeat ex. "Keep her safe, Jack. You hear?" I knelt in front of Hayley and took her hands. "I know, munchkin, but you have to. So the zombies can't grab it." So I wouldn't be able to grab it.

Black curls fell to the rhythm of snipping scissors as I walked away from our makeshift camp, the bite mark on my arm beginning to burn.

Jasmine Arch lives in a rural corner of Belgium with two horses, four dogs, and a husband who knows better than to distract her when she's writing. Her love of the written word in all its forms and incarnations is only superseded by her deep abiding passion for caffeine. Her work has appeared or is forthcoming in Illumen Magazine, ParABnormal Magazine, and Scifaikuest.
Website: jasminearch.com
Twitter: @jaye_arch

Where Z-Go, We Go
by Evelyn Benvie

Ronda had gotten the notification at eight that morning. Small family, two kids, pet dog.

Urgent pickup.

The young families always were.

She frowns at the clock. It's nearly dark now. Families always waited too long to call, thinking walls and quiet were safety enough.

They weren't.

She arrives at the coordinates around seven. Zees are there already, swarming the walls of the two-story house. She watches, numb and angry.

The first rule of Z-Go is to never leave the vehicle.

A child jumps from the window, stumbling toward her. The zees follow him.

She opens the door. And hopes.

Evelyn Benvie is the woolly jumper in a family of black sheep. Both a cynic and a romantic at heart, she writes diverse, queer-positive fiction and poetry that have been published online and in print. Her first novella, Something to Celebrate, was recently published by Mischief Corner Books and is available on Amazon.
Website: evelynbenvie.com

Peace and Quiet
by Jason Holden

As far as James was concerned, the best part about the end of everything was the peace it brought. No more people milling around aimlessly with their phones strapped to their heads. He had never liked people. Now it was just him and his dog, walking the empty roads together.

Noise hit his ear as he walked; a motorcycle engine. He unslung his rifle and took up position, aiming down the scope towards the growing growl emanating from the oncoming bike. From time to time, it wasn't so bad coming across another person. After all, a man's got to eat.

*After giving up a full-time job as a quarry operator so that his wife could follow her dream career as an academic in the field of chemistry, **Jason Holden** and his family left England and temporarily moved to Spain where they currently reside. While there, he took on the role of full-time parent and began to create stories for his daughter. Now that she is in school, he creates stories for himself and hopes to share those stories with others.*

BLACK HARE PRESS

The Seventh Seal
by Ali House

The blood moon dominated the sky. The end of times had finally come, the world ablaze with war and disease.

The white outfits of Saul's Disciples glowed red as they gathered in their holy field and prayed. They welcomed the divine cleansing, rejoicing in the deaths of non-believers. Soon they would receive their reward and ascend to an eternal heaven.

A white-winged angel landed in front of them. Her clothing was bloody and she held a large sword.

"Is it time?" Saul asked eagerly.

The angel nodded.

"Have you vanquished all the profane?"

The angel readied her sword. "Not yet."

Ali House is the author of sci-fi/fantasy novels The Six Elemental and The Fifth Queen, along with various short stories in the "From the Rock" series published by Engen Books. She is a traveller, baker, and fan of the Oxford comma. You can find her various thoughts on writing on her blog.
Website: engenbooks.com/tag/house-blog/

Vortex
by Nerisha Kemraj

The vortex of wind tore through the town, uprooting everything in its wake. They huddled together underneath the table, Sammy shaking against Tom's chest. It was only a matter of time before it moved down their street. With no idea where David was, they prayed for his safety. The winds howled outside, mourning the death of those it saw. The loud crash outside meant it was time, but instead of the tornado ripping them to shreds, their front door flew open and David staggered in.

"Oh, David!" Sammy ran to hug him, just as flying debris pierced through them both.

Nerisha Kemraj resides in Durban, South Africa with her husband and two mischievous daughters. She has work published/accepted in various publications, both print and online. She holds a Bachelor's degree in Communication Science, and a Post Graduate Certificate in Education from University of South Africa.
Amazon: amazon.com/author/nerisha_kemraj
Facebook: Nerishakemrajwriter

World War III: a brief history of Man's Best Friend and the Apocalypse War
[Entry 23: from the journal of Francis Lloyd]

by Cameron Marcoux

It started with Mudge. Our sweet golden Pekingese. One day she just…started barking and didn't stop. Like a fit of uncontrollable laughter. *Yip! Yip! Yip!* Incessant.

Mind grating.

Yipping!

Neighbours glared at us from windows and mailboxes. *Shut that damn dog up!* (Trust me, Fred. We've tried).

After two full nights without sleep, I was ready to give the anklebiter the boot myself, when… Silence!

"Mudge?"

On her side. Glassy eyes. No rise and fall of breath.

She was dead.

And so was every dog on the planet.

I blame the Russians. Or maybe those guys at the Pentagon.

Cameron Marcoux is a writer of stories, which, considering where you are reading this, makes a lot of sense. He also teaches English to the lovely and terrifying creatures we call teenagers. He lives in the quiet, northern reaches of New England in the U.S. with his girlfriend and scaredy dog.

Behold! I Saw a Red Horse
by Cecelia Hopkins-Drewer

"Get out the spike strip," ordered the corporal.

An adaptation of the caltrop, once used to disable cavalry charges, these spikes were supersized to deflate the tires of enemy trucks.

"Yes, Sir!" The Squadron raced to obey.

The spikes were laid, and the soldiers ducked for cover. Strangely, they could see no drivers in the cabins.

The corporal presumed visibility was poor. "Activate!"

The tires had been packed with explosives. The entire area flamed with napalm. Most of the men were incinerated. A few suffered carbon monoxide poisoning.

"We set it off!" the corporal groaned as he died of asphyxiation.

Cecelia Hopkins-Drewer lives in Adelaide, South Australia. She has written a Masters paper on H.P. Lovecraft, and her weird poetry has been published in THE MENTOR (edited by Ron Clarke), and SPECTRAL REALMS (edited by S.T. Joshi). Her novels include a teenage vampire series commencing with MYSTIC EVERMORE. Short stories have been published in WORLDS, ANGELS & MONSTERS, BEYOND, STORMING AREA 51, and UNRAVEL. (Dark Drabbles anthologies edited by Dean Kershaw).
Amazon: amazon.com/Cecelia-Hopkins-Drewer/e/B071G968NM
Website: chopkin39.wixsite.com/website

A World of Chaos
by Destiny Eve Pifer

On a dirty mattress the young girl lay, staring up at a cracked ceiling. Silently, she prayed for it to all be a dream, a horrible nightmare that she would soon wake up from.

In the corner of the room, a rat scurried across the dirty floor. Food was scarce, even for the rodents. In just one night, the world as she knew it had ended. The fire that had shot across the sky left a world full of ash. There was chaos and tears. A world covered in fear.

Those who had survived that night would wish they hadn't.

Destiny Eve Pifer is a published author whose work has appeared in Angel's: A Divine Microfiction Anthology, and has been accepted into the Unravel Anthology. Her work has also appeared in Single Mothers Anthology, River Tales Anthology, Kiss and Tell and Summer Fling. Her work has also appeared in FATE Magazine, Spotlight on Recovery, Country Magazine and True Confessions. She resides in Punxsutawney, Pennsylvania with her son Dartanyan.

Mottled Skin
by Rhiannon Bird

"I'm fine," she said, and stomped further into the warehouse. Thankfully they didn't follow her, and when she was out of sight, a sigh of relief escaped her. Wincing, she unwrapped the bandage from around her arm. The skin had gone from a purple blue to a greenish yellow. Tears spilled silently from her eyes as she looked at the bite and the mottled skin around it. There was no stopping it now. She refused to end up like those disgusting things. She took a steadying breath and reached for her gun.

A woeful shot rang out through the warehouse.

Rhiannon Bird is a young aspiring author. She has a passion for words and storytelling. Rhiannon has her own quotes blog; Thoughts of a Writer. She has had 4 works published. This includes 3 short stories and 2 poems. These are published on Eskimo pie, Literary yard, Down in the Dirt Magazine and Short break fiction. She can be found on Facebook, Instagram, and Pinterest.

Mr. Omega
by Brandy Bonifas

The electricity shut off the same day I got the eviction notice. Three children, and a husband who'd left; what else could I do?

Mr. Omega—not his real name—offered cash for what I could smuggle from the research centre where I worked. Alpha-PVP, immortal jellyfish DNA, rare strains of rabies—like a shopping list for Dr. Frankenstein.

Later, the news reported a man found dead, hotel room trashed. I knew what they'd stolen.

The news called it Bioterrorism. The violent pandemic spread worldwide in weeks, unstoppable. As the T.V. cut to static, I held my children and cried.

Brandy Bonifas lives in Ohio with her husband and son. Her work has appeared or is forthcoming in anthologies by Clarendon House Publications, Pixie Forest Publishing, Zombie Pirate Publishing, and Blood Song Books, as well as the online publications CafeLit and Spillwords Press.
Website: www.brandybonifas.com
Facebook: brandybonifasauthor

Egyptian Gold
by Matthew M. Montelione

Long ago, I awoke to the sound of screaming strangers. They choked on poisonous air, turning yellow before they died.

Only I remain.

I wander through the silent halls of the dusty museum, longing for home. I admire the gold, the jewels, the art of the ancient past. Still, it is not home.

The poison gave me life, yet, I have no one to share it with.

I am Nesmin. I return to my coffin; my amulets glow in the sulfuric air. I lay my mummified body down to rest, and pray to Min for deliverance from this devastated world.

Matthew M. Montelione is a horror writer born and raised on Long Island in New York. His stories have been published in Quoth the Raven: A Contemporary Reimagining of the Works of Edgar Allan Poe, Thuggish Itch: Devilish, and other titles. Matthew is also an American Revolution historian who focuses on the local experiences of Loyalists on Long Island. His work on the subject has been published in Long Island History Journal and Journal of the American Revolution.
Website: maybeevils.com
Twitter: @maybeevils

The Fish and the Fury
by Austin P. Sheehan

Our world fell apart overnight; the desperate, furious hordes cut through the cities and towns, leaving only ruin.

Abandoned factories, towers reaching the clouds, all now little more than tombs.

On the dust-covered mantle of a dilapidated suburban house lays a faded photo. A man and his son, captured in a brief moment of joy, bonding over a bass on the end of the child's line.

A survivor—starving, weak and alone—cradles the frame in his hands, looking at it with envy. It's been a decade since he last saw his son, but all he wants is the fish.

Austin P. Sheehan *is a writer of speculative fiction, a lover of language, literature and '90s TV. Armed with a psychology degree, he went into the world to study humanity, and now prefers the company of his wife and their greyhounds. He grew up in the valleys of Victoria's high country, and despite living in Melbourne, always feels at home amongst the mountains. You'll often find mountains in his stories, whether they're sci-fi, fantasy or alternative history.*
Website: austinpsheehan.com
Twitter: @AustinPSheehan

Week One
by D.J. Elton

Monday. It's beginning, screens have dropped out. Communicado nil, damn it! Could be worse, but…I could get lonely out here in the APY lands with dogs and two thousand cattle. Will take a look tomorrow, more light.

Tuesday. All signals are out. Generators not working either. At least there're cans and water for six months. I'll take the plane out tomorrow.

Wednesday. Some earth tremors! Cattle are rumbling, restless. Plane got damaged in the land cracks. Hell! Big earthquake?

Thursday. Can't move my legs. Fridge on top of me?

Friday. Hell…pain. God, if you exist…!

Saturday. Silence.

Sunday. Nothing.

Monday…

D.J. Elton writes fiction and poetry, and is currently studying writing and literature which is improving her work in unexpected ways. She spends a lot of time in northern India and should probably live there, however there is much to be done in Melbourne, so this is the home base. She has meditated daily for the past 35 years and has worked in healthcare for equally as long, so she's very happy to be writing, zoning in and out of all things literary.
Twitter: @DJEltonwrites

Urban Jungle
by Cameron Marcoux

They grew out of cracks in the sidewalks first. Small green tendrils. Slithering snakes of ivy or somesuch. Small, not of much consequence. But then they began to grow out of sewer grates, kitchen sinks, and toilet bowls; creeping, demanding. The plants covered houses and cars, roadways and telephone poles. The National Guard was called. Then the Army. In days, the invasive flora had conquered cities. Soon, entire continents. Nature had come to claim what was its own. Most folks resigned themselves to a life of tree and vine, to the primitive ways of the ancients. The animal kingdom thrived.

Cameron Marcoux is a writer of stories, which, considering where you are reading this, makes a lot of sense. He also teaches English to the lovely and terrifying creatures we call teenagers. He lives in the quiet, northern reaches of New England in the U.S. with his girlfriend and scaredy dog.

Necrotizing Fasciitis
By Eddie D. Moore

After four months of isolation, five men and five women boarded the Last Chance and left Earth behind. A decade ago, the lights of major cities could have been seen from orbit, but no longer. The mutated flesh-eating bacteria that evolved twenty years ago devastated the human population.

Phil and Karen stared at the dark planet below while the others sealed themselves into their cryo-units.

Phil sighed and said, "Maybe we'll have better luck in the next solar system."

Karen nodded and waited until the others were all in stable cryogenic stasis to explore the purple patch between her toes.

Eddie D. Moore travels hundreds of hours a year, and he fills that time by listening to audiobooks. When he isn't playing with his grandchildren, he writes his own stories. You can find a list of his publications on his blog or by visiting his Amazon Author Page. While you're there, be sure to pick up a copy of his mini-anthology Misfits & Oddities.
Website: eddiedmoore.wordpress.com
Amazon: amazon.com/author/eddiedmoore

Noxious Clouds
by Kent Swarts

An asteroid struck California while JJ piloted a submersible in the Mariana Trench. The parent vessel, the *Bracken*, heard about the apocalypse on the radio.

Thick, noxious clouds covered the planet. As the temperature plummeted, the ship headed to Manila. There they found a nation of zombies, although a few living people congregated on wharfs.

JJ stood on the *Bracken*'s deck next to his captain.

"Are we going to save anyone?"

"Do you honestly think we will survive?" He emphasised, 'will.'

"I figured we would."

"JJ, you figured right," said the captain. "We'll go ashore to live a reanimated life."

Kent Swarts is a retired aeronautical engineer and is an enthusiastic astronomer. He edits the astronomy club's newsletter. He has been published in four anthologies and has one published novel, The Fate of the Charles Wilkes, a sci-fi story. He lives in Waco, TX.

The Farmer
by Susanne Thomas

The dirt had turned to granite crumbles, but Bri'lara tilled it.

The seeds were hard pebbles and she sowed them with care.

There would be few sprouts and fewer full-grown plants. Bri'lara shook her head and hummed to herself. When a thousand years had passed no one would remember when corn could not grow.

She worked on. The meltdown of every government, every country, and every land had left a lot of problems for the people.

She glanced down at her hands, one sporting seven fingers, the other eight, before lifting her gear and moving on to the next field.

Susanne Thomas reads, writes, parents, and teaches from the windy west in Wyoming, and she loves fantasy, science fiction, speculative fiction, poetry, children's books, science, coffee, and puns.
Website: www.themightierpenn.com
Facebook: SusanneThomasAuthor

Alien Barbeque
by Kelly Matsuura

"You're really eating that?" The guys were roasting a little sprinter alien they'd caught earlier. Even before cooking, Leila thought it smelled like an old, sick cat.

"Hell, yeah!"

The three boys tucked in. Only Michelle, a vegetarian, and Wallace, the group's Collie, kept Leila company.

Minutes later, the boys all turned green and barfed vile black gunk. Then they all choked. Leila noticed Scottie's eyes fell right out of his skull.

Michelle rushed to help, but Leila couldn't see the point.

"How did you know?!" Michelle cried.

"Wallace didn't want any, did ya boy?" Leila scratched his ears, unaffected.

Kelly Matsuura writes diverse YA, fantasy, and literary fiction. She is the Creator of 'The Insignia Series' anthologies (Asian fantasy themed) and has had stories published with Ink & Locket Press, A Murder of Storytellers, Crushing Hearts & Black Butterfly, and many more. Kelly lives in Nagoya, Japan with her geeky husband. She loves traveling, knitting, cooking, and of course, reading.
Website: www.blackwingsandwhitepaper.com
Twitter: @KellyMatsuura

Dietary Unrestrictions
by Raven Corinn Carluk

She moved with the rest of the herd, picking through the remains of the old world. They were safer together, though none of them had weapons. No practical skills to earn them a place inside one of the enclaves, the barest instincts geared toward survival.

Most had forgotten they were even human.

She remembered more than most. Grocery stores, and smartphones, and distressed jeans. Pumpkin spice lattes and appletinis.

Now, they ate anything they found. Grubs and mushrooms were common. Dead animals were a bounty, jealously gobbled up by whomever found them.

She missed having the choice to be vegan.

Raven Corinn Carluk writes dark fantasy, paranormal romance, and anything else that catches her interest. She's authored five novels, where she explores themes of love and acceptance. Her shorter pieces, usually from her darker side, can be found in Black Hare Press anthologies, at Detritus Online, and through Alban Lake Publishers.
Twitter: @ravencorinn
Website: RavenCorinnCarluk.Blogspot.Com

Dwindling Topography
by Chip Houser

In a collapsed hall, an echoing crunch truncates panicked screaming.

Later, a wrinkled sheet of parchment skips corner over corner across the heaving stones of an empty plaza, catching on a clattering stand of dry stalks rising from a russet mound that was once a fighting machine. The bones of its soldiers were scavenged long ago. Crimson splashes dapple the parchment in a delicate arc like the islands of a whimsical archipelago. A map describing the mysterious geography of a small violence.

Its cartographer is feasting now, alone in the darkness, an artless crunching amid a shifting landscape of bones.

Chip Houser's fiction has appeared in Daily Science Fiction, New Myths, The Drabble, 101 Fiction, 50 Word Stories, Every Day Fiction, Rosebud, Gemini Magazine, and others. He has an MFA in Creative Writing from The University of Missouri in St. Louis, attended the Odyssey Writing Workshop, and is a practicing architect. When he isn't working, he turns the tiny, ill-shapen horrors of the modern world that cling to his soul into dark morsels of fiction.

The Circus Comes to Town
by Terry Miller

The war was over. Homes and buildings were flattened, vegetation scorched, and bodies were extra crispy. Some people retreated to the caves in the hills, some just watched in disbelief as the shockwave expanded ever-farther until it was too late.

A tiny car drove out from the second cave on Pine Mountain, swerving frantically down the dirt road. It reached the bottom, stopped, and the passengers began to exit, and exit, and exit; there were ten in all. They skipped down the streets with merry smiles and red noses, leaving balloons tied to the charred corpses of the town's children.

Terry Miller is an author and 2017 Rhysling Award-nominated poet residing in Portsmouth, OH, USA. He has self-published a dark poetry collection on Amazon and one short story to date. His work has also appeared in Sanitarium, Devolution Z, Jitter Press, Poetry Quarterly, O Unholy Night in Deathlehem, and the 2017 Rhysling Anthology from the Science Fiction and Fantasy Poetry Association.
Facebook: tmiller2015

The Hunt
by Jennifer Hatfield

With teary eyes Mother said, "The gun has two barrels; a shotgun with rock salt and a rifle on top. Be careful out there, shoot anything that moves. Bring animals home, leave bodies behind."

At only 8 years old, I hoped to make Mom proud. I stepped out for the first time ever into a landscape of rotting bodies, bright light that hurt my eyes, and dying trees.

Just before dark, I spotted a rabbit; rushing back to the bunker with my prize held high.

Momma smiled when I returned. "Good girl," she said as she took her last breath.

Jennifer Hatfield spent a large portion of her life being a dedicated mother and wife. She managed her epilepsy diagnosis, and handled the loss of her husband. Grateful to find comfort in the ability to write in an effort to express her feelings, thoughts, and struggles. She's published 5 poems.

Redemption
by Terry Miller

For miles, the facility stretched. Rows and rows of bodies stuck in pods and drained of their water which proceeded through the filtration systems. This is how we survived. We are sixty percent water, after all.

It had been a year since the aliens scorched the surface to ash. If we had not downed some of their ships, we would never have had this technology; a blessing amidst the chaos. The dregs of humanity came to serve a purpose to the elite after all. Each meal, we raised our glasses to toast those who redeemed us through their bodily reservoirs!

Terry Miller *is an author and 2017 Rhysling Award-nominated poet residing in Portsmouth, OH, USA. He has self-published a dark poetry collection on Amazon and one short story to date. His work has also appeared in Sanitarium, Devolution Z, Jitter Press, Poetry Quarterly, O Unholy Night in Deathlehem, and the 2017 Rhysling Anthology from the Science Fiction and Fantasy Poetry Association.*
Facebook: tmiller2015

The Final Christmas
by Charlotte O'Farrell

A humming drone flew over ruined cities the morning after the extinction event.

"It's just such a shame," said the pilot to her assistant, operating it remotely light-years away. "I thought they had a chance."

The drone captured snapshots from the rubble of tinsel, indoor trees and abandoned meals.

In the "mythology" section of her Lost Species Report, the pilot sketched the doomed creatures' apparent god: a bearded, alarming man in a red suit. Icons of him appeared all over the scattered wastelands, grinning.

"We've been watching them a while," replied the assistant, yawning. "They were always heading this way."

Charlotte O'Farrell is a lifelong horror fan who writes about all manner of the weird and wonderful. Her work can be found at the Drabble, the Rock N Roll Horror Zine and Horror Tree, among other places.
Twitter: @ChaOFarrell.

The Rider on the Black Horse
by Matthew M. Montelione

Lightning flashed as the dark-haired rider on his mighty black horse stormed towards the dilapidated house. He held a pair of scales.

Little Julia looked up at her father, Mason. "Do we have enough this time, Daddy? I'm so hungry!"

Mason lovingly combed his fingers through his daughter's curly hair. "I know, honey. Go inside with Mommy."

Julia smiled and obeyed; she didn't truly grasp their dire situation.

The primeval horseman halted before the man. "Coins for grain!"

Mason dropped his money on the empty scale; the other dish held bread.

It wasn't enough. Again.

Famine cackled and rode off.

Matthew M. Montelione *is a horror writer born and raised on Long Island in New York. His stories have been published in Quoth the Raven: A Contemporary Reimagining of the Works of Edgar Allan Poe, Thuggish Itch: Devilish, and other titles. Matthew is also an American Revolution historian who focuses on the local experiences of Loyalists on Long Island. His work on the subject has been published in Long Island History Journal and Journal of the American Revolution.*

Website: maybeevils.com
Twitter: @maybeevils

Not My Jenny
by Terry Miller

Nuclear Winter came and snow cream was off the menu. In fact, the only thing on the menu was what we had stored underground. A few that had sheltered in the bunker with us went atop to explore what was there. I suspect they quickly regretted their decision.

I didn't want Jenny to go. She never listened, ever. When she returned, her face was badly burned. Skin was peeling from her forehead and cheeks, plus she didn't act right in the head. She wanted to make love, I couldn't. It wasn't Jenny, not my Jenny; she didn't look like that!

Terry Miller is an author and 2017 Rhysling Award-nominated poet residing in Portsmouth, OH, USA. He has self-published a dark poetry collection on Amazon and one short story to date. His work has also appeared in Sanitarium, Devolution Z, Jitter Press, Poetry Quarterly, O Unholy Night in Deathlehem, and the 2017 Rhysling Anthology from the Science Fiction and Fantasy Poetry Association.
Facebook: tmiller2015

A Disaster Waiting to Happen
by Brianna Witte

Humans: one of the few species that will turn against their own kind at the drop of a hat.

We fight, kill and thrive on violence. People said they could change; that we will not make the mistakes that our ancestors did. Humans could never keep their word. History always repeats itself.

Now we have finally paid the price. We have destroyed one another; our planet no longer liveable nor safe.

When the nukes soared through the sky, I knew it was over. Our savagery and violent hearts had finally killed us. In the end, we were our own demise.

*As an up and coming writer from Ontario, Canada, **Brianna Witte** has a passion for spinning tales of adventure and fantasy. She enjoys taking readers on a ride through the realm of fiction by weaving magical and mystical stories that materialize from her wildly creative dreams and vivid imagination.*

Keep Moving
by Neen Cohen

There were always pockets in the cities I travelled through. Small pockets of survivors making the most of the shitty existence that was left behind.

Some asked me to stay, some didn't let me pause.

Sometimes I lingered, but never long.

When the world ended, sticking to the same reasons of staying put felt completely alien.

I saw families decimated, friends turn on each other. But I respected the pockets, all members were survivors.

I survived by moving, and wearing my father's clothing, hiding what little femininity I possessed.

When you move, the old demons found it harder to follow.

Neen Cohen lives in Brisbane with her partner, son and fur babies. She is a writer of LGBTQI, dark fantasy and horror short stories and has a Bachelor of Creative Industries from QUT. She can often be found writing while sitting against a tombstone or tree in any number of graveyards.
Facebook: Neen-Cohen-Author-424700821629629
Website: wordbubblessite.wordpress.com

Elephants
by Kelly Matsuura

Mum showed me a video online once, of a man who took a piano to an animal sanctuary and played to the rescued elephants. God! Remember elephants? And going to the zoo? All those incredible animals. All gone now, of course.

We see small creatures around: lizards, snakes, rabbits; things that move fast. Things that can get away from The Sick. They mostly get away from us too.

No elephants here, but I have a piano. I moved it close to The Locker Room and I play for the lost ones inside; the ones In-Between. They seem to like it.

Kelly Matsuura writes diverse YA, fantasy, and literary fiction. She is the Creator of 'The Insignia Series' anthologies (Asian fantasy themed) and has had stories published with Ink & Locket Press, A Murder of Storytellers, Crushing Hearts & Black Butterfly, and many more. Kelly lives in Nagoya, Japan with her geeky husband. She loves traveling, knitting, cooking, and of course, reading. Website: www.blackwingsandwhitepaper.com Twitter: @KellyMatsuura

The Glow
by Andrew Anderson

We spent so long underground during my childhood that I developed a crippling fear of the dark. In the pitch-black, listening to the war rage above our heads, those months were filled with many sleepless nights.

Once the bombs stopped Father scavenged the wasteland for supplies, returning to the shelter at night. Late one evening, Mother stopped by my bed and pointed. "Look Julie, you don't need to be scared of the dark anymore."

She was right.

Turning to look at Father in the neighbouring bed, his irradiated body glowed, acting as a human nightlight.

I slept well that night.

Andrew Anderson is a full-time civil servant, dabbling in writing music, poetry, screenplays and short stories in his limited spare time, when not working on building himself a fort made out of second-hand books. He lives in Bathgate, Scotland with his wife, two children and his dog.
Twitter: @soorploom

Global Brain Wasting Disease
by Vonnie Winslow Crist

The rabbit beneath Kelly's porch was not cuddly and cute—it was dead.

She stepped back. Global Brain Wasting Disease had originated with insects, then moved up the evolutionary ladder. Humanity was its endgame.

Kelly grabbed her garden rake. Still, the raggedy rabbit crept towards her.

"Stay back," she warned.

The rabbit gnashed its teeth.

Surprised at how much larger bunny teeth appeared without skin around the mouth, she thought, *those cuspids could do real damage.*

She heard clicking behind her—whirled around.

Dozens of zombified rabbits approached.

Kelly screamed as the colony jumped on her—teeth biting, tearing, chewing.

Vonnie Winslow Crist is author of The Enchanted Dagger, Owl Light, The Greener Forest, Murder on Marawa Prime, and other award-winning books. Her fiction is included in "Amazing Stories," "Cast of Wonders," "Outposts of Beyond," Killing It Softly 2, Defending the Future - Dogs of War, Midnight Masquerade, Chaos of Hard Clay, and elsewhere. A cloverhand who has found so many four-leafed clovers she keeps them in jars, Vonnie strives to celebrate the power of myth in her writing.
Website: www.vonniewinslowcrist.com

Sky Fall
by Allen Ashley

Rex was shouting, "We're all doomed. The rock from the sky will destroy our way of life."

Nobody was listening.

Eventually, Topsy said, "I saw it blaze across the firmament, but it must have fallen half the world away. We're safe now."

"You don't understand," Rex answered. "The crash will send up so much dust and debris into the atmosphere that everywhere will turn dark. For ages."

"And?"

"Nothing will grow. You vegetarians will starve."

"You'll just have to learn to eat carrion, Rex."

She trundled away. Rex let out a growl at the wilful hubris of his fellow dinosaurs.

Allen Ashley is a British Fantasy Award winner who works as a creative writing tutor and critical reader in London, UK. His most recent book is as co-editor (with Sarah Doyle) of the anthology "Humanagerie" (Eibonvale Press, 2018) — a collection of short stories and poems exploring human-animal liminality. He has stories due soon in "Shoreline of Infinity", "BFS Horizons" and the NewCon Press anthology "Once Upon A Parsec". He is the founder of the advanced science fiction and fantasy group Clockhouse London Writers.
Website: www.allenashley.com

Ragnarok
by Cindar Harrell

The nine realms were in flames, a spark ignited by prophecy and fanned by the winds of Odin's wrath. The inferno grew by the heated intensity of Loki's revenge.

For their sins the world would pay.

The world tree served as kindling for this foretold apocalypse and all I could do was sit back on my throne of death and watch my father play his role to perfection. Helheim was flooded with new guests. We sat, waiting for the world to begin anew, although we would never be part of it.

As such was our destiny. As such was Ragnarok.

Cindar Harrell loves fairy tales, especially ones with a dark twist. Her stories are often fairy tale inspired, but she is also working on a mystery series. Her stories can be found on Amazon and in various anthologies. You can follow her on Facebook and visit her blog, which she promises to try and update more often,
Website: cindarharrell.wordpress.com
Facebook: CindarHarrell

The Man from Above
by Stephen Herczeg

"Where did he come from?"

"He says from outside, from above."

"Impossible. Nothing can survive out there. Has he been checked?"

"Yes. No radiation. No disease. He's healthy."

Stern looked at the man, concern on his face.

"If it's true, we can't let it get out."

"Why? If it's clear above ground then we can finally leave this place."

"No," snapped Stern, "Our society is built on the belief that there is no outside world. It would breed mutiny."

"But—"

"No buts. We can't have fake news like this get out."

Stern cocked his gun and stepped into the room.

Stephen Herczeg is an IT Geek based in Canberra Australia. He has been writing for over twenty years and has completed a couple of dodgy novels, sixteen feature length screenplays and numerous short stories and scripts. His horror work has featured in Sproutlings, Hells Bells, Below the Stairs, Trickster's Treats #1 and #2, Shades of Santa, Behind the Mask, Beyond the Infinite; The Body Horror Book, Anemone Enemy, Petrified Punks and Beginnings. He has also had numerous Sherlock Holmes stories published through the Belanger Books - Sherlock Holmes anthologies.

Chivalry Ain't Dead Yet
by Gregg Cunningham

I stood watching the ritual from the shadows.

Six of them lusting after the helpless traveller, groping after her like hungry hens scratching for corn in their pen.

When they finally forced the young woman to the ground and surrounded her, I sighed again, dropping my cigarette.

Slowly, and without a sound, I made my way over to the scrum and lifted one of the attackers from the pack. The grateful eyes of the hysterical woman stared back at me.

"How many times have I told you guys?"

My gunshot echoed across the barren highway.

"Don't play with your food!"

Gregg Cunningham 48, is a short story writer from Western Australia who has had to pick up his game since stumbling into facebook writer's groups. He has stories published by 559 Publishing in in 13 Bites volume 3,4,5, Plan 9 from Outer space, Other Realms, Heard It on The Radio, 559 Ways to Die, short stories publishing by Zombie Pirate Publishing in Relationship add Vice, Full Metal Horror, Phuket Tattoo, World War four and Flash Fiction Addiction (flash) with Zombie Pirate Publishing, and also in Daastan Magazine Chapter 11 and Brian,Rich and the Wardrobe. Amazon: www.amazon.com/-/e/B016OTHX0K

Ghosts of the Apocalypse
by Stacey Jaine McIntosh

Keeley lowered her gun. Bullets weren't effective against zombies, but it did stun them for a moment, which was enough time for Keeley to reach for her machete. Decapitation was the only way to kill a zombie. Not everyone had the strength or the mental fortitude. Most ran screaming, but not Keeley. She'd seen too much. It was kill or be killed.

Once, she'd had a brother. Jensen had been infected and she'd been forced to kill him.

She'd cut down zombies before, but nothing had prepared her when she looked into his eyes and saw ghosts from the past.

Stacey Jaine McIntosh was born in Perth, Western Australia where she still resides with her husband and their four children. Although her first love has always been writing, she once toyed with being a Cartographer. Since 2011 she has had over two dozen short stories and drabbles published both online and in various anthologies. She has also had two poems accepted for publication. Stacey is also the author of Solstice, Morrighan & Lost and she is currently working on several other projects simultaneously. When not with her family or writing she enjoys reading, photography, genealogy, history, Arthurian myths and witchcraft. Website: www.staceyjainemcintosh.com

Munch
by D.M. Burdett

As apocalypses go, this one ain't too bad.

I mean…there's no Macey's, no Pret a Manger. No electricity, no internet.

But, I'm alive.

And I still have my special edition iPhone MMXXX. I keep it hooked up to my solar charger, keep the battery juices filled up. Always ready.

I still take pictures of my dinner. I've got hundreds of photos ready for when Facebook is back online.

I'm lining up a shot now; I get the angle right, shade the lens from the sun, snap the girl as she runs.

Then I raise my gun and shoot again.

D.M. Burdett *initially roamed as an army brat, but now lives in Australia where she spends her days avoiding drop bears and killer spiders. She has published a Sci-Fi series, has short stories in various anthologies, and has published two children's series. She is currently working on the first book in a dystopian series.*
Website: www.dmburdett.com
Facebook: DMBurdett

Survival
by Stacey Jaine McIntosh

The world had ended the same way it had begun. With a glorious bang and a rain of fire and ash. A massive meteor had nearly wiped out the Earth and made the land uninhabitable. Humans had retreated underground, seeking shelter from the elements, the heat and acidic rain that battered the continents on a daily basis.

Loris opened the hatch and peered out through her visor. It wasn't raining, which meant she was free to scavenge. Despite the harsh conditions, some vegetation had managed to adapt to live above ground, and with careful preparation, it was edible.

Humanity survived.

Stacey Jaine McIntosh was born in Perth, Western Australia where she still resides with her husband and their four children. Although her first love has always been writing, she once toyed with being a Cartographer. Since 2011 she has had over two dozen short stories and drabbles published both online and in various anthologies. She has also had two poems accepted for publication. Stacey is also the author of Solstice, Morrighan & Lost and she is currently working on several other projects simultaneously. When not with her family or writing she enjoys reading, photography, genealogy, history, Arthurian myths and witchcraft. Website: www.staceyjainemcintosh.com

Apocalypse Support Group
by Michele Freeman

"It's the same dream," I said. "Mom and Dad, covered in bloody sores, try to infect us."

My older brother Sean nodded. "I dream about that, too."

"C'mon, you guys," sniped Cheryl, our younger sister. "The apocalypse was a whole year ago."

"Trauma doesn't have an expiration date." Counsellor Rick smiled at us from behind the Plexiglass. "Remember, you're in a safe space."

Safe? *Hah.* Trapped in an underground bunker. Poked and prodded by scientists. Questioned by government officials.

No one understood why three teenaged siblings were immune to the virus.

It never occurred to them we were the cause.

Award-winning author **Michele Freeman** *writes horror and dark fiction. She loves crochet, chocolate, and zombies. She lives in Texas with her Viking husband and their adorable fur babies.*
Website: www.authormichelefreeman.com

Judgement
By Eddie D. Moore

We were ten miles away from the Air Force base when the missiles launched. Dozens of them took to the sky riding upon the flames of Hell. The smoke trails they left behind gleamed a brilliant white as the setting sun cast long shadows around us. Tears fell from my cheeks as I held my family close.

I barely registered the words as my wife said softly, "Though your sins are as scarlet, they shall be white as snow."

A chill ran down my back when I recognised that the missile's top-secret engines sounded like the call of a trumpet.

Eddie D. Moore travels hundreds of hours a year, and he fills that time by listening to audiobooks. When he isn't playing with his grandchildren, he writes his own stories. You can find a list of his publications on his blog or by visiting his Amazon Author Page. While you're there, be sure to pick up a copy of his mini-anthology Misfits & Oddities.
Website: eddiedmoore.wordpress.com
Amazon: amazon.com/author/eddiedmoore

Caution Radiation Area
by J. Motoki

Years ago, I ran the Anti-Population Movement. Humans were maggots eating through the earth's corpse. Now I run with an infant.

Howls. My pursuer sprints on hands and knees. Tumours sprout from his face.

Before me, the fence. The yellow sign. Black flower with three petals.

I smile at the baby's screams. Strong lungs.

A hand pokes out of the fence, waves frantically. She gestures and I understand. There's no time left to climb. I kiss the baby once. So smooth, unblemished.

This one will survive.

Baby over the barbed wire, still screaming.

I turn around.

I face my pursuer.

J. Motoki is the Short Story Editor of Coffin Bell Journal and the Strange Editor of Rune Bear. Her works have been published or are forthcoming in Blood Song Books, The Other Stories Podcast (Hawk & Cleaver), Coffin Bell Journal, and others.
Website: www.jumotki.com

Cubes
by Nicola Currie

I suppose I'm spinning, but I can't tell in the infinite blackness. When I last glimpsed another cube it was tumbling wildly. That was months, years ago. Perhaps only minutes. I can't tell time now either.

At first there was a crowd of cubes, each sustaining one not chosen to take shelter amongst the few thousand beneath earth's surface, away from the scorching sun, but luckier than the billions left to burn. A million self-sustaining cubes, sent in a million directions, tasked with finding a home for all humanity.

Until then I drift. Awake. Asleep. Alive. Dead. I can't tell.

Nicola Currie is 34, from Cambridge, UK where she works in educational publishing. She has published poetry in literary magazines, including Mslexia and Sarasvati, and has also completed her first novel, which was longlisted for the Bath Children's Novel Award.
Website: writeitandweep.home.blog

Vallee de la Mort
by Jo Seysener

Bodies littered the field everywhere I stepped. A battlefield of death, where no one was fighting.

At least, not anymore.

Some fresh, some older, and I wondered if I had been this way before.

I had walked so many steps, been to so many places.

Everywhere it was the same.

I would cry tears, but I had none to give the empty corpses, their souls gone.

Now there were no souls left, the last had departed. So I found my horse, stiffly climbing onto her back. I patted her mane.

An ethereal pair: a pale rider on a pale horse.

Jo Seysener is a mum of three crazies, a scatter of chickens, a decrepit kelpie and a rambunctious GSD. She lives with her husband near Brisbane, Australia. When she is not exposing her kids to cult story books from her childhood, she can be found in the kitchen experimenting with new flavours and pairings. She adores alpacas.
Facebook: joseysener
Website: www.joseysener.com

APO Eclipse Inc.
by Joachim Heijndermans

Are you looking to clear out prime real estate planets of its ruling species, be it on your own world or on that of a neighbouring one? Don't know where to start and in need of guidance? Then let us be that helping hand. With APO Eclipse Inc., we offer services that range from infernal decimation through firestorms, to the re-animated dead hunting the living, to just too many weasels.

You need an apocalypse fast, efficient and most importantly, with results? Then call us, and we'll bring the end times to you.

Because you deserve the best ending. Call now.

Joachim Heijndermans *writes, draws, and paints nearly every waking hour. Originally from the Netherlands, he's been all over the world, boring people by spouting random trivia. His work has been featured in a number of anthologies and publications, such as Mad Scientist Journal, Asymmetry Fiction, Hinnom Magazine, Ahoy Comics's Edgar Allan Poe's Snifter of Terror, Metaphorosis and The Gallery of Curiosities, and he's currently in the midst of completing his first children's book.*
Website: www.joachimheijndermans.com
Twitter: @jheijndermans

Solitude
by Cathy Hinkle

The Santa Ana winds whip dust and trash around the cars and fallen motorcycles cluttering Wilshire Boulevard. Weeks of solitude and silence slice into my soul.

I crave noise like I crave companionship; my frustration prompts me to hurl a rock through a window.

A silhouette disrupts the boutique's shadows, and hope pulls me forward.

"Stay back!"

I move anyway.

Thin steel stabs my chest, the pain knocking me to my knees while crimson stains the sidewalk.

A girl drops beside me, tugs out the knife she'd thrown. "I'm sorry..."

The light fades, but her presence is enough.

I smile.

Cathy Hinkle is an editor for Havok Publishing and an emerging author of futuristic science fiction. She has a degree in English Literature and currently lives in Ohio with her family.

Digital Divide, No More
by Maria J. Estrada

Harry awoke to the loud alarm. Blood rushed to his head, eyes adjusted to darkness. His automated Virtual Reality companion warned: Only two days of nutrients left. Restock.

He struggled out of his sleeping chamber, infuriated to be pulled from his recent battle victory in Space Vikings. A #5 ranking, crushed. He had been in the arms of a voluptuous redhead, soon laid.

Plugged in for over two weeks, he had missed the end of the world. He parted the blinds.

Harry saw charred skies and toxic streets.

Social media was a corpse.

He thought.

Reclining, he commanded, "Restart game."

Maria J. Estrada grew up in the desert outside of Yuma, Arizona in a barrio comprised of new Mexican immigrants and first-generation Chicanos. She has published poetry, fiction, and essays in Blaze: The Inner Circle Writers' Group Flash Fiction Anthology 2019, Spillwords Press, Dastaan World Magazine, The Inner Circle Writers' Magazine, and A Language & Power Reader: Representations of Race in a "Post-Racist" Era. She lives in Chicago, IL.
Facebook: drmariajestrada
Website: barrioblues.com

Acceptance
by G. Allen Wilbanks

I sit on my front lawn and watch the sun setting in the east. There isn't much else to do. I've decided I will just let it happen. No fuss, no muss. My friends think I'm crazy because I won't even try. I think the same thing about them.

They're fooling themselves.

I've seen the movies, read the books. No, thank you. I want nothing to do with what comes next.

I see a flash of light off to my left. *Still too far away,* I tell myself as the mushroom shaped cloud blooms and grows. Maybe the next one.

G. Allen Wilbanks is a member of the Horror Writers Association (HWA) and has published over 50 short stories in various magazines and on-line venues. He is the author of two short story collections, and the novel, When Darkness Comes.
Website: www.gallenwilbanks.com
Blog: DeepDarkThoughts.com.

Alone
by Maxine Churchman

I was with him when he died; the man who started it all. Had he known how painful and ugly his death would be when he chose to unleash his manmade virus on the world?

He told me "It was too virulent to be useful to the military; they wanted it destroyed and I couldn't let that happen."

He really believed he was doing the right thing to save the planet and therefore mankind. He thought 15% of people would be immune and be thankful to him.

Six months on and I am still searching for even one other survivor.

Maxine Churchman lives in Essex UK and has recently started writing poetry and short stories to share. Her interests include leaning to improve her writing, reading, knitting, walking and teaching yoga. She is also planning a novel.

The Search for Walter
by Nicole Little

First came the heat, then the fires. This is what we're told each time we ask what happened to this godforsaken land. For generations now we've watched as our people die of The Thirst. There is hydration serum if you can afford it. Most cannot.

Rapt, we listen to the legends. We hope that there is truth to the story of one who dwells underground; he who can end the drought. Though memories have faded with time, the elders believe his name to be Walter.

And thus, we begin our pilgrimage. The search for our salvation. The search for Walter.

Nicole Little is an award winning short story writer who lives in St. John's, Newfoundland, Canada. Her publishing credits to date include Sweet Sixteen (Kit Sora: The Artobiography, 2019), The Market (Dystopia from the Rock, 2019) and Last One Standing (Dystopia from the Rock, 2019). Her short story Doxxed placed favorably in the Writers Alliance of Newfoundland and Labrador's "A Nightmare on Water Street: Scary Story Reading". In her spare time, Nicole can be found with either a pen in her hand or her nose in a book. She is married with two daughters.

Jerusalem
by Abigail Linhardt

Crusaders had been marching towards the Holy Land for years. The general was not surprised to see a fresh army slowing making its way towards his walls. It was time for prayer. His rug was missing. East was faintly visible through the ashen fallout.

The knights were leading the army, red crosses on a field of white. They had come a long way to take back a city they had never set foot in.

"Prepare the missiles," the general called. They were too close for more nukes. The city would no longer be holy. But maybe it was worth it.

Abi Linhardt has been a gamer all her life but is a teacher at heart. When she is not writing, you can find her slaying enemies online or teaching in a college classroom. She has published works of fiction, poetry, college essays, and even won two literary awards for her short stories in science fiction and horror. Abi lives and writes in the grey world of northern Ohio.

Fight or Die
by Stuart Conover

"Listen up, you bottom dwellers. This is it, you fight or we die!"

The Major shouted orders to his troops, knowing they'd be his last.

His men were the final defence for what remained of mankind.

How do you fight aliens that could tear you apart with their claws let alone vaporise you with their weapons?

The bunker wouldn't hold.

He could hear the outer shielding already beginning to fail.

"Hold the line" he belted out as they fell.

The President came on the line, offering a prayer for their souls.

It was the last thing any of them heard.

Stuart Conover is a father, husband, rescue dog owner, published author, blogger, journalist, horror enthusiast, comic book geek, science fiction junkie, and IT professional. With all of that to cram in daily, we have no idea if or when he sleeps or how he gets writing done! (We suspect it has to do with having evil clones.) Stuart is a Chicago native and runs the author resource Horror Tree.

The Last
by Wendy Roberts

Sophie drives the knife through the side of her brother's forehead, stifling a sob as the last breath leaves his body. She ignores the oozing sores covering his neck and face. The same flesh eating disease that's eaten most of humanity has just taken the last of Sophie's family.

She wipes the blood off on her sleeve, wincing as the rough fabric rubs against the fresh boils climbing up her arm. The wounds will soon be festering from the inside and she rests her head against the wall, wondering who'll be around to drive the knife through her own head.

Writing short stories and novels started as a past time for **Wendy Roberts** *and has now become a fully fledged passion. She posts short stories on her website and can be found most days on Twitter.*
Website: flippinscribbler.wordpress.com
Twitter: @_WARoberts

Day 626
by Stephen Herczeg

Day 626

I finished the last of the food yesterday.

The water ran out a month ago. I store all my urine. It tastes sweet and sticky, but you get used to it.

I keep looking at the door. It leads out there. Surely it's safe by now. The gizmos keep telling me the rad levels are death, but so is staying in here.

Smithers kept saying your skin would slough off within a few minutes. I didn't like his skin, it was tough. His leg tasted better.

I look at the door again.

I think it's time to leave.

Stephen Herczeg is an IT Geek based in Canberra Australia. He has been writing for over twenty years and has completed a couple of dodgy novels, sixteen feature length screenplays and numerous short stories and scripts. His horror work has featured in Sproutlings, Hells Bells, Below the Stairs, Trickster's Treats #1 and #2, Shades of Santa, Behind the Mask, Beyond the Infinite; The Body Horror Book, Anemone Enemy, Petrified Punks and Beginnings. He has also had numerous Sherlock Holmes stories published through the Belanger Books - Sherlock Holmes anthologies.

Warming
by N.M. Brown

You notice how summers get hotter every year? I've studied it for the past year, and you need to know why.

It's not your imaginations or age. The Earth's been moving infinitesimally closer to the sun with each rotation for decades.

Within fifty years, all snow on Earth will be gone. It will be melted into boiling waters that flood all lands. Crops will fail to thrive due to overexposure to heat and sun. Our skin will blister and burn the second we step out of our doors. Our planet will turn into a global oven; no one will survive.

*Since **N.M. Brown** made her first post to a popular Internet forum, she's taken the horror community by storm. Her ability to create, terrify, and drive home her stories is insurmountable. Sinister Sweetheart's published works can be found in multiple anthologies for all to read, but be forewarned, if you do... you may want to call your therapist after, her stories are terrifying, disturbing and devilishly unsettling. She is not only a fright visually, but also has a creepy tentacle in horror podcasting as well. Sinister Sweetheart writes, voice acts and is the media director of the Scarecrow Tales podcast.*
Website: Sinistersweetheart.wixsite.com/sinistersweetheart
Facebook: NMBrownStories

Piece de la Resistance
by Joachim Heijndermans

I stand among them in Dixon Street as I announce the reveal of my greatest artwork yet.

Flash. The ignition of white light leaves them blinded. None have the chance to even scream, instantly vaporised by the shockwave. A woman beside me cradles her child as they become ash and are blown away, with only their shadows left to mark their existence.

The city crumbles. Fire rages. Everything but me dies, their flesh roasted by my piece de la resistance. I did this. Beauty in carnage. The end brought forth by my weapon.

I'll think I'll make this a series.

Joachim Heijndermans writes, draws, and paints nearly every waking hour. Originally from the Netherlands, he's been all over the world, boring people by spouting random trivia. His work has been featured in a number of anthologies and publications, such as Mad Scientist Journal, Asymmetry Fiction, Hinnom Magazine, Ahoy Comics's Edgar Allan Poe's Snifter of Terror, Metaphorosis and The Gallery of Curiosities, and he's currently in the midst of completing his first children's book.
Website: www.joachimheijndermans.com
Twitter: @jheijndermans

Stick to the Plan
by Crystal L. Kirkham

"Let me in!" came the desperate cry from outside the walls of my refuge. I could see that she'd been scratched. I didn't know if it was by a zombie, but it didn't matter. What mattered was survival. I had a plan, and I was sticking to it.

"Please," she begged, her voice cracking with emotion.

I could hear creatures moving through brush. A figure stumbled into the clearing—there was no mistaking *that* monster for what it was.

"Sorry, Mom." I aimed my rifle and squeezed the trigger. She didn't need to suffer because I couldn't let her in.

Crystal L. Kirkham *resides in a small hamlet west of Red Deer, Alberta. She's an avid outdoors person, unrepentant coffee addict, part-time foodie, servant to a wonderful feline, and companion to two delightfully hilarious canines. She will neither confirm nor deny the rumours regarding the heart in a jar on her desk and the bottle of reader's tears right next to it. Her paranormal urban fantasy series, Saints and Sinners, is available on Amazon and her YA Fantasy, Feathers and Fae will be released October 11, 2019, from Kyanite Publishing.*
Website: www.crystallkirkham.com

Rabbit Sailboat Dragon
by Cameron Marcoux

You sit cross legged on the top of Gallant Hill, the tallest in your town. It's a small town. Rural, folksy, quiet. From the top of the hill, like a Touist monk at the watchtower, you watch the lands beyond. Most people chose to leave, head higher into the mountains up north, the Dakotas and such. Canada. Last-ditch hopes. Desperation.

You chose to remain. You were born here after all. Might as well die here too. The day shifts, the clouds float by in characterisations of your youth: Rabbit. Sailboat. Dragon. Until night falls and fire burns the world away.

Cameron Marcoux is a writer of stories, which, considering where you are reading this, makes a lot of sense. He also teaches English to the lovely and terrifying creatures we call teenagers. He lives in the quiet, northern reaches of New England in the U.S. with his girlfriend and scaredy dog.

Bunker 10
by Jem McCusker

The stark white room hummed and buzzed to the rhythm of technology. A parade of technicians filtered in and out.

I brought up the reactor on screen and entered in my manual override code. Removing a thumb from my pocket, I pressed it over the keypad.

The screens lit up, with red warnings flashing and the evacuation bell ringing. I engaged the locks.

White lab coats threw themselves against the doors. I watched, unmoved.

Opening a case, I held the eyeball to the biometric screen. Bunker ten opened for me.

"Welcome to the new world." A smile filled my face.

Jem McCusker is a middle grade fiction author, living near Brisbane with her two sons and husband. Her first book Stone Guardians the Rise of Eden was released in 2018 and she is working on the sequel. She is releasing a Novella for the Four Quills writing group, A Storm of Wind and Rain series in July, 2019. She longs to be a full-time author, won't wear yellow and loves rabbits. Follow Jem on Twitter, Facebook and Instagram. Details on her website...

Athlete in the Apocalypse
by Emily Fluke

I hated mother for forcing me into gymnastics. "You'll go to the Olympics, baby girl." I refrained from spitting on her face. The Diseased took care of that for me.

I perched on our rain gutters and watched a Diseased chew at mother's chin like beef jerky. They came for me next, drooling at the sight of my juicy gymnast muscles. I leapt to the next building and clung to the window railing. A Diseased snapped at my feet. I pulled up and whispered an apology to mother before leaving her half-eaten corpse behind.

Survival is better than the Olympics.

*Congenital Heart Defect survivor, **Emily Fluke**, finds joy and peace through the expression of writing. She engages and has been published in many formats from poetry to short stories to flash fiction. Emily and her husband spend their free time wrangling two children and playing video games in their busy California lifestyle.*

Nine Nights
by David Bowmore

Who'd have thought a zombie apocalypse would actually happen? Not me.

Perhaps the dead will rip each other to shreds, before we starve to death.

For nine nights, ten of us have been holed up in this museum. We're armed to the teeth with ancient weapons, and committed to doing the right thing should anyone's time come. I've already re-killed and maimed so many people; the merciful death of a comrade does not bother my conscience.

My dog becoming infected hurt the most. Fortunately, there was no recognition in his eyes as I beheaded him with a seventeenth century cutlass.

David Bowmore has lived here, there and everywhere, but now lives in Yorkshire with his wonderful wife and a small white poodle. He has worn many hats in his time; head chef, teacher and landscape gardener. His first collection of short stories 'The Magic of Deben Market' is available from Clarendon House.
Website: davidbowmore.co.uk
Facebook: davidbowmoreauthor

White Light
by V. Mylynne Smith

I wore a crown of human teeth atop my head. A necklace of finger bones was strewn around my neck. Knives of various lengths hung from my belt.

When the white light came, it turned our town to rubble. My friends were taken, and I was left alone with my enemies. All of us were starving, and it was my life or theirs.

A crowd gathered as I struck down my first foe. They cheered and buried their teeth in the meat I'd provided. Supporters began to follow me. Though the world was next to empty, our stomachs were full.

V. Mylynne Smith is from Northwest Arkansas where she lives with her husband and two pets. She's had stories featured in issues #21 and #24 of Dark Dossier Magazine. Premeditated, her first novel, was self-published last year. Her story "Pearl" was featured in Salty Tales by Stormy Island Publishing, and "Melinoe's Curse" is featured in Divinity by Iron Faerie Publishing.
Website: vmylynnesmith.wordpress.com
Facebook: vmylynne

I Tried to Warn You
by Jacob Baugher

To Whom It May Concern,

I tried to warn you. I sent you prophets with "Inconvenient Truths."

Vegans warned you about methane. You mocked, ate beef.

Environmentalists warned you about carbon, but alternatives were too expensive.

Scientists warned you about the "2 degrees," but you called it cyclical.

But when the oceans rose up and swallowed your cities; when storms ripped down skyscrapers and famine starved your land because honey bees went extinct, you shook your fists skyward and asked God, "WHY?"

I tried to warn you. But change was too damn inconvenient.

Enjoy the apocalypse, assholes.

Love,

Mother Earth

Jacob Baugher teaches Creative Writing at Franciscan University of Steubenville. When he's not teaching or coaching the track team, he can be found in the Cuyahoga Valley hiking with his wife and son or brewing beer on his front porch. He's received honourable mentions for his work in the Writers of the Future contest and he co-edits a series of Fantasy and Science Fiction anthologies titled Continuum.

La Señora y El Niño
by Ximena Escobar

She never smiled but she liked that boy. He'd go places.

He took the shopping from her hand, dragging it up the bleak building's stairs.

She hated having to fill the silence; that's why she liked him, because he didn't matter; she didn't have to bother and just listened for the keys in her pocket (he for the coins). But then, both heard the distant gun shots.

Shooing him away, she gave him a few pesos. But a loud roar filled them with emptiness, lighting the windows red. She clasped his wrist, their lives flashing to an end between them.

*Ximena Escobar is an emerging author of literary fiction and poetry. Originally from Chile, she is the author of a translation into Spanish of the Broadway Musical "The Wizard of Oz", and of an original adaptation of the same, "Navidad en Oz". Clarendon House Publications published her first short story in the UK, "The Persistence of Memory", and Literally Stories her first online publication with "The Green Light". She has since had several acceptances from other publishers and is working very hard exploring new exciting avenues in her writing.
She lives in Nottingham with her family.
Facebook: Ximenautora*

Lastwoman of the Red Bird Pack
by Joshua D. Taylor

The Lastwoman of the Red Bird pack ran for her life down the abandoned road, passed crumbling homes with rusted vehicles. She would rather take her chances with the wild beasts and the elements than be devoured by her packmates, the growlers. Now that her daughter was old enough to replace her, there was no reason to feed and protect two lastwomen.

The growlers might not even bother to pursue her. If she could just make it to the mountains, it was rumoured that others lived there, free of the packs. Then she saw a paw print in the mud.

Joshua D. Taylor is an amateur writer who started writing a few years ago when he realised he was too old to play make-believe. He lives in southeastern Pennsylvania with his wife and a one-eared cat. He enjoys gardening, comic books, ska-punk music, Disney World, and travelling with his wife. Raised during weirdness that was the late 20th century Josh's eclectic interests produce eclectic works. He loves to mix-n-match things from different genres and stories elements to achieve a madcap hodgepodge of the truly unexpected. His short story 'the Obelisk' appears in Salty Tales by Stormy Island Publishing.
Facebook: authorjoshuadtaylor

The Final Step
by J.S. Carnes

Travis walked through the wasteland in a trance, surrounded by remnants of a world fallen to silence. The overlapping signs of life that once filled the world became echoes across a desolate landscape.

Grass sprouted defiantly through cracked concrete; Mother Nature reclaiming her rightful place.

The world will renew itself. Travis could hear Samantha telling him as if she was walking with him.

The hazy silhouette of the tree he came for stood on the road's edge.

"Samantha, my love, I promised you I would make it home." His words cracked in his dry throat. "I love you."

Travis collapsed.

J.S. Carnes enjoys the sites and sounds of Austin, TX. He enjoys good music, good coffee, good spirits, and good people. He finds inspiration from the unique places he's experienced and the quirky people he's interacted with, then throws in a twist.

Rise of the Underworld
by Ann Christine Tabaka

Thomas looked out the window at the dark clouds closing in. He wasn't sure what to make of it all. Everyone was standing outside staring at the sky in dismay. No one wanted to believe the worst. Life has had its disasters before, but somehow it seemed more serious this time. It wasn't just war, famine, pestilence, and death. This time it was something bigger, on a global scale.

The ground shook and heaved. Heat and flames rose from the underworld. Thomas fell to his knees, shaking in in fear, as the four horsemen mounted up and prepared to ride.

Ann Christine Tabaka was nominated for the 2017 Pushcart Prize in Poetry, has been internationally published, and won poetry awards from numerous publications. She is the author of 9 poetry books. Christine lives in Delaware, USA. She loves gardening and cooking. Chris lives with her husband and two cats. Her most recent credits are: Burningword Literary Journal; Ethos Literary Journal, North of Oxford, Pomona Valley Review, Page & Spine, West Texas Literary Review, The Hungry Chimera, Sheila-Na-Gig, Pangolin Review, Foliate Oak Review, Better Than Starbucks!, The Write Launch, The Stray Branch, The McKinley Review, Fourth & Sycamore.

Final Tweet
by Debbie Wingate

"Sir, it's time to go." The agent looked to the chief of staff for assistance.

"Mr. President, everyone is waiting to hear your outgoing speech."

"No sir, your executive order to make you president for life was blocked."

"Yes sir, many appreciated your leadership, but it's the will of the people to elect someone new."

"Um, yes sir, the entire world reads your tweets."

"Yes sir, the last one said you are the greatest and the last president of the United States. Was that a typo, sir?"

"Yes sir, I saw the thumbs up and laughing emojis from North Korea."

Debbie Wingate has two self-published books, *News From the Northwoods*, a memoir, and *Truthfinder*, a work of fiction about finding one's path. She does payroll by day, and writes when the urge strikes. She admits to not being very disciplined. Debbie lives in Gresham, OR with her partner of 15 years, and Annie, the rescue cat.

Last Resort
by Gabriella Balcom

"I could never do that," Marilyn insisted.

"You *must*," her mother Linda stressed. "There's no food."

Marilyn hugged her parents. "We'll find another way."

Her father merely shook his head.

Three weeks later, she stood alone on the Dead Grounds. Dad had died yesterday, Mom today. Marilyn had hidden their bodies instead of burying them.

Looking around, she saw many graves had been opened. Clearly, others who'd survived the Great War had come up with the same solution as her parents, because bodies lay everywhere. Even though they were decomposing, their fleshiest parts had been eaten right off the bone.

Gabriella Balcom lives in Texas with her family, loves reading and writing, and thinks she was born with a book in her hands. She works in a mental health field, and writes fantasy, horror/thriller, romance, children's stories, and sci-fi. She likes travelling, music, good shows, photography, history, interesting tales, and animals. Gabriella says she's a sucker for a great story and loves forests, mountains, and back roads which might lead who knows where. She has a weakness for lasagne, garlic bread, tacos, cheese, and chocolate, but not necessarily in that order.
Facebook: GabriellaBalcom.lonestarauthor

Three Boys And...
by Sue Marie St. Lee

Joe, Chris and Mike were up to their usual shenanigans that Saturday morning. Packed with loaded BB guns, chips, cans of Coke, lanterns, and Mom's binoculars, they headed to the abandoned mine shaft.

Tearing down the "Do Not Enter" sign, they entered and explored deep within it until the earth shook, rocks fell, loud noises stung their ears and the air became thick with dust.

Huge rocks blocked their escape. While arguing about how to escape, they saw green eyes staring at them.

The ant-like creature walked into the light of their lanterns, "Yellowstone took your world. Welcome to mine."

Sue Marie St. Lee writes dark, twisted tales. Her favourite genre is horror with tinges of the supernatural and macabre. Ghosts, black magic, time travel, and all things weird feature in her stories. Sue also writes non-fiction on subjects ranging from healthcare, aging and caring for diabetic pets. When Sue is not writing, she enjoys getting physical with home renovations and landscaping projects. Her favourite way to relax is with a glass of wine, cat on her lap, and reading her Kindle.
Website: suemariestlee.home.blog
Amazon: amazon.com/author/suemariestlee

Better Than I Thought
by Glenn R. Wilson

It's not so bad. Really, it isn't.

I always heard those that survived were the unlucky ones.

I disagree.

The pandemic was swift. A week—two at most—and it was over.

Now, there's a few of us left. Unaffected by the virus. Just a lot of bodies, burning all the time. But that's on the outskirts of town. Downwind, too. I made sure of that.

Everything else remains as it was. The store shelves are full. Plenty of petrol. And all the animals and plants are still here.

We'll start again. We have the books to show us how.

***Glenn R. Wilson** has come full circle. Making a point to mature, like fine wine, before diving head-first into his long list of writing projects, he's approaching them with a plan. That strategy is to build with one brick at a time. He's accumulated a few bricks already and is adding more. Over time, with persistence and determination, he'll have a home. But for now, a solid foundation is the goal. Please, enjoy the process with him.*

The Last Question
by Ximena Escobar

If she had a fear of anything, it was space. Not even if they paid her a billion dollars would she contemplate going out there; not even craving—as she craved—to know the answers to all the questions, would she find herself in that enormity; not even if all the answers were proven to be there, and it was guaranteed she'd return 100% safe.

But as all the lights went out, every single one in the world, she didn't have a choice.

In the empty desolation of the ruins, all alone amongst the stars, she could only ask 'why'.

Ximena Escobar is an emerging author of literary fiction and poetry. Originally from Chile, she is the author of a translation into Spanish of the Broadway Musical "The Wizard of Oz", and of an original adaptation of the same, "Navidad en Oz". Clarendon House Publications published her first short story in the UK, "The Persistence of Memory", and Literally Stories her first online publication with "The Green Light". She has since had several acceptances from other publishers and is working very hard exploring new exciting avenues in her writing. She lives in Nottingham with her family. Facebook: Ximenautora

The Old Man Dirge
by E.L. Giles

Across a desolate and windswept plateau travelled the echoes of a guitar, transported on the mournful wind with no ears to hear its complaint.

Restlessly the old man played, walking the barren land, his fingers stiff and painful.

Relentlessly he strummed the same chords, sang the same lines of the dirge, again and again for the dead world, a hymn of solitude and desperation.

"Take me," he sang. "Take me, God, for I can't bear this loneliness anymore. For the pain is too great, and I am too weak. For I can't endure the sight of this dead world anymore."

E.L. Giles is a dreamer, passionate about art, a restless worker and a bit of a weird human. He started his artistic journey as a music composer until the need to put his thoughts and stories down on paper grew too strong for him to resist it any longer. He lives in the French Province of Quebec, Canada, with his girlfriend and two boys.
Facebook: elgilesauthor
Website: www.elgilesauthor.com

BLACK HARE PRESS

ACKNOWLEDGEMENTS

Huge thanks to all the authors who have contributed to APOCALYPSE, the sixth book in the Dark Drabbles series and our tenth publication.

We saw a whole new batch of emerging writers submit to this anthology—it was a popular theme—and you all nailed it. So, well done.

We are lucky to be surrounded by great authors who are willing to submit to our anthologies, and we'll continue to showcase their work for as long as they allow us.

As always, a very special *thank you* to you, our loyal and dedicated readers, who continue to support our work.

www.blackharepress.com

BLACK HARE PRESS

Stories of new worlds, new creatures, alien colonisation, humanity's new home, space accidents, alien snackcidents, evil planets, military mashups, alien autopsies, and much, much more.

Beatific angels, holy wars, kitty saviours, epic battles between good and evil, devils and demons, fallen angels and many more tantalising tiny tales.

BLACK HARE PRESS

Wendigos, vampires, things that go bump in the night or hide under the bed, witches, demons, upirs, kelpies, toad people, zombies, sirens and hundreds of other tiny terrifying tales.

Micro myths of the paranormal;
poltergeists, spirit boards, ghosts
and ghouls, avenging apparitions
and horrifying hauntings.

BLACK HARE PRESS

Murder mysteries, criminal chronicles, whodunnits, revenge, suspicion, mayhem, intrigue, and lots more.

www.ingramcontent.com/pod-product-compliance
Lightning Source LLC
Chambersburg PA
CBHW060945190726
48286CB00005B/1431